THE KNIGHT'S REWARD

BORDER SERIES ~~~~~~ EN

CECELIA MECCA

ALTIORA
PRESS

I will never be able to properly thank you, Angela, for helping to bring the Border Series to life.

CHAPTER 1

*W*indsor Park, August 1274

Neill blocked out the murmurs and shouts of the crowd, concentrating on the position of his opponent's lance. Making a slight adjustment to his shield, he vowed to defeat the Flemish champion in one pass. For his surrogate mother and father. For the Waryn family name.

For the king's honor.

This was his chance to make a difference, to do his part to silence the murmurings of trouble along the border between England and Scotland.

Waiting for the knight marshal's signal, he loosened his grip on his own lance just slightly, adjusting his stance as needed so he could take down both man and horse. The fact that no other knight had managed such a feat even once in the past three days meant nothing to him. He had decided he would do it, and so he would. When the horn blasted and he spurred his destrier forward, Neill held his position steady despite the movement under him. Despite the hundreds of pounds of horseflesh hurtling toward him.

One chance.

Lance straight over the horse's head. Hit first. Hit hardest.

He repeated the words over and over in his head until the deed was done, his opponent unseated.

Slowing his mount, still breathing heavily from the effort that had lasted only seconds yet nearly shattered the bones in his hand, Neill tore off his helm and then his gauntlets. Handing both to his squire, he finally allowed the roar of the crowd to penetrate his ears.

Turning toward the stands, he searched the bright blues and greens, ladies' gowns clashing against the red and yellow banners that hung on all sides. Finding Cora, Neill raised his hand and was acknowledged with a wave in return. She knew what he was about to do. They both did. And so, after accepting his opponent's payment—his horse and armor, which Neill would give to a young knight in need of both—he joined the marshal in front of the most important man in the crowd. The one who stood in front of his makeshift throne in the stands, towering over his companions, and silenced the rowdy audience with the simple raise of his hand.

The king of England tended to have that effect.

"Sir Neill Waryn," the marshal called out, "son of the late Lord Thomas Waryn of Bristol Manor and ward of Sir Adam Dayne and his wife, Lady Cora Maxwell."

The latter Neill had insisted on adding despite the marshal's protestations to the contrary. If his dead father would be acknowledged, then so too should the man and woman who'd helped raise him from a petulant young boy to the man that he'd become.

"Your Tournament of Peace champion," the marshal finished.

Neill dropped to his knees and waited. When King Edward finally indicated that he should stand, Neill did so, bracing himself for the question he knew would come.

"Congratulations, Sir Neill. Your boon?"

The boon. The crowd remained quiet despite their numbers,

each person leaning forward to hear what was said. Until this day, the Tournament of Peace had been the one tournament Neill had not yet won. Of them all, it offered the biggest prize—a boon from the king of England.

Neill darted a glance at Adam, who stood near the stands, before giving his full attention back to the king. Proud and unapologetic, King Edward was exactly as Neill remembered him from the last tournament. Power exuded from him—from the way he held his head to his upright posture. Damn if he wasn't the only man Neill could remember intimidating him in a long, long time.

"My thanks," Neill said, his voice strong and loud. "It has been a pleasure to serve my king and my country, a privilege bestowed on me by the grace of God," he started, acknowledging his very pious leader. "But if you would grant me a boon beyond that privilege, I will gladly ask for it."

More than one in the crowd gasped. Rightly so. Although he and Adam had agreed on this course of action, Neill almost regretted the words now that they'd left his mouth. By acknowledging the pleasure of serving his king as his prize, he was taking a huge risk. Edward could very well accept the offering and forgo the greater request he intended to make.

Reminding himself regrets served no purpose, he waited for the king's response.

"Your answer pleases me," King Edward said. "Your adherence to the very chivalric code I have vowed to uphold prevents me from accepting this"—he gestured to the list on which Neill still stood—"as your prize. Ask for your boon and you will have it."

Had he pleased the king enough by that gesture to see his unusual request granted? He was about to find out.

"If it pleases Your Majesty, I ask that Lord Caxton be removed from his position as Warden of the Middle March."

Neill's previous comment had stirred the crowd, but his

request inflamed them. When his words finally penetrated, the low murmur of conversation burst into loud chatter. Everyone was staring at the king and the young knight who'd petitioned him, but Neill didn't pay them any mind. He never shifted his gaze from the one man who possessed the power to protect his family.

Lord Caxton seemed intent on breaking the peace at the border rather than upholding it, as was his job, and each day he served as warden brought the situation closer to a breaking point. The monthly Day of Truce, which had staved off battles along the border, had fallen apart under his rule. The Scottish wardens refused to attend the meetings until he was removed. Without the Day of Truce, reivers and murderers met with no justice as long as their crimes crossed over the border.

In other words, anarchy reigned, just as it had before the Treaty of York drew the first line between England and Scotland some thirty years ago.

Although Neill now resided in the south of England, the politics of the borderlands were never far from his mind. His two brothers and sister all resided along the border. The disintegration of the Day of Truce affected his family directly.

The king did not so much as flinch. Watching him, unwavering, Edward leaned over to speak with his second in command. Although Neill longed to glance at Adam and Cora, he didn't dare look anywhere but directly at the king.

Holding his breath, he waited. And waited.

The crowd grew impatient, stirred into a frenzy by the boldness of his request and the length of time it was taking the king to grant it. He'd never once denied a boon requested by a Tournament of Peace champion, although there was always a first.

Finally, Edward raised his hand once again.

"Your boon shall be granted, with one condition."

He had been prepared for this too. Neill braced himself, maintaining eye contact with Edward, who now lowered himself into his makeshift throne. Even sitting, he was still high above Neill.

"You and your guests are invited to dine at the king's table tonight," said the king's chancellor, surprising him. That, he'd not expected. "Congratulations, Sir Neill."

With that, he had been dismissed.

Bowing, knowing he'd need to take a victor's lap down the length of the list before he joined his squire and spoke to Adam and Cora, Neill walked back to his mount.

A condition.

Whatever it was, this condition must be met. Once it was, Neill would take the good news to his brothers. It was time to go home.

But first, his victor's lap and requisite meeting with the marshal. Only later, as he sat in the great hall of one of the most impressive castles in England, did Neill allow the king's condition to trouble him.

They'd eaten, drank their fill, and still the king and queen sat quietly on the raised dais. Finally, he was called before them once again. With a final glance back to Adam and Cora, he made his way to the dais. Bowing deeply, he stood only when the king advised him to do so.

"When I have my renewed oath from Alexander, Caxton shall be removed. After—" he exchanged a look with the queen before continuing, "—you will take the Lady Alina deBeers as a bride."

"WE'LL BE NEEDING you downstairs, Kathryn," Magge shouted from the other side of the door.

Shoving the innkeeper's books back inside the desk Magge had procured for her the month before, Kathryn stood, shook out her well-worn dress, and grabbed an apron hanging near the door.

"On my way," she called, putting it on and entering the dimly lit hallway.

"Yer hair," Magge cautioned before she shuffled away.

Kathryn reached back, quickly braided her hair and secured it with a ribbon from the pocket of her apron. Sometimes, to avoid notice, she wore a headcovering as well, but Magge seemed in a hurry this eve. Saying a silent prayer she'd not regret it later, Kathryn headed belowstairs, following the sounds of men deep in their cups. Darkness had already fallen, the only light now from the hearth and tallow candles casting their dim glow on the men feasting at the rows of trestle tables.

Her first job would be to refresh the candles.

"Keep yer hands to yerself." Magge swatted old MacAdder as she walked by him. Sure enough, the Scottish reiver's eyes widened when he saw her. Although he seemed harmless enough, she wouldn't tempt fate by walking near him, so she navigated around him to start her duties at the far side of the hall.

Seeing a candle that needed to be replaced, Kathryn leaned between two men, careful not to touch either of them. She took the candleholder with her.

"She's the one I told you about," one of the men said to the other.

Uh-oh.

"Fine speech for a barmaid."

Ignore them, Kathryn.

She tried to move on to the next table, but the young knight grabbed her hand. Kathryn sighed. For months The Wild Boar had been her sanctuary, but she'd made a mistake last night, slipping into French to respond to one of the men, and it would seem she'd made an impression.

While most inns of this size catered to nobles, or at least

gentry, this sole inn along the border attracted a wide array of men. Nobles and knights, reivers of both the English and Scottish variety. Magge knew how to handle them all, which was how The Wild Boar had earned its reputation as the sole location on the border where peace still reigned and where men could meet to discuss important matters that affected both the English and the Scots. The Wild Boar and its proprietor were known far and wide.

Magge had proven a fine teacher. Although her figure was stout, her hair greying, she was still quick with a dagger and a fine flirt. She knew the best approach for each of her patrons, and she'd taught Kathryn the same sense of discernment. Kathryn had come to her knowing little of the daily activities of an inn. She'd frequented them, of course, but until she'd come to Magge for help, she'd never worked a day in her life.

"Too fine to address her patrons?" the knight asked.

He stood close enough for her to smell the ale on his breath. Kathryn glanced up and caught the innkeeper's eye from across the room. *Ignore, play along, defend. In that order.* Magge had given her that piece of advice the day she'd come here seeking sanctuary, and she'd realized its worth a dozen times over.

"Not so fine as that, sir," Kathryn said, spinning around and winking in a perfect imitation of Magge. No one dared to enter The Wild Boar and give Magge anything but the respect she deserved. This inn did not simply survive—it turned away patrons nearly every night of the week—and if the guests did not behave, she could and would make them leave.

The man who'd accosted her was an English knight, though not titled if the condition of his armor and roughness of his speech were any indication. His companions watched her as she smiled politely at each of them.

"A pitcher of ale for your troubles?"

The apology rolled smoothly off her tongue, as if it were her fault she spoke "so finely" or wanted to avoid the attentions of three men who'd likely been drinking ale all evening. But none would guess her thoughts by the smile she offered them. That was a lesson she'd learned well.

"What's your name?" one of the Englishman's friends asked.

Bearded and a few years older than the man who'd addressed her, this one was likely the leader of the group. Also untitled, most likely, but she'd guess he had a bit more coin than the others. None of which he'd spend this night as Kathryn had just offered to serve them free drink.

Magge wouldn't be pleased, but she'd be even less pleased if a fight broke out.

Kathryn had inadvertently started more than one, and there was nothing Magge despised more. She'd built The Wild Boar's reputation on maintaining peace, but even the innkeeper knew violence was unavoidable at times.

Like the time a Scots chief's son had attempted to drag Kathryn deep into the stables for "a bit of fun." That particular incident had ended with a local baron dumping the man and his father in the nearby river on Magge's orders. The innkeeper had no shortage of muscle to assist her when it became necessary.

All of the locals loved Magge, as they did this inn, and they would fight to protect what was hers, including Kathryn. Unfortunately, those who were new to the inn, or too bold or drunk to care about the rules, sometimes had to learn the hard way.

"Kathryn, sir."

"Does the maid have a surname?" he asked. Perhaps he simply asked out of curiosity, but Kathryn always expected the worse.

That he might know her, or her father. Might suspect the truth.

"Baird," she lied. "Kathryn Baird."

"Where are you—"

"The ale?" the third companion interrupted. Kathryn could

always count on at least one person caring more for ale or wine than for her.

"Of course," she murmured, hurrying off and breathing a sigh of relief. She'd not be back to their table this eve. When she reached Mary, she said, "Can you bring a pitcher of ale to the three Englishmen—"

Mary rolled her eyes, the young maid already knowing what she needed. It happened at least once a night when Kathryn worked the hall. Which was why Magge only brought her down here when necessary.

"Aye, I'll trade yer tables," the normally good-natured Mary muttered.

Kathryn blew her a kiss.

"Pucker those lips again," Magge said, catching up with her and giving her bottom a little swat, "and ye'll be givin' ale to every goddamn man here."

Kathryn couldn't help but laugh at Magge's expression.

"I learned from the best," she teased. The older woman was a more notorious flirt than even the most skilled courtiers. And Kathryn would know. She'd spent more time in the English and French courts than she had anywhere else in her twenty years. Although her duties at The Wild Boar were a long way from attending the queen, another duty of her past life, navigating overly-amorous men and sometimes jealous ladies here in The Wild Boar was not overly different than being at court.

Only then, she'd had her father to protect her.

Now that he was gone, Kathryn had to protect herself . . . and her father's legacy. Which someday, between ordering brews and swatting away prying hands, she vowed to do. Someday, she would learn who had killed him. Who had forced her into this life of hiding.

CHAPTER 2

"Just a bit lower," Cora instructed.

Back at Langford Castle from Windsor, Neill stood with the woman who had been a host, mother, and confidante to him these past seven years. She'd challenged him to one final contest at breakfast, and since he could no sooner refuse her than he could ignore a challenge, here they were in the training yard.

This time, Neill was determined to best her.

Though his senior by nearly thirty years, Lady Cora had no parallel with the longbow. No matter that he was one of the most decorated tournament knights in all of England.

"Offering advice to the competition," her husband said from Neill's other side. "One might think you will the boy to win."

Neill's hands froze in place. "Neither the constant chatter nor your reference to my age will take me off this mark."

Adam tsked, clearly disagreeing.

Cora's arrow had skewered the target just slightly off-center, enough of a miss for him to capitalize on. Listening to her instructions, he did lower his aim ever so slightly, and let loose.

Every head in the training yard turned to watch Neill's arrow land just outside Cora's.

"Well met," she said. "Though it seems you'll be forced to return to Langford for more lessons."

Neill turned to Cora and forced a smile, but her words had pained him. He'd known no other life but Langford and tournaments since he'd arrived here as a young, and very lost, boy. Adam and Cora had not just fostered him into knighthood, they had become his parents these past years.

But they weren't his only family, and his siblings needed him now. They needed him to fulfill the end of the bargain he'd made.

"Perhaps on the way back to court I will come for a rematch."

Cora frowned as Neill handed his bow to a squire. "She is lovely."

"That hardly matters."

"From a good family."

"I did not choose her."

Since returning from Windsor, he and Cora had gone round and round on this very topic. At least Adam had spoken up for him, though now he remained silent.

"Few choose their spouses," Cora continued. She glanced at Adam, a small smile on her lips.

"Not true," he interrupted, the sound of clanging swords punctuating their conversation. Now that they'd finished their competition, the men's training resumed around them.

"Adam and I—"

"Were not ordered by the king to marry."

"The queen," Adam offered at last. "I do believe the match was her idea. DeBeers is only a minor baron, but the daughter serves the queen. Likely this is her doing."

"King. Queen. What does it matter? Either way, Lady Alina will be my wife."

Though he argued against it, Neill's only choice was to make peace with that fact. A small price to pay, to marry a woman he knew only from description, for the boon King Edward had granted him.

A small price to pay for peace.

"More importantly," he said as they made their way back to the keep. "Caxton will be removed as warden." He'd planned to go home months ago, back when the Day of Truce had first fallen apart, but the Tournament of Peace had been announced. It was then he and Adam came up with this plan. Ask for the one thing that could restore peace along the border.

Caxton's removal.

"That should have happened long ago," Cora said.

"Aye," he agreed. But now Edward had finally ascended as king, and it seemed he was willing to make some changes. "Once it's done, the Day of Truce restored—"

"You will visit often." Cora stepped over a mud puddle in the center of the courtyard.

Neill laughed. "Your daily reminders to come back are unnecessary." He stopped walking and turned to face his foster parents. "I will never forget what either of you have done for me."

Under Adam's tutelage, he'd become a champion.

Under Cora's, a gentleman.

"When Geoffrey sent me here . . ."

He didn't need to continue. All three of them were aware of Neill's past, as was the entire Langford household. His brothers, Geoffrey and Bryce, and his twin, Emma, had stayed in the north. Together. He had been sent south to Langford. He'd raged against their decision at first, feeling he'd unfairly been sent away. But Neill had come to recognize that his brothers, already knights and well into adulthood, had done the best possible thing for him at the time. They'd ensured he would get the training he needed to become the knight they knew he could be.

"Thank you."

The words hardly seemed adequate, and as Cora wrapped her arms around him, he ignored the looks they were receiving from the men in the training yard and hugged her back.

She never had cared about appearances. A more unconventional lady couldn't be found anywhere, with the exception of in the north among his own family.

"Give your siblings our regards," she whispered. "And Lady Sara too."

"I will," he promised.

"And Neill . . ." She pulled away slightly but still held his hands. "Please remember what I told you."

"The greatest knight in Christendom is nothing without his family." He winked. "Although I suspect you say that only to remind me to return."

She didn't deny it.

Neill turned to Adam.

Lord of Langford, a man who knew very well that not all family was related by blood. Adam himself had been the ward of Spencer Caiser, the former Earl of Kenshire. Neill wished he could have known the great man, the grandfather of his sister-in-law Sara. "You are my Richard Caiser," he said.

He embraced the man who'd acted as his father after his own father was killed. He vowed, as he'd done so many times before, to continue to make him proud. To uphold the virtues Adam held dear. Strength with humility, honor and family above all.

And he'd start by saving the very borderlands that would be his home, apparently with Lady Alina by his side.

KATHRYN WAS GRATEFUL FOR MAGGE.

For The Wild Boar.

For her new life.

But she was really not having a good time of it.

Four of the Scottish king's men had come to the inn, and she'd thought it her chance to learn something about her father's murder. But when she'd tried to question them, Magge had promptly shooed her out of sight.

Later, she'd berated her for a fool.

"You always talk about stayin' out of sight. And here you are, doin' everything but proclaiming yourself a lady to the very same men you've been warned away from."

Kathryn reminded her it was the English court, not the Scottish one, she was afraid may harbor a traitor. But the innkeeper had insisted that she remain abovestairs until they left.

Three days had passed.

Three long, miserable days of nothing but a view of The Wild Boar's stables, hours spent poring over the books, which were completely up to date, and the orders, which Magge came for each night. At least she knew now not to complain about working down in the hall.

Unsolicited flirtation was preferable to boredom.

As she left her room to take inventory at the stables—the men in question had finally left—she heard someone whisper, "Psst, Kathryn."

Groaning, she stopped at the top of the stairs. Should she pretend she hadn't heard Mary's plea?

Too late. She'd been seen.

Mary's head, and only her head, peered at her from behind the closed door of her room. As Magge reminded them frequently, they were fortunate to each have a private space. "If Magge asks for me, tell her I cannot come down."

"If you have a man in there again . . ." She shook her head but couldn't help but smile at the other girl's audacity.

"Please?" Mary blinked, her big brown eyes pleading. "I'll owe you a boon."

"Very well," she said. The quick flash of a smile was the last thing Kathryn saw before Mary closed the door.

If she'd found the women at court bawdier than expected, well, they had nothing on Mary. Her well-meaning friend had hardly believed her when she'd explained she was still a virgin, and Mary was eager to see Kathryn initiated into womanhood. She didn't understand the expectations of Kathryn's past life, and her inability to throw them off.

Not that she would make a good marriage now.

Even if her situation were to reverse dramatically, her reputation was likely ruined beyond repair for the simple fact that she'd been working here these past months. But she cared about neither of those things, really. Staying alive was her primary concern.

Even so . . .

"Have you seen Mary?"

Of course it was the first thing Magge asked her when she passed through the hall.

Busy, though not unmanageably so, the inn not quite at capacity. They could easily get by without her for a time.

"She'll be along. In the meanwhile—"

"In the meanwhile, fetch a pitcher of ale, and make it quick." She nodded to a lone man sitting apart from the others in the corner. His head was down, so Kathryn couldn't see the reason for Magge's urgency. The innkeeper typically wasn't quick about anything unless a royal visitor or important noble was underfoot. There were a few exceptions, this man obviously one of them. Well-dressed but not, by appearance, one of the king's men.

Doing as she was bid, Kathryn filled a pitcher and grabbed a tankard, not seeing one already in front of the guest. Which was when her backside was rudely assaulted.

"Give it here," said the reiver who'd swatted her so openly.

As she'd been taught, Kathryn took his measure. Hardened, strong, and more than a bit intimidating, he was not the sort who'd be put off by a few honeyed words. The only course of action here was to acquiesce, as much as it pained her.

Leaning down to place both the pitcher and tankard on the table, Kathryn gritted her teeth when he reached up to touch her breast, bold as could be. He'd gone too far. Slapping his wrist, she stood, prepared to make a hasty retreat amidst the howls of laughter from his friends.

But she wasn't quick enough.

Kathryn found herself on the man's lap, his padded gambeson the only soft thing about him, as she struggled to free herself.

"Let her go."

She couldn't see where the voice had come from, but something flickered in the reiver's eyes—fear?—and he tossed her to the side and drew a dagger.

"Put 'em away, gentlemen."

Magge.

Kathryn had leapt to her feet, but she still could not see the man who'd saved her. His back was to her, his stance rigid as he faced off with the reiver.

"Robert, you don't want to be messin' with a Waryn. Now sit down, keep your hands off my ladies, and drink your ale."

A Waryn. Was it the earl or the lord of Brockburg?

The fact that the reiver instantly complied was a testament to the innkeeper's reputation.

Magge's attention turned to the newcomer. "Kathryn will be along shortly."

He didn't move, obviously reluctant to walk away from the fight. But Magge shooed him away, and he finally complied.

"Many thanks," he said to Magge. His voice was as deep as his hair was black, curling just slightly at the nape of his neck.

He wore only trews and a tunic, so she couldn't tell his exact status just yet. But a glance over at the empty table confirmed this was the man she'd been bid to serve.

She watched as he walked back to the table and sat. When he did, Kathryn could see his face clearly. This must be the youngest brother. She had heard he was handsome, but that was hardly an adequate description. Striking. Intense. Godlike with a face to make a woman forget herself. But handsome? Nay, he was much more than that.

And from his expression, he saw her clearly too.

CHAPTER 3

*N*eill was surprised to see the serving maid reach across the man who had just assaulted her and snatch the pitcher of ale from his table. He tried not to smile, knowing, as the reiver continued to glare at him, it would only inflame the situation.

He had noticed her the moment she'd stepped into the hall, as if a force beyond his control had pulled his attention to her. Or maybe it was that the other heads had already turned in her direction.

Either way, she was difficult to miss.

Two things had struck him about her at once.

She was beautiful. Brown hair fell down her back in waves, tied away from her face on both sides, giving him a clear view of her determined expression. As if she were preparing for battle, determined to win.

Second, she was no serving maid.

Shoulders back, head held high, this was a highborn woman if ever he'd seen one.

So what was she doing here, getting fondled by fools reliant on Magge's reputation for a conflict-free inn? He may have been a young man the last time he and his brothers had graced her hall, but the innkeeper had changed little. As such, he let the matter go for now. She wouldn't thank him for bringing conflict to this hall—but that didn't mean he couldn't retaliate later.

The reiver would be taught some manners before the night was through.

Though she'd taken back the pitcher of ale, the maid skirted out of view, presumably to fetch him a new tankard. Watching for her old, cream-colored gown to reappear, Neill finally spotted her.

As she approached, he noticed something else about the maid.

Despite the initial spark of interest he'd noticed in her eyes, her expression was now quite neutral. Where had she learned such a skill? Here at the inn? Or from whomever had trained her to walk with such grace?

"Sir," she said, correctly guessing his title, "your ale. And a thank you for your assistance back there."

Her correct speech and courtly accent confirmed his suspicions.

"It was my pleasure to serve you." He paused and watched her carefully. "My lady."

Though her shoulders stiffened, the maid gave no other indication his address disconcerted her in any way.

"Your ale, courtesy of Mistress Magge," she said, placing both pitcher and tankard on the board in front of him. This particular table was set on two empty ale kegs, although sturdy enough to serve its purpose.

Her scent drifted to him as she leaned in close.

Lavender.

Neill breathed in deeply, the fragrance continuing to linger as she stood.

"May I serve you anything—"

"Who are you?"

Bold, perhaps. But Neill had never pretended to be anything but. Besides which, his time at The Wild Boar was limited. His eldest brother, Geoffrey, would be joining him at any moment, and once he did, they would leave at once for Bristol Manor to meet up with their other brother, Bryce. After visiting with his new nephew, all three intended to make their way to Brockburg Castle in Scotland to take part in a council there. Typically reserved for Scots border lords, their presence would be welcome as Neill planned to relay his king's message.

This was, of course, if all went according to plan. Geoffrey's wife Sara was due to give birth soon, which could alter his brother's intention.

"I am—" she frowned, the tiniest of lines appearing on the edges of her very full lips, "—Kathryn."

She'd deliberately misunderstood. Interesting.

"Kathryn," Magge crooned from the other side of the room.

"I must go."

And so she did.

Kathryn.

He turned the name over and over in his head, though he knew very well that he should not do so. He definitely should not watch her move from table to table, effortlessly avoiding overzealous patrons as she served them food and drink. Despite himself, he was impressed by the ease with which she handled herself. Fascinated by her self-assurance. He passed the time trying to imagine why Lady Kathryn passed herself off as simply "Kathryn."

It was only when the reiver stood to leave that Neill did the same, following the man wordlessly into the night. Three companions accompanied the man, but Neill was not put off— he simply waited for his moment. He needed to catch all four of them unaware if he had any hope of coming away from this with his body parts intact.

They entered the stables, and Neill, knowing the quarters

were too close inside for him to make a move, waited near the entrance. The mostly pleasant smells of the hall, lamb pie and ale, were replaced with the stench of hay and manure. Two men stumbled from the entrance of the inn, looked his way, and then quickly moved off when his hand drifted to the hilt of his sword.

A whiff of lavender preceded the sound of soft footfalls. How had she come from the inn without his notice?

"I suspected as much," she said as Neill turned and stared straight into a pair of clear green eyes. Though the only light beamed down from the moon, it shone uncommonly bright this eve.

"Please let the matter rest." She glanced nervously toward the stables. "'Tis not good for business. Magge will be upset and—"

He nodded, placing his finger to his lips.

Knowing she must have left the inn through a back door, he circled the stables and headed back toward the larger building. He spotted the back door then and walked toward it.

"Stay here," he instructed, fully intending to ignore her request.

"Please." She grabbed his hand as he turned back toward the stable. The shock of such a bold gesture wore off quickly when he realized they were still connected, her small fingers wrapped around his much larger ones.

Fighting the temptation to hold on, Neill allowed her hand to drop. The loss of her touch made him regret his foolishness.

What would she have done if he had attempted to do so just a bit longer?

"I cannot allow him to leave—" he began. But even as he said it, Neill watched as the men exited the stables with their hobblers—another indication they were, indeed, reivers—and mounted the small horses.

"Please, sir, I implore you—"

He spun on her so fast, Neill worried he may have startled her. But she must have known his intentions were honorable, for she stood tall and did not flinch.

"Tell me who you are, and I'll not pursue them."

This time, there was no mistaking the flash of panic in her eyes before her calm composure was restored.

Looking over his shoulder, clearly stalling for time, she cleared her throat.

Allowing her to believe she'd bested him, Neill crossed his arms and waited. He hated to allow the reivers to escape without more than Magge's scolding, but it would be worth it to speak with her. Although he knew better than to expect he'd get the truth from her, he was nonetheless anxious to hear what she'd say.

"My name is Kathryn Baird, the daughter of Richard Baird of Bondgate-in-Darlington."

His lady, though spirited and uncommonly fair, was a liar.

"Hmmm. And that is all you'll give me, I suppose?"

"What else do you want?"

Realizing what she'd said, Kathryn looked at him with wide eyes, and even though Neill considered himself a gentleman, he purposely goaded her.

"Shall I answer that honestly?"

Her mouth parted, those full lips tempting enough for his mind to consider the possibilities. And then she promptly closed it.

"Since you are very much a lady," he said, hurrying to finish before she could argue that point, "I'll not do so. Instead, I'll ask only for your true identity." He frowned. "It intrigues me to learn why a highborn lady such as yourself is serving men like the one who just left here with his person fully intact."

She intrigued him too, although he'd do better not to think it, let alone say it. He was, after all, no longer free to pursue relations with the fairer sex.

Pity.

"It intrigues me," she finally shot back, "to know if you are who I suspect."

This would be interesting.

"And who do you suspect me to be, my lady?"

He was sorry his use of her title annoyed her, but getting a rise out of Lady Kathryn was proving too much fun for him to desist.

"Magge called you Waryn—"

"And indeed, she hit her mark."

"I've seen both of your brothers at the inn, and know you are neither the husband of the beloved Countess of Kenshire nor Bryce Waryn, who frequents The Wild Boar quite often on his travels from Brockburg to Kenshire Castle."

Neill waited, leaning against the wall of the inn, wondering if she was being missed inside. Magge seemed to rely heavily on the young woman who was as much from Bondgate-in-Darlington as he hailed from France.

"Which means you are the youngest of your family. The great Neill Waryn who has supposedly been crowned champion of more tournaments than any other before you. The black-haired 'beast of the list' whose jousting lance has never been broken."

Though it was true, the nickname was not one he relished, simply because Cora abhorred it. He also would not self-identify as "great" for his performance in the tournaments. He'd only participated in so many of them because the real test of a man's mettle, the battles for which the tourneys were meant to prepare the king's men, were so few. Adam had begged him not to take up the Crusades as his cause, reminding him that his true purpose was to rejoin his family in the north and help keep peace along the mercurial border. Though relative peace had reigned in recent years, Lord Caxton, an English warden, abused his post, taking bribes for allowing men to go free.

Because of it, the Scots refused to attend the monthly Day of Truce, where criminals from both sides were brought to justice. Without it, chaos now reigned once again.

He'd only participated in two actual battles, hardly making him one of the greatest knights in Christendom as some would claim.

"I am Neill Waryn," he said instead, bowing. "At your service. Though my elder brother, with whom you are apparently acquainted, should be along any moment. We're headed north—"

"This eve?"

Neill couldn't tell if her tone was hopeful or just the opposite.

"Aye, though the hour is late, we've a council to attend."

Kathryn smiled for the first time that night, though it faltered for a moment, and damned if Neill's knees did not buckle just a bit.

"You are as I suspected." She curtsied as prettily as if he were the king. "My thanks again for your assistance earlier, Sir Neill."

With that, she fled through the back door and into the inn.

She'd flitted in and out of his life like a beautiful butterfly, alluringly elusive, never to be seen again.

A good thing, for she was a woman for whom a king would give up his kingdom.

CHAPTER 4

"Come in."

Picking her head up from the parchment, the letter she'd taken from her father's belongings, Kathryn sat back in her seat when she heard a knock at the door. She'd read it so many times, looking for clues, that she knew it likely would not help her anyway.

Mary had taken longer than usual to apologize.

"I'm beggin' your forgiveness—"

"For abandoning me in the hall or forcing me to lie to Magge?"

"Both," Mary said, looking anything but sorry. Smiling so broadly it looked as if her cheeks may crack at any moment, she sat down on Kathryn's modest bed.

"Maybe someday I'll be lyin' for you."

She could feel the heat in her cheeks. Kathryn had spent a sleepless, torturous night thinking not of the violence and terror that had driven her to the inn but of Sir Neill Waryn.

Every time she closed her eyes, she saw him leaning against the inn, arms crossed, lips curled up ever so slightly. What was the matter with her? Plenty of men as handsome as Neill Waryn had wandered into The Wild Boar.

Well, maybe not quite that handsome.

Still, there had been other guests she'd admired. Some she'd even imagined kissing.

The men at court were not shy with their attentions, and Kathryn had in fact been kissed before. Both times, however, she'd felt only mild curiosity and very little in the way of excitement. Neither kiss had been her idea, although she'd been curious enough to play along. The first time, because she'd never been kissed before. The second, to know if the first was typical or not.

But neither time had she lain awake in bed imagining scenario after scenario in which the man swept her into his arms and—

"About time."

Mary forced her attention back to the present.

"Pardon?"

"Who is he?"

So much for being coy. Although Kathryn had known from the start she was no card player. Magge had told her as much when they'd first attempted to conceal her speech, attempting to turn her into a simple country maiden and disguise the fact that Kathryn was, in fact, the daughter of one of the most favored men in the English court.

Magge had eventually told her to give up the ruse, do her best not to attract attention, and if asked, simply refuse to divulge her background. Sure, plenty had wondered, but few dared to outright ask as Neill Waryn had. Most wanted something more from her, and when they realized they would not get it, they lost interest in the serving maid, highborn lady or not.

But not him.

"Never mind." Mary stood. "I already know."

As her friend turned to leave, Kathryn practically shrieked, "Wait!"

"Yes?" the younger woman said, her eyes sparkling.

Oh. She'd been goading her.

Kathryn glared at Mary. "How do you know?"

"You think a man like him don't attract attention?"

"But you weren't in the hall last eve . . ."

"He's breakin' his fast even now."

Kathryn's heart pounded faster in her chest. He hadn't left yet? She'd told herself he was long gone, that she'd never see him again. She paused, trying to regain control over herself, then said, "He said he was waiting for his brother and that they were leaving immediately."

Mary shrugged. "I must be wrong then."

Clearly, she didn't believe so.

"Is he an Englishman?"

"Aye. A knight by the looks of him."

"Black hair?"

"Aye."

"Blue eyes?"

"Didn't see them."

"Is he—"

"Handsome as the devil?"

Kathryn nodded before she realized she'd been utterly and completely trapped.

"Ha! Come down an' see for yerself." Mary threw her a saucy wink and flounced out of the room, shutting the door behind her.

Though she wanted nothing more than to follow her, Kathryn didn't move. The man was too perceptive, by far. As much as the famed knight intrigued her, nothing was more important than remaining unseen. Unnoticed.

Unidentified.

Instead, she remained where she was, staring at the blank

parchment on her desk. Still, there was no denying the thought of him being just belowstairs made her restless. Standing, Kathryn moved to the window and opened the wooden shutters. Nothing to see except for the very same stables where he'd found her the night before.

After a few moments, Kathryn actually realized she was waiting for him to appear down below. If indeed it *was* the famed tourney knight. But if so, why was he still here?

Another knock.

Despite what Mary had said, Kathryn would not go—

"Magge!"

The innkeeper opened the door and stood in the opening, staring at her.

"Is something amiss?"

Magge looked as if she were about to cry. And Magge never, ever, ever cried. Railed against cheaters, swatted men twice her size for their boldness, yelled out orders with as much confidence as the king.

But cry?

Nay.

"This is your chance." The innkeeper pushed into her room and shut the door behind her.

"What do you mean?" Kathryn asked, disconcerted and out of sorts.

"I overheard young Waryn . . ."

Her heart leapt. So he *was* still here. The man she'd dreamed about last night was right below her.

"I hear he's headed to Brockburg Castle, in Scotland." Magge planted her hands firmly on her large hips. "And you're going with him."

Going with him? Had Magge bumped her head?

"Pardon?"

"There's to be a council meeting. All of the Scottish wardens will be present, along with one of the English wardens and some of the more important border lords from both sides."

"Magge, I fail to see—"

"The Earl of Bothwell will be there."

She immediately understood. This time, her heart lurched for a very different reason. This was the chance she'd hoped for. She needed access to Bothwell, the last man who'd seen her father alive.

"I do worry if you leave you may never return."

Kathryn grabbed the older woman's hands, knowing Magge was right. She had to take this chance. "I will come back."

The older woman did not look convinced.

"But you are right. I have to go. It may be my best chance to get to Bothwell."

"Sir Neill cannot know your purpose."

"Of course not."

"Ye better think of a good reason to accompany him, and quickly. I overheard 'im talkin' to one of his men. They'll be leavin' as soon as his brother arrives. From the sound of it, he'll be here any moment."

Kathryn began to pace the room, frantic for a viable explanation for why this man who did not know her should take her on such a journey.

"He'll never do it. I've no chaperone, no reason why he should—"

Magge cleared her throat. Her expression left no doubt as to what she was thinking.

"Oh no. No, no, no . . . Magge, how could you even suggest it?"

"He's as fine a man as any. Nay, more so."

"Are you suggesting I . . ." She could not even say the words. Every part of her rebelled at the idea. "He'll not take me if I *flirt* with him."

"Gah! Flirt? Give yourself to 'im, more like."

"Magge! I will not."

She was not a good mentor in many ways. To think this was the woman her father had told her to seek out should anything happen to him. If he were here now, certainly he'd have second thoughts.

Shrugging, unapologetic, Magge walked toward the door. "Then stay. I'll not argue against keepin' the best helper ever to grace The Wild Boar. 'Tis you who have lamented these past months, saying how much you long to learn the truth. Well, if yer hopin' it walks through the doors of the finest establishment, I fear you'll die as ignorant as ye are now. If you can live with that—"

"There must be another way to convince him. I can tell him . . ."

What? What could she tell him? Not the truth. She knew too little of the man to guess where his loyalties lay—and to lose such a wager would be costly indeed. She could simply ask him to bring her to the council meeting? Nay. He would most certainly demand an explanation.

One she did not have to give.

"Yer the prettiest maid I ever seen, the most well-read too. And yer body . . ." She shrugged again. "I don't doubt ye can convince him without offering him what every man wants, but time is wasting."

Kathryn could not believe she was considering this.

Bothwell will be there.

"You forget, I was raised in the English court, lady to Queen Eleanor herself."

"I never forgot it, my lady. Ne'er for a moment."

It was the first time Magge had used her title.

She had to go with him. Whatever it took. If she could get him to accept another explanation, she would, but either way, she was leaving here with him.

"I may be ill," she said. And meant it.

"You might think to wait until after you convince Sir Neill to take you with 'im to do that."

And then, with no warning, the woman who had, quite literally, saved her life, wrapped her arms around her.

"I'll miss you, my lady," she said, using her title again. For some reason, though she'd been addressed as such her whole life, it felt odd coming from the innkeeper. Too formal.

"I *will* be back."

"Nay," she said. "I don't believe you will."

Kathryn had no time to ask what she meant, for a disturbing sight caught her attention out of the corner of her eye.

Neill Waryn was entering the stables.

He was leaving.

And she aimed to go with him.

* * *

"Lord."

Neill spun in his saddle, still unaccustomed to the courtesy title. Aylmer, his closest confidant at his surrogate family's home in Langford, had accompanied him north, along with two other men. Both Neill and Aylmer were third sons, something that had strengthened the bond they'd forged under Adam's tutelage. Assuming the king kept his word and replaced Lord Caxton, restoring peace at the border, they planned to return south after the council meeting, whence Neill could collect his bride and return to Kenshire with her.

Geoffrey and his wife, Sara, had invited Neill to Kenshire many times. Their castle rivaled in strength and size any other fortress in England. He looked forward to seeing it again, although he'd not thought to return for an extended stay so soon.

Nor had he expected to take a bride.

Seeing Aylmer nod to something behind him, out of his

31

view, Neill immediately halted his mount. He turned to see what had caught his friend's attention, and the relief he felt surprised him.

Kathryn.

When Neill had received word from a messenger that his brother would not be joining him after all, he and his companions had decided to stay the night. He'd looked for Lady Kathryn in the hall this morn, but to no avail. The innkeeper had acted oddly coy when he'd inquired about her. Still, he'd left soon after sunrise, eager to get to Brockburg.

Although he'd originally intended to make his way to Scotland through Bristol Manor so he could see his young nephew —Bryce's wife, Catrina, had given birth to their first son the year before—he could no longer afford the delay. He needed to make haste to Brockburg so he could arrive in time for the council.

Neill would be offering his account of the king's reward to the border lords there, and since the king had assured him the new warden would be fair, unlike Caxton, he was happy to give it. While he had been playacting battles on the tournament circuit, his brothers had been fighting real battles, ones that would protect their families.

Finally, he'd been able to make a difference.

"Kathryn," he murmured.

A vision in yellow, her hair hanging down her back in a long brown braid, she approached him hesitantly.

"Go," he said to the other men. "I'll be along shortly."

She looked . . . different somehow. Less guarded.

"Good morn, my lady."

"I am no lady," she said, anticipating his greeting.

"If you insist." Neill dismounted to speak to the maid properly. "You are well? No further incidents?"

"In fact . . ." She looked down to the ground, which was when he noticed the satchel at her side. "Earlier, in the stables . . ."

She didn't finish. "Was it the same man?"

"Nay," she said. "But 'tis a daily occurrence, and I can no longer stay here."

So she was leaving The Wild Boar. "Where will you go?"

She looked at him and blinked. Which was when Neill suddenly realized her intent. He shook his head regretfully.

"I cannot take you with us."

"I beg you . . . I am accustomed to travel and will not hinder you in any way. I've saved some coin."

"I am not traveling toward Bondgate-in-Darlington."

"My destination is north. Dunbar, perhaps."

Dunbar was just north of Brockburg. Even still. And yet . . . Neill stopped to consider his next words. Although he doubted she could keep the pace they had intended to set, they could afford a short delay. One or two days at most. And he'd never before refused a lady in need. After what he'd witnessed the night before, he thought it best for her to leave the inn. "Who would serve as your escort?"

"My escort?"

He knew her answer before she gave it. No one would accompany her, which meant she cared little for her reputation. Perhaps she was not so gently bred as he'd thought.

"I have none," she confirmed.

"Your mount?"

She stared blankly at him.

No escort. No mount.

"Dunbar." He sighed. "The border is no place for a lady."

"The Wild Boar is no place for a lady. Though I am but a simple serving maid."

Unlikely.

"The Wild Boar has been fortunate to avoid the turmoil happening all around, yet I cannot stay here."

After what he'd witnessed, Neill could not blame her. But neither, under the circumstances, could he take her with him.

"I plan to attend a council in Brockburg and will be heading straight there, staying on the open road."

"I've traveled as such many times before."

"The pace will be brutal."

"I will not slow you down."

"You have no mount."

"Perhaps I can share yours?"

She asked much of him. Too much.

"I'm sorry." And he truly was. Something about the maid pulled at him. Nevertheless, the council was too important for him to risk that she could not travel as well as she claimed. "Good day, my lady." Using the title he knew to be hers, Neill nodded in parting, wishing he could be of service.

He should not have looked back. Had he not done so, he would have missed her crestfallen expression, her appearance of defeat. That one look sealed his fate. And perhaps hers too.

Neill held out his hand, cursing himself for a fool.

The lady intrigued him and was much too beautiful for the close proximity they would be sharing. He was all but promised to another lady. And yet, he could not deny that he'd spent the night thinking of this woman, who did indeed mount behind him as if she'd done it many times before.

Kathryn Baird had at least been honest about her ability to ride. Only someone who had been raised around horses could maneuver one so well.

So many mysteries surrounding this woman, but it was not his place to learn them. She'd asked for an escort to Dunbar, and he would take her there, but he would not involve himself in any further intrigue.

He had a job to do and could not be distracted.

CHAPTER 5

"*L*ord?"

Neill watched as Kathryn bent down to the river, the hem of her gown no doubt wet by now. He'd warned her not to get too close.

"Lord."

He spun about, not having heard Aylmer approach.

"I've been shouting for you."

"And I've asked you to use my given name."

Although he and Aylmer had been fostered together, his friend had resorted to using his honorary title from the moment they'd left Langford. His brother, now Earl of Kenshire, was a lord in truth. Bryce had inherited Bristol Manor and the feudal title that came with it. But as a third son, Neill was no lord. He had no property of his own, no title to speak of save the one Aylmer insisted on using.

"You are more lord than most."

"Use Neill, if it pleases you." He watched Kathryn out of the corner of his eye.

"In public spaces, it does not."

Neill rolled his eyes, grateful for his friend's loyalty and the service he'd pledged, even if he considered it misplaced.

"The men are ready to leave."

"I know we planned to stay on the road, but with Lady Kathryn"—he ignored Aylmer's grimace—"I wonder if it would be possible to make it to the Anvil Inn instead?"

"That will take at least a full day from our travels."

He knew as much, and it had pained him to make the suggestion, but she would need a proper rest. They could afford a one-day delay.

"If I might ask." Aylmer looked toward the vision that was Kathryn. He hadn't offered the men an explanation for her presence and had merely told them that she would be coming with them. But after nearly a full day of riding, he expected the respite had come to an end. They deserved to know what he'd agreed to.

"She needed an escort."

Neill looked down to meet his friend's eyes. Aylmer was a short man, although any fool who'd underestimate him would soon learn that what he lacked in height, he made up for in ferocity.

"I have a favor to ask," he said as Kathryn walked toward them, reminding him of the uncomfortable journey so far. The maid was much too lovely for him to ignore the proximity of her supple body when they rode together. The contact was unintentional, of course, and every time she found herself too close, the lady moved away from him. As far as possible given the circumstances.

Which was not far at all.

Her arms had also been permanently wrapped around his waist. A difficult fact to ignore.

"Once we arrive at Brockburg, I'll ask for you to continue to Dunbar with the maid. 'Tis her final destination."

"Dunbar?"

"Aye, sir," Kathryn said, joining them. "I've heard the market in the small town has escaped the border troubles."

"None have escaped them completely," Aylmer replied, looking at Kathryn as if she might lunge at him with a knife at any moment.

Neill laughed at his friend's expression. He was normally quite affable with women.

In turn, Aylmer shot him an odd look.

"If we plan to stop at the Anvil Inn," Neill said, "we should leave now."

Aylmer looked anything but pleased about the prospect, a fact poor Kathryn seemed to notice.

"Please do not do so for my sake. As I said, I am accustomed to being on the road."

She seemed to mean it, but why would a lady such as herself be accustomed to such a journey?

He would not ask. But Neill could tell Aylmer was just as curious. Instead, he nodded to his friend to ready the others.

"We considered it before you chose to join us," he lied, knowing she would not relent otherwise. Neill did not want her to feel badly about the decision. "And we have some time before the council," he said, holding out his hand. That, at least, was true.

She took it and allowed him to help her mount the jet-black destrier that had been a gift from Adam to celebrate his elevation to knighthood.

Pulling himself up in front of her, Neill settled in and tried his best to ignore his body's reaction to Kathryn's arms around him. Just like he had ignored the feel of her soft hand in his as she mounted.

They'd spoken little, Neill afraid to care about her situation more than he did already, but his curiosity was too great to be ignored. As they traversed the open moorland that was northern England, the hot summer's day giving way to a typically cooler evening, he allowed himself one question.

"How did you come to work at The Wild Boar?"

He hadn't expected her to be truthful, or to say anything at all, but as his horse moved to his accustomed position at the front of the men, she answered him.

"My mother died in childbirth. My father . . . died suddenly. With no other family, I had no choice but to find my way there."

"So far from your home?"

Most people Neill had met on his travels did not venture far from where they were born. He and his sister and brothers were an exception, although they hadn't left Bristol Manor willingly. They'd been driven out by a family of Scots—the Kerrs. It felt like one of life's greatest ironies that the Kerrs were now tied to them by marriage, the greatest of alliances. "And you said you were accustomed to the open road?"

Another question. Damn if he hadn't promised himself just one.

"Aye. Magge was very accommodating."

Despite himself, Neill turned in the saddle just enough to see her profile. Kathryn raised her chin ever so slightly, and he could not help but smile.

She was not easily intimidated, his lady.

He turned back toward the road. They'd be forced to stop before long, and Neill wished to make good time.

Another question was on his lips, damn his curious soul, when he heard the distinct sound of riders approaching from around the bend in front of them. When they did finally appear, the strangers were immediately flanked by his own men, who knew without being told that Kathryn should be protected.

The men with him were knights, like himself, sworn to a conduct of honor Adam had insisted was more than a string of words. For him, and for Neill and the other men, gallantry was a way of life.

"Reivers," he muttered.

"Take the reins," he said to Kathryn as he dismounted. He'd not have done so if he'd been alone.

But he was not, and so a change of strategy was needed.

Looking back at her to offer a reassuring smile, Neill was surprised at her expression.

The lady had no fear.

———

KATHRYN REALIZED her mistake too late.

She supposed it would have been appropriate to show fear, but she and her father had met plenty of reivers on their travels. Three mounted men had come upon them, aye, and from the small hobblers they rode and their distinctive style of armor, she knew them for reivers. But she traveled with four seasoned knights—odds that seemed much better than the ones she and her father had faced, even if her father had worn the seal of the king. Sometimes a knight or two had accompanied them in their travels, but more often than not they had traveled alone, as was customary for a royal messenger.

Too late. Sir Neill was already walking away from her. The reivers' leader had also dismounted, apparently not at ease with Neill making his way toward them so brazenly. As if he could not be run down at will.

Brave? Or foolish?

Her father had often told her the two were indistinguishable. Although she hadn't known Neill long, she did know him and his brothers by reputation. The Waryns were brave—brazenly so—and the youngest brother was the most daring of all.

When one of the reivers skirted forward, so did the man Neill had called Aylmer.

They were preparing to fight.

She'd known this trip would be dangerous—journeys along

the border were notoriously difficult. But since the Day of Truce had fallen apart, tales of increasingly violent acts had reached the inn. Even Magge had begun to worry. "An' I've lived through the worst of these parts, mind you," she had said many times.

Kathryn kept careful watch on Neill's hands, as well as those of the reivers' leader. None seemed inclined to raise a sword. Yet. That was good. Her father, who'd trained with the king's own men, had always told her to run if he reached for the sword at his side. She'd only needed to follow that precaution twice. The first time she'd returned to see the slain body of her father's adversary—her first time witnessing death. The second time was the only occasion upon which Kathryn had truly feared for her life, with the exception of their final, fateful visit to the Scottish court.

Two men had come upon them that day, not reivers but warriors both, and so she'd obeyed her father's caution to run. The dagger skills she possessed would do her little good against a sword. After a time, the sound of swordplay faded and Kathryn returned to the road. Thankfully, her father's injuries had not been fatal, though the other two men had not fared so well. Her papa's leg had been broken, however, though with her help he'd made it to the closest inn.

The incident had shaken her father enough that he'd sat her down and explained what she should do if he were killed. She'd hated to entertain the possibility, but he had insisted. Kathryn knew where to go at each new place they traveled. But she'd not listened. Instead, she made her way to The Wild Boar, waiting for an opportunity to get back to Scotland. To learn the truth.

After that fateful day . . .

It appeared there would be no quarrel today, however. Neill's show of strength had been enough to intimidate the men, and he was making his way back to her even now. He mounted in front of her once again, and they watched as the reivers passed. She let out a breath the moment the rough men disappeared from sight.

Once again, they were on their way, as if nothing had happened.

Holding on to Neill's tunic, his armor hung at the sides of a packhorse nearby, she swallowed hard. He was exactly as his reputation suggested. "The greatest knight" some called him. And though she'd not seen him fight, Kathryn suspected the reivers would not have fared well in a quarrel with Neill Waryn.

She knew she would not fare well either, should he continue asking her questions. The intensity of the man demanded the truth. Thus far, she'd navigated his questions easily enough, remaining, as her father had instructed, as close to the truth as possible.

He turned to look at her, his profile accenting a strong jaw and high cheekbones that no doubt sent the ladies at court aflutter. Having spent time at the court herself, she could well imagine how he was received there. Especially as the champion of the great King's Tournament, a title she knew he'd once claimed.

"Scottish reivers," he said, although she'd not asked for an explanation. "On the move earlier than normal."

Kathryn knew from her time at the inn that reivers typically traveled at night.

"Have you seen many of them, then?" she asked, curious.

He twisted toward her then, giving her a full view of his handsome face.

Aye, the ladies she knew would all have vied for this man, she was sure of it. She took some pleasure in the knowledge that, for the briefest of moments, he was hers.

"Aye. Though it's been some years since I've been home, I grew up in the borderlands."

She knew his story, in broad strokes. He'd lost his parents to violence too—a not uncommon story for those who lived along the border. His eldest brother later married Lady Sara of Kenshire. His other brother, Bryce, had reclaimed their ancestral home from Clan Kerr, although he'd gone on to marry the chief's sister. But she'd not ask him to speak of that.

After holding her gaze for a moment longer, Neill finally turned back around. Kathryn loosened her grip around him, realizing belatedly she'd tightened it as he spoke.

"I've not met your brothers, but I did see them pass through the inn. Magge spoke highly of them."

Even though she could only see the side of his face, Kathryn saw enough to know his smile transformed his face. It was hardly fair for a man to be so handsome.

"I've a sister too. Emma."

Kathryn knew all about her. Everyone along the border did. She had married the Earl of Clave, a powerful man on both sides of the border.

"All along the border know your family's story," she acknowledged.

"I suppose they would. 'Tis quite a tale, enemies becoming family."

Kathryn had never really thought of it that way before. There was a certain beauty to the statement.

"So you truly hold no grudge against Clan Kerr?" Then, realizing the question was rude, especially since she did not intend to share her history with him, she said, "I'm sorry. I did not mean to overstep."

"And you did not."

He stopped then, the men riding up behind them. "We will stop here?" he called back to the others.

The man called Aylmer, who was clearly wary of her, nodded. "Aye, my lord."

Neill stiffened. She'd not have noticed if her arms were not still wrapped around his waist. She remedied that now that they were stopped.

"I will answer your question tonight." He dismounted and held a hand up to her. "Provided you answer one of mine as well."

Before she could refuse, he grinned, and Kathryn nearly fell from the massively large destrier. The smile he'd given before had moved her, but this smile . . . She was pretty sure no woman had ever refused him in the face of such a grin.

And Lord save her, she probably would not be the first.

CHAPTER 6

𝒦athryn slowed her breathing, something she'd learned to do whenever this familiar feeling assaulted her. The attacks of breathlessness had started not long after her father was murdered. One had assailed her the very day she'd arrived at The Wild Boar. Kathryn had stood in the hall of the inn, not moving, unable to answer Magge's questions. When it happened, it was as if a pair of invisible hands held her pinned to the spot.

In those moments, she could not breathe. Or, more accurately, she could not catch her breath. Try as she might, she could not slow her heart to a normal pace either. But now, after so many months, she had learned to sense the attacks before they came.

Although she'd feared Neill would prevail upon her to talk the previous evening, he was not the one who had thrown her into a panic this eve. Indeed, she had not suffered an attack since meeting him. His presence calmed her, which seemed ridiculous given the way her pulse skipped whenever he was near.

His promise to question her last eve had fallen by the wayside. Just as they'd settled in around the fire for a meal of roasted rabbit, one of his men had called for him. She'd eaten quickly, watching as the two spoke from across their makeshift camp, and then retired to the bedroll he'd laid out for her.

It wasn't difficult to fall asleep, despite the hard ground beneath her. Kathryn had not exaggerated about her experience with traveling, although it had been some months since she'd spent this much time on the back of a horse.

She'd awoken with the sunrise, surprised the others were nearly ready to leave. Kathryn had assumed she'd be riding with Neill again, but the packhorse had been saddled, the equipment disbursed to the other men, who did not seem well pleased by the prospect. Though Neill had been polite all day, he had not spoken to her beyond "Good day" and a few words when they stopped to rest the horses.

Nay, her panic was not for him. If anything, she'd been . . . disappointed. Part of her had looked forward to his questions.

They'd stopped for the night, this time at the Anvil Inn, which Kathryn had only visited once before. She and her father had stopped here a year earlier, the night after he'd delivered a message to James Douglas, Lord Warden of the Marches, one of the most feared men in all of Scotland.

Douglas!

How had she not considered him before? Of course he would be at this council meeting, and he *knew* her. Although she'd never actually met the other wardens, even at the Scottish royal court, she had dined with Douglas, who would most certainly recognize her.

That thought was what had at last driven her into a panic.

"My lady?"

Neill walked toward her as the other men left their horses and made their way toward the inn. Those two words were

45

more than he'd spoken to her over the last day. Why couldn't he leave her alone now if he'd decided to keep his distance?

Deep breaths.

"Something is wrong—"

"Nay, all is well," she lied. "Shall we go inside? And it is Kathryn, if you please."

Though she was very much a lady, her mother the only daughter of a minor baron whose lands had been forfeit to the crown upon her parents' death, she didn't wish to call any attention to that fact.

She attempted to walk past him, but he stopped her.

Night had fallen, the only light coming from two open shutters at the front of the inn and the moon above them.

"Tell me," he said, so gently it should have comforted her. But his kindness had the opposite effect.

This attack would not be held off. Like it or not, it was happening.

She allowed him to guide her around to the side of the building, a similar one to The Wild Boar, just two structures, the inn and stables directly next to it. They stood on the far side of both, the area silent but for the sound of her gasping for air and the trickling of a stream not far into the trees beyond them.

The inn was surrounded by thick forest, hidden from view of the road, odd for an establishment that relied on the business of travelers.

As she struggled for breath, Neill watched her with a pity that was worse than anything.

"I will be fine," she said as soon as she could manage it. When it finally felt she could breathe without her chest feeling as if it would explode, Kathryn tried to get him into the inn.

"Your men are waiting."

He took her hand, reminding her of their encounter outside The Wild Boar.

"Let them wait."

He let go of her hand but continued to look at her with a combination of concern and sympathy. This would not do.

"It happens from time to time. Please, there's no cause for concern."

He didn't believe her.

"Whether or not there is a cause matters little. I am concerned. You were unable to breathe."

"And am now breathing quite well."

The arrival of a small riding party caught their attention, and Kathryn thought to use it as a distraction. She once again walked toward the entrance to the inn.

Neill had other plans. "Wait. Has this happened before?"

She shrugged, frowning, but she didn't wish to lie to him. Not about this. "It has."

Why did he appear so concerned now, when he'd taken pains to avoid her for the past day? She'd not intended to mention it, but . . .

"You ensured I had my own mount today."

It came out like an accusation, which was absurd. Surely she should be thanking him for his pains. She turned away. "I should not have mentioned it."

He grabbed her hand again, pulling her back. It didn't take much convincing. Kathryn hadn't wanted to leave him.

"Not for the reason you think."

This time, he did not let go, his warm, callused hand engulfing hers. Those calluses had been born of hard work.

"How can you possibly know what I'm thinking?"

"Because . . ." She sucked in a breath as he stepped closer. To anyone walking by, they would appear to be talking casually, side by side, but Kathryn knew otherwise. His hand, though concealed from view, hadn't moved.

"I know the assumption I would make, if I were you. But you're wrong."

Her first assumption was that he'd wanted to distance himself from her. Could she have been wrong?

"Have I offended you? When I asked about Clan Kerr?"

It was the only other possible explanation that had come to mind during the long ride that day. But Neill shook his head vigorously.

"No. God no, I don't offend easily."

He smiled again, that devastating smile that made her forget he was reputed to be one of the most fearsome knights in all of England.

"I can only offer the truth," he said, his thumb rubbing her palm. Did he even realize what he was doing?

"I am much too curious about you," he continued.

Oh my.

"I want to know how you really came to be at The Wild Boar. I want to know if you truly are as well-bred as I believe you to be. And if so, how a lady such as yourself came to be at The Wild Boar with Magge as a mentor. I want to know why you're able to ride for two days straight as skillfully as one of my men, all of whom were trained to do so. And why you weren't afraid when we met those reivers."

This time, she couldn't breathe for very different reasons. As he spoke, the low pitch of his voice cut through her like a knife through Magge's freshly baked bread.

"You could have asked," she said quietly, fully aware she'd not have answered. He'd warned her he would ask, hadn't he?

"And be pulled toward you more than I am already?"

So he felt it too.

"I . . . I don't know what to say."

As if he had just now realized what he was doing, Neill dropped her hand for the second time.

She felt the loss immediately.

He stood there, the sound of his breathing capturing her

attention more than the distant sounds coming from inside the inn.

"To answer your question about the Kerrs, I hate them . . . and love them too," he said finally. "Toren. Alex. Reid. Catrina. They are family now, and I love nothing in this life more than my family. But I hated them for so long that it's hard to forget, especially when I allow myself to remember the raid. My parents were both killed that day, and although Toren and Alex did not slay them themselves, Clan Kerr men were responsible. I'm not sure I can ever forget that fact." He took a step back. "But, like my siblings, I have forgiven them. We have moved beyond it."

She'd asked, and he'd answered. Was he waiting for her to do the same?

After what he revealed, the lies Kathryn had been preparing would not form on her lips. Instead, she remained silent.

"Are you hungry?"

She was taken aback by the abrupt change in topic. She'd expected him to press her.

"Aye."

He nodded toward the front of the inn.

"This is the last real meal and bed we'll have until we arrive at Dunbar. Shall we?"

This time it was she who stopped him. It didn't feel right to give him nothing when he'd given her so much. Kathryn could not share her secrets, but she could at least address what he had shared.

"You are a better person than I." She shifted her weight from one foot to the other. "I do not think I could forgive, were I you. But I admire you for it."

That, at least, was true. When she finally learned who killed her father, forgiveness would not be foremost on her mind.

"As I admire you," he said, startling her.

"For?"

"For your strength. I know not what you are about, Kathryn, but I can tell you have undertaken a quest most ladies would not dare consider, one that requires you to leave one dangerous place to seek another. My sister, Emma, and my sister-in-law, Sara, would admire you very much indeed."

To that, Kathryn had no response, so she followed him inside instead.

CHAPTER 7

*N*eill remembered Bo and Berit, the brothers who ran the Anvil Inn, from his youth. The inn was less than a four-day ride from Bristol Manor. The bulky brothers appeared older, understandably, and more hardened. As did all of the borderers in the months after the Day of Truce had fallen apart.

As the men on each side of him filled their stomachs, Neill put thoughts of the past behind him, wondering how Kathryn was faring. He'd attempted to secure a private room for the night, but by the time he got around to asking, his resourceful companion had already made her own arrangements. Bo had informed him, "Your sister-in-law's cousin is already abovestairs, her room paid for."

Catrina's cousin. A likely story for why she was headed to Scotland, and why he might be escorting her. Since they hadn't originally planned on stopping here, Neill had never agreed upon an explanation for their situation. He'd meant to discuss the matter outside, but he'd been distracted. By Kathryn. By the raw fear he'd seen in the unusually resilient lady. By her graceful movements, which seemed so contrary to her simple attire. By the way she held her shoulders high and straight despite the fact that she was at the mercy of men she hardly knew, traveling to a place she'd never been before.

And, if he were honest, by her beauty. Though she wore her hair in a lone, long braid at her back, Neill could not forget the one time he'd seen it loose. Not one color, but with brown and blonde strands woven together as if she'd not been stuck inside an inn all summer working for a woman who terrified knights and reivers alike.

"Caxton is the worst sort of bastard."

The sound of the English warden's name from the table behind them forced Neill back to the present. Immediately, Aylmer caught his eye. They wordlessly conveyed to the others to stop talking so they could listen.

"Aye. Openly taking black mal now that the Day of Truce is no longer."

"Berit," one of the men, a Scot, called to the innkeeper. "Have ye heard about this council? There'll be borderers from both sides there."

"Ah, won't do any good," the innkeeper said, waving him off. "Another pitcher?"

Neill broke the silence at his own table. "Say nothing."

It would serve no purpose for them to bring attention to the fact that they were headed to that very council.

"Piss on your king for keeping Caxton in power."

Though Neill's back was to the men, Aylmer's expression confirmed his suspicion. The insult was directed toward them.

"Say nothing," he said again, looking from one man to the next, his hand held up.

"You've been warned before, MacDuff," Berit said.

Neill moved his hand slowly down. And waited.

"Are you not ashamed to call the man your king?"

Privately, Neill had no love for King Edward, who had taken two years to return home from the Holy Lands after his father's death, leaving his country to regents, but neither could he and his men continue to ignore the treasonous words much longer.

And they all knew it. They were prepared, as he was, for the worst. But it had not yet come to that, and with any luck, it would not. Neill shook his head again, ever so slightly.

"You've had too much ale," Berit said. "Stop inciting trouble or leave."

Bo, even bulkier than his brother, caught Neill's eye as he walked past him to join his brother.

Neill sighed. This was one of the reasons they avoided inns. Unlike The Wild Boar, most inns along the border were not known for being peaceful. He should not have stopped here. But the thought of Kathryn going without a proper bed or meal for four, maybe five nights . . .

The sound of benches scraping the wood floor, rushes so thin they hardly did their duty, meant there'd be no peace this night. Hand gripping his sword, Neill moved just slightly toward the edge of his own bench.

"I'll take that pitcher now," the man called MacDuff growled.

"No."

Neill couldn't tell which of the brothers had denied him, but when the sound of scraping metal reached his ears, he did not hesitate.

This was his homeland, his king, and Bo and Berit needed assistance.

So he gave it.

Neill stood, twisting away from his men, and pulled out his dagger, opting to leave his sword sheathed. The smaller weapon allowed him to escape notice until he stood directly behind the instigator. Arm wrapped around the man's neck, the tip of his dagger pressed to his man's throat, he issued his only warning.

"Do as you've been instructed and leave. Or you will lose men this night."

Both sides stood facing each other now, Bo and Berit in the

middle looking at Neill with a combination of hesitation and gratitude. He couldn't see the eyes of the man he held at knifepoint, so he watched his men instead for an indication of how this might proceed. He could see they were preparing to fight.

"The man with a knife to your throat is the younger brother of Geoffrey and Bryce Waryn," Bo said. "Think carefully on his words."

Not the approach he would have chosen. His success at the tournaments had led to an unfortunate side effect—many men wished to challenge the "great" Neill Waryn. And though he was not as well-known here in the north, the skills he'd learned defending himself had traveled with him.

Neill's victim lifted his head ever so slightly. Neill tightened his grip on the man's arm—watching, waiting. The air crackled with the promise of a brawl. All other activity around them had ceased.

"Waryn," the drunk Scot growled. "You're the reason for the council."

"Aye."

"We are headed there as well."

He loosened his grip ever so slightly. Only border wardens, clan chiefs, and selected elders would attend, along with a few English border lords. If this man was on his way to the council, Neill had no fight with him.

"Ferguson MacDuff, Chief of Clan Kern, ally to deSowlis—"

"DeSowlis," he said, "is an ally to my family."

"Aye, the Kerrs. I know them well."

Neill realized he'd heard of this very man from his brothers. Although not a warden, he was well-respected along the northeastern border. And notorious for his temper.

He lowered his arm, and MacDuff turned to face him.

"You may be the younger brother, but you are no boy."

"And you may be a friend to deSowlis, but you've insulted my king. As well as the owners of this fine establishment."

MacDuff, a robust man whose beard hid most of his face with the exception of his bulbous red nose, laughed. "Not so fine as that."

Neill glared at the insolent chief, his meaning not so subtle.

MacDuff rolled his eyes. "My apologies, sirs," he said to Bo and Berit, "for any insult I've caused."

Even though he'd silently demanded that the man issue an apology, Neill was surprised MacDuff had been agreeable. So too, apparently, were the Scotsmen's fellows, who grumbled their displeasure.

MacDuff merely slapped Neill on the back. "Ale for the Waryn boy and his men," he bellowed to Bo and Berit. "We were just on our way out."

His men did not seem appeased, but they followed their clan chief out willingly enough. What were they doing this far south? He was curious, but the question would have to wait. For now, Neill wanted to ensure the men truly were leaving. The last thing he needed was for one of MacDuff's men to retaliate for his treatment of their chief.

So while his men enjoyed more ale, courtesy of the Scotsmen, Neill found himself standing guard near the front of the inn, watching as MacDuff and the others entered the stable.

And that was when he saw her.

***

KATHRYN COULDN'T SLEEP.

She'd told Neill she wished to go to Dunbar, and now he aimed to bring her there. Soon. That would not do. She had to get him to agree to bring her to the council.

Noise from the inn reached her on the second floor, and rather than attempt to block it out, she did something quite foolish. She broke her self-imposed exile and left her room.

Although she had already damaged her reputation past saving,

Kathryn absolutely did not wish to be accosted by drunk and inappropriate men—which was why she immediately began to rethink her decision as she made haste toward the hall. The stairwell from her room led directly outside, the lock on her door the only impediment to an intruder. Kathryn knew it was a typical arrangement for an inn but was grateful Magge's was not similarly situated.

Hurrying along, eager to reach the relative safety of the hall, Kathryn came to a stop when a group of men walked out of it. Unfortunately, she'd caught their attention.

Kathryn knew their kind well. Far along in their cups. Eager for an argument. Magge always said when the sun went down and the moon rose high in the sky men lost themselves. Kathryn believed it had more to do with the consumption of ale than some ancient legend about men turning into beasts under the influence of the moon, but Magge was more superstitious than most.

"Kathryn?"

The men moved on.

Neill stood in the doorway of the hall. He looked just the same as when they'd parted ways earlier, but for some reason, he appeared foreboding now. As she continued her approach, she knew the reason for it.

He had been responsible for those men leaving.

Kathryn had witnessed more brawls than she'd ever thought possible, even though Magge expressly forbade them, and she'd come to recognize the telltale signs.

The men who'd left the hall were clearly drunk.

Neill clutched a dagger in his hand.

She couldn't help but voice her observation.

"You?" She nodded toward the stables, where the men disappeared.

"Aye."

"Dare I ask what happened?"

"Dare I ask why you're out here, wandering about alone at this time of night?"

He moved them away from the doorway.

"I'm not alone, not any longer."

"It is not safe for you out here."

"And yet, I've never felt safer." As soon as the words were out, Kathryn wished them back. She hadn't meant to say such a thing, even if it were the truth. What would he think of her?

"Why?" he said, holding her gaze, and she knew he wasn't asking her why she felt safe with him. He wanted to understand why she'd gone into hiding, why she'd asked him to help her. "Tell me, Kathryn."

Her answer was immediate. "I cannot."

Even those words were probably a mistake, for Kathryn had effectively admitted to having a secret. Of course, Neill knew that already. He'd known it from the start.

"You cannot?" He cocked his head to the side.

"Nay."

"If you cannot tell me what ails you, then perhaps you can explain why you would see to your own welfare and safety, then come back down here all alone. It makes no sense."

"I am rash," she admitted.

"Pardon?"

"Rash. My father used the word often to describe me. 'Tis the reason I'm down here when I should not be."

That smile. Kathryn was sure she would say, or do, just about anything to see it.

"As am I, at times."

"Is that so?"

"Aye. According to Adam, the man with whom I fostered. And my brothers too." He frowned. "So you will admit coming out here was not the best idea."

"Mayhap, but I'll not say I regret it."

When he turned serious, his smile faltering, Kathryn realized how foolish she'd sounded. "I didn't mean . . ."

Only she had. He was the reason she didn't regret venturing where she should not have gone. She'd wished to speak to him about Brockburg, aye, but that wasn't the only reason she was happy to see him.

His lips parted, just slightly. She couldn't stop staring at them, wondering what they would feel like on hers. What a proper kiss, from him, would feel like.

Something told her such a kiss wouldn't be merely passable.

The men who'd entered the stables rode past them, interrupting the tense moment. One of them inclined his head to Neill before they rode off into the night.

The moment had passed. Thankfully. Kathryn needed to focus on the task at hand. Convincing Neill Waryn to take her to Brockburg.

"What do you regret?"

The question took her aback. She blinked, considering her answer.

"I regret not saying goodbye to my father."

"Was his death unexpected?"

Kathryn should not have told him the truth. But she had, and there was no way to take it back. "Aye."

But she needed to turn the conversation to him.

"I would imagine the great Neill Waryn has no regrets?"

The look he gave her said otherwise. At first, he didn't answer.

"I've spent the past few years fostering with a great man by the name of Sir Adam Dayne. He and his wife, Cora, have taught me many things." He sighed. "Regret, he said, is a thief, and only we can allow him to steal from us."

He shrugged.

"I've never wasted time on the sentiment . . ."

She sensed there was more, but he stopped talking.

"You are fortunate to have been fostered with them, it seems?"

"Aye, fortunate indeed."

They fell silent.

"So what happened?"

Neill slipped his dagger into the leather pouch at his side. "If you'd like, I can tell you inside."

"Will it be difficult to explain why I am unescorted?"

That smile was back, and she felt her heart throb in response. "We shall say your escort was run through by a reiver."

Her eyes widened. "But—"

"I jest," he said, laughing. "If anyone should ask, I will simply run them through myself." With that, Neill turned toward the door, expecting her to follow.

She did laugh then at the pure outrageousness of his suggestion. With any luck, none would inquire after her. Kathryn would not like to be the cause of an argument between Neill and the other guests, and something told her he would not hesitate to defend her honor.

CHAPTER 8

*K*athryn had never gotten around to making her request at the Anvil Inn. Or in the two days since. Perhaps it was simply that she thought he'd deny her. Or maybe, and she feared this was true, she simply enjoyed his company too much to endanger the connection they'd formed.

She was brooding over the matter a couple of evenings later when Neill called out, "Hold."

When Neill stopped, the men did as well, Kathryn's borrowed mount falling in line with the others. After four days, Kathryn had worked out that although Neill was not the group's official leader, the others looked to him for guidance.

And although Kathryn would be hard-pressed to find anything disagreeable about Neill, she had noticed a failing of his—something her father would have cautioned her against. Aylmer disagreed with the spot Neill had picked for their camp, saying it was much too close to the road. But Neill had quickly dismissed the other man's concerns, saying they would be perfectly safe.

Noble? Aye. Handsome? Certainly.

But the gallant Neill Waryn, called the greatest knight in the kingdom of England, was not accustomed to being questioned.

Perhaps stupidly, Kathryn had hoped an act of God would resolve the problem of Dunbar. She'd left the request so long in the hopes there'd be an unexpected delay and they'd have no choice but to put off the trip until after the council meeting. But it hadn't rained even once, despite her vigilant observations of the sky.

One of the men, Burns, had even remarked on it that day, asking how she managed to stay atop her horse as she constantly looked up rather than forward. Laughing at the observation, Kathryn had challenged him to a race, the wide-open field around them perfect for a little competition.

The knight truly hadn't had a chance. She'd almost felt sorry for him, for his loss had given his companions, including Neill, a source of amusement for most of the day.

Which hadn't gotten her any closer to making her request of Neill.

"I'll take him," Burns said as she dismounted her horse.

Kathryn handed the reins to him. "A boon for my win?"

Even Aylmer chuckled at her little jest.

"Aye, my lady," Burns bit back, though he was still smiling.

They'd taken to calling her such at Neill's insistence. At Brockburg, there would be others around, and so she'd be sure to correct them. For now, she was happy for them to make her feel like Kathryn, the young woman who'd been trained by her father and educated by royal tutors, rather than Kathryn the bar wench.

Sighing, she followed the men into the woods, the thicket likely one of the reasons Neill had chosen to stop here. But then she spied the other reason.

"What is that?" she asked him. "It looks like a farmhouse made of stone."

61

"Bryce told me of it, an abandoned bastle house so old none know its name or origin."

Actually, two tall but narrow stone buildings stood side by side in a clearing only large enough for the two structures. What might have once been open field around them was now overgrown with trees and bushes.

"Early reivers built them, likely. Though now they house travelers like us."

"And reivers too?" she asked, raising an eyebrow.

While they spoke, the men walked past them with the horses, which meant a river or stream must be nearby.

"Aye."

He studied her much as he had these past days, as if trying to learn something of her without asking. And there was something else to his expression. A certain interest Kathryn could not afford to explore.

"If you want to wash—"

"I'll follow the men," she finished, suddenly feeling awkward. She didn't look back, though she wanted to see his face. Those serious eyes. That mouth that could transform his face with a simple smile. Instead, Kathryn put the handsome knight out of her mind as she followed the men to the stream. Slow-running with more rocks than water, it would do for her purposes. She bent by the side and started to wash her face.

"Where did you learn to ride like that?" Aylmer asked from over her shoulder.

She'd expected someone to ask and had prepared an answer.

"My father was once a stable master, before he passed." She looked up to the heavens. It had gotten dark so quickly. Standing, Kathryn took the rag she'd brought to dry herself with and wiped her face and hands.

Aylmer merely grunted, but it must have been enough to pacify him since he didn't press her.

"Will Burns hear of this for some time, then?"

She couldn't tell in the waning light of dusk, but Kathryn swore she spied a smile. A small one, aye, but she'd count it as progress. She knew Aylmer had not been pleased to bring her along on their journey.

"A question you could have asked," Burns said, approaching them, "before trouncing me so thoroughly."

The way he grinned at her, teased her, made her feel like one of the men. Even so, she couldn't help but wonder what these men thought of her. Surely they knew how unusual it was for a lady to accompany a group of men on such a journey. She reminded herself that didn't matter.

Like the previous nights, she sat with the men around a fire, listening, not saying much. They talked of being graced with good weather for the journey—though she would disagree—as well as the upcoming council meeting. Kathryn had learned much about what was to come, including Neill's part in the final effort at peace.

It was no small thing to force a king's hand, but apparently that was what he had done by asking for Caxton's removal as his boon. A bold, brave move that seemed so indicative of the man she knew.

It was Lord Caxton's underhanded dealings that had prompted the Scottish wardens and clans from attending the Day of Truce. Because of Neill, the borderlands would see the removal of a warden Kathryn knew most despised, including Magge, except for the small few who benefited from his corruption.

She watched as the fire was doused, a nightly practice, and wondered about their sleeping arrangements. She caught Neill's eye, but he immediately looked away.

"Lady Kathryn will take the southern tower," he announced, "further from the road."

Looking at the two buildings standing nearly side by side, Kathryn shivered. Though she welcomed shelter, the thought of sleeping alone in the abandoned building was not a prospect she anticipated with pleasure.

Taking a deep breath, Kathryn bade the men goodnight and walked toward the abandoned building.

When she entered the open doorway, it took her a moment to acclimate. It was just as she might have expected of a stone farmhouse. One room. More like a stable than anything, with a wooden ladder leading to a loft high above her head.

"We sleep up there."

She spun, startled, only then realizing Neill had followed her.

"We?"

He cocked his head to the side. "Did you believe I'd have you sleep in there alone?"

She had thought that very thing and was relieved to learn it wasn't so.

"Kathryn, have you been so mistreated . . ." He stopped. "Nay, do not answer that."

"Why?"

"'Tis not my concern. But you're under my protection now." He nodded toward the ladder. "I will follow you in a moment."

She blinked, realizing he was giving her time to prepare her pallet. Though they'd slept in close proximity before, it seemed more . . . intimate without the presence of his companions. But she supposed it did make sense. If they were attacked . . .

"Your companions do not mind the prospect of being attacked first?" she blurted, stepping off the ladder.

The wooden floor creaked beneath her feet.

Kathryn dropped her belongings and laid out the bedroll, wishing she had straw or grass to stuff it with. They may be sleeping indoors, but the hard floor would be no more forgiving than the dirt mattress on which they'd been sleeping.

"Nay," he called up, laughter in his voice. "They rather enjoy it."

Well, it had been a silly question deserving of a silly answer. She had just enough time to remove her tunic, kirtle, and boots before the sound of the creaking ladder reached her ears.

She quickly scrambled atop her bedroll and pulled the thin blanket to her shoulders. Though her shift still covered her arms, Kathryn felt bare, as if she wore nothing at all. Especially under his gaze.

When Neill carried his belongings toward her, laying his own bedroll down not far from hers, Kathryn turned and curled to the side . . . as if she could ever possibly fall asleep. She listened to the sound of his sword hitting the floor, the straps of his leather boots being undone.

"I can move further away," he said, as if sensing her uncertainty.

"No, 'tis fine." She did not have to turn to look to know where he was lying now. She could sense his warmth, his presence.

"I didn't wish to be too close to the ladder."

She shifted carefully toward him, the blanket still to her chin.

He was exactly where she'd sensed him to be, positioned directly between her and the entry point for any possible attack.

"I suppose you've learned to consider strategy?"

Despite herself, she found her eyes lowering to take him in. His loose shirt covered a pair of linen braies, neither covered by a blanket. The opening of his shirt exposed just enough for Kathryn to see a glimpse of his bare chest under it.

"I have."

"No blanket?" she blurted.

"None."

Neill turned onto his side, facing her, and propped his head in his hands.

"You're preserving enough modesty for both of us."

Kathryn gasped.

"Apologies for saying so, my lady." But those words had been accompanied by a grin that said the very opposite.

"Kathryn," she corrected. "And when we . . ." She'd almost said, *when we get to Brockburg*. Although their current situation was admittedly awkward, their privacy did afford her the perfect opportunity to do what she'd been avoiding and discuss her final destination with him.

"Yes?" he prompted.

"I would like to discuss something with you . . ."

"*Neill.*"

She'd not yet called him by his given name.

"Neill."

He smiled. This one was not a mocking or teasing smile. It was intended to put her at ease.

"I worry taking me to Dunbar may delay your arrival to Brockburg."

He seemed surprised by her observation, as if he'd expected her to say something else.

"I will have you escorted there by Aylmer, so you need not be concerned."

Hm. She had worried he might say that. Unfortunately, she could think of no other reason for him to take her to Brockburg. Kathryn had thought of many excuses, but none seemed viable.

She was left with just one possible approach:

The truth.

Or part of it, at least.

"I wish for you to take me to Brockburg with you."

There, she'd said it.

Just as she'd expected, Neill shook his head. "'Tis not possible, Kathryn. Men from both sides of the border will be at the council, but their wives will not."

"I am not your wife."

Although the thought had occurred to her. She'd never seriously considered marriage before—the men she'd met at court were vapid and uninteresting—but it would be a wonderful thing to marry a man such as Neill Waryn. Whomever he did marry would be a lucky woman indeed.

"A companion, then."

Suddenly, the very air around them changed. She wondered if their relationship was something he'd thought of as well.

There are no relations between us. He is my escort and that is all.

"What are you hiding?" he asked, putting words to the dance between them—one based on concealment and pursuit.

Kathryn sighed. "There is a man there I would like to speak with."

Neill tensed. She could see it in his shoulders, the hard line of his lips confirming he had interpreted her words very differently than how she'd meant them.

Kathryn had intended to tell him about her father. Not his occupation or the circumstances around his death, but the fact that he had been murdered—enough truth that he would agree that it was harmless enough for her to speak with the man who'd last seen him alive.

But instead, he thought she meant . . .

Kathryn's cheeks flushed with heat.

Why had she not considered how he would interpret her words? Especially given Magge's advice, which she'd discarded, on how to convince Neill to escort her.

"I am sorry for my deception. But I'd worried you might not have agreed to escort me had I told you the real reason." She looked down, her embarrassment not a ruse.

It was very, very real. The thought that she was willing to leave England, leave The Wild Boar, to chase after some man . . .

"You would have been correct."

His voice hard, Neill rolled onto his back, ignoring her. This was not the man she'd come to know. Kathryn had rarely felt this embarrassed, this conscious of her every breath and movement, but she could not let it go.

"Will you take me, then?"

He didn't look at her.

"Who is this man?"

She hated the censure in his voice. The anger. But Kathryn could not give up. It would be better for her to allow him to think as he did. If he knew the truth, that she courted danger, not romance, he might not relent.

"I cannot say."

He was quiet for so long, Kathryn was sure he would refuse her. Neill rolled over then, giving her his back.

"I will take you to Brockburg."

She waited, but he did not continue. She wasn't even sure if he heard her "thank you" because he did not address her again.

It took her some time to finally fall asleep. Sadness, guilt, and a tinge of regret kept her mind active until finally, sometime later, she drifted off into a fitful rest.

CHAPTER 9

a man. She had wanted to come here to meet a man.

Neill attempted to push the thought from his mind, but he was all too aware of her presence behind him. At least she rode separately.

They'd arrived at Brockburg Castle.

Most outsiders tended to discount the seat of Clan Kerr as a minor holding due to its size, but Neill knew otherwise. The castle, nestled high up on a ridge, had never been taken. While Bristol Manor had changed hands many times over the years, Brockburg was just far enough north that no one disputed it was firmly in Scotland and on Clan Kerr land. That, along with the high defensive walls and elevated position, Brockburg had been the seat of more than one council meeting during the past year.

He'd missed so much, but Neill was past regretting his time in the south. Being away from his family had enabled him to win that tournament. Gained him the ultimate prize.

Regret was a bitter bedmate, and he'd sooner sleep with . . .

Nay, not her.

Kathryn had someone already. And he'd taken her right to him.

Neill had lain awake the night before mulling over that bitter irony, only calming himself by remembering he was not free to think such thoughts.

He was all but a promised man.

Though there had been no time for a betrothal ceremony, he was right and stuck with Lady Alina deBeers. The queen's lady-in-waiting. A woman he'd never met. But one who nevertheless played a vital role in bringing peace to the border.

And yet...

He'd done everything possible to distance himself from Kathryn. But somehow, at every turn, he found himself in her presence. Sitting beside her at the inn, her easy handling of his men a testament to the time she'd spent at The Wild Boar. Watching her race Burns with the skill of an expert horse-woman. Traveling beside her on the road as she attended to herself without complaint, leaving him with no doubt that she was indeed accustomed to life on the road.

Despite himself, Neill wanted to know more about her. He wished to understand her, to know her secrets, and to play a role in her future.

"Stay close," he said to her now as she rode up beside him.

As usual, her hair was tied back in a braid. Her well-worn though serviceable riding gown would not attract attention on its own, but he did not doubt she would be noticed. No ragged gown could conceal she had the face of an angel.

They rode into the courtyard, already a flurry of activity with the council beginning in two days. Word of his arrival must have reached the castle, for the one man he most wanted to see strode toward him now.

His brother Bryce strode toward him, an unapologetic grin on his face. He waited until Neill dismounted before pulling him into an embrace.

He'd not seen his brother in years, the travel time and instability along the border keeping him "where you belong for now,"
according to Geoffrey. He'd missed weddings, births.

Neill had missed his siblings.

And although he was a man full-grown, he felt more like a
boy in the presence of his older brothers.

"Thor's teeth," Bryce said, pushing back. "You are a man."

Neill laughed as the others fell in around them. "And you are
. . . older."

In truth, he looked much the same. Maybe a bit thicker in
the chest and arms.

"Not so old to challenge you, youngling. What say you,
brother?"

"We've much to discuss. And the training yard seems a
perfect place to do it. But—" He turned toward Kathryn,
intending to see to her well-being.

She was . . . gone.

He looked at Aylmer, who held the reins of the horse she'd
abandoned, and his friend nodded to the main keep. Had she
truly left without a proper farewell?

*The man she came to meet. She's gone off to find him. Your
purpose for her has ended.*

"Neill?"

He shook off the unease that had crept up his back. Bryce
was here. He could not continue to distract himself with
thoughts of Lady Kathryn. Their time together was apparently
at an end.

"'Tis nothing," he said.

Bryce peered behind them.

"Where's Geoffrey?"

"He sent word to The Wild Boar, where we were to meet,
that I should continue on without him. Something has held him
at Kenshire."

Bryce frowned. "Hmmm."

"The young pup returns."

Toren Kerr, chief of Clan Kerr and Brockburg Castle, approached him.

The man looked as ferocious as he remembered. But by the look Toren and Bryce exchanged, their bitter enemy truly had become an ally.

"Chief." He extended his hand, but Toren took his forearm instead, a more intimate gesture signaling they were more than simply allies.

They were family. Bryce had seen to that.

Speaking of which . . .

"I hear we all have news to celebrate," Neill said, pulling his arm back. "I am remiss in my congratulations, Bryce. I had hoped to stop at Bristol Manor to see your son, but I was delayed."

This time, it was he who initiated the embrace. It had been far too long since he'd seen his family, and although Neill already missed Adam and Cora, he could not deny he was glad to be back in the north. Back where he belonged.

With luck, Lady Alina will have no qualms living in Northumbria. As long as the border was secure . . . he pushed aside the vision of a future with Kathryn. It was not to be, for many reasons.

"Come," Toren said. "Most are already here in the hall." He greeted the other men, raised his hand for a stable boy to take their mounts, and began to guide them toward the main keep, but Bryce shook his head.

"We go to the training yard first."

"Tell Lady Juliette," Toren said to the boy who'd followed them. A squire, presumably. "I will be along soon. First—" he turned back to Neill, "—I shall test my skills against the man they say cannot be bested in the joust."

"Or," Bryce added, looking more than a little proud, "with a sword. Your reputation has reached the border, brother."

"I wonder how that came to be?" he said, one corner of his mouth inching up. His sister, Emma, wrote to him often, and she'd told him that their brothers bragged of Neill to nearly every person who'd listen.

Bryce shrugged. "You were always the quickest of us, brother."

As they walked the length of the courtyard, servants and guests alike stopped to stare.

"Are they always so reverent of their chief?" Neill asked as they skirted the stables. He glanced inside. No sign of Kathryn.

He hadn't realized both Bryce and Toren had stopped. He turned and cocked his head at their shared expression of disbelief.

"Does he really not know?" Toren asked.

"Apparently not. Though Neill was never one to boast, like other Waryn men."

"You mean like *you*," Toren teased.

Teased.

It was odd to see the two like this. They'd gone from bitter enemies to brothers-in-law who had obviously forged a close bond. What else had happened while he was away?

"I was talking of Geoffrey," Bryce said.

"I know."

Neill cut in. "Will someone please explain what the two of you are going on about?"

"They aren't looking at their chief, Neill," his brother said. "They are looking at you. I told you, your reputation has reached the borderlands. I assumed you would be accustomed to such a reaction."

He sighed. In truth, he was, though Neill had not expected it this far north. Which meant he would be challenged at every turn. He'd been hoping to avoid that.

Immediately contrite, knowing he should be grateful for his skills *and* the respect they afforded him, he smiled at the pair.

"Shall we see if I can uphold my reputation, then?"

Bryce slapped him on the back.

"I've no doubt you will do so, against all others. But I know your weakness and mean to exploit it. Come."

This would be interesting.

CHAPTER 10

*B*rockburg Castle was large, though not large enough she could escape notice for long. With so many guests, most would assume she traveled with another party. But avoiding Neill, his men, and the Scottish lord warden was another matter. Even though it had been nigh on two years since she and her father dined with Douglas, he'd no doubt recognize her.

Her plan was simple.

Find Bothwell and interrogate him about her father. Although she had no notion of what she'd do after that, she meant to focus on her goal until she saw it through. Would he have seen someone from the English court, perhaps, that may have raised suspicion? Was that why her father had advised her not to return there if something happened to him? It seemed the last person to speak to him would have as many answers as any.

Sitting on the hay bale behind Brockburg's handsome stables, Kathryn tore at the piece of bread she'd received from the kitchen. Luckily, it was a separate building from the main keep, and acquiring the food had been a simple matter. She'd asked for a piece of bread for "her lord," and none had thought to question her. She looked very much like a servant, of which there were plenty mulling about for the council.

You *are* a servant.

Kathryn forgot, at times, she was not playing a part. This was her life now, at least until she could learn more about her father, and she'd best become accustomed to it. Only then would she consider making her way south to her only surviving relatives. Though distant, her father's instructions had been clear.

Except . . . he'd not accounted for his own murder. And she would not leave the north until she learned what had happened to him.

It took her a moment to realize the space was eerily empty. Earlier, there had been people everywhere—now, she saw only animals grazing on patches of grass and a stray servant or two milling around. In the distance, cheers and shouts went up. The others had gathered to watch something, and her impulsiveness bade her to make her way toward the distant sound. At least she took care to walk near the buildings in case she spotted someone who would force her into hiding. Silently thanking her father for the many times they'd slid in and out of castles such as this one, Kathryn followed the noise.

When she made it past the armory, the sound of hammering steel a familiar one, she finally understood. Although she could see only the gathered crowd from this vantage point, Kathryn could tell there was a large open space between the east bailey and the chapel to her right. Aside from the courtyard, the only area that large without buildings was typically a training yard of some sort.

Making her way through the crowd, Kathryn edged to the front.

And stared.

She had lived among kings and queens.

She had traveled further than nearly every person she'd ever met.

But she had never seen anything quite so extraordinary as Neill Waryn dueling with his brother. They were so evenly matched, Kathryn was sure the contest would go on for some time. Though it wasn't their skill with swords or the way each ducked and whirled in between clashes that had her enthralled.

She'd seen many well-built men, and indeed, Bryce was as fit as one would expect of a knight. But Neill. Was he even human?

The greatest knight in all of Christendom.

She supposed the moniker had been earned, and the discipline needed to fight as he was now, to look the way he did . . . where did it come from?

Kathryn was much too interested in the answer to that question. In the man who fought his brother, drawing a crowd that likely included every man, woman, and child at Brockburg.

"'Tis a sight, for certain."

As was the lady who'd appeared next to her.

Though her own hair mixed light and dark, never certain of its true shade, this woman's hair was like pure gold—a stark contrast to the navy blue kirtle she wore so elegantly.

"Indeed, it is," she agreed, looking away from the very beautiful Englishwoman back toward the yard.

"Who do you believe will win?" she asked.

Kathryn thought carefully. "The younger brother, I understand, rarely loses a contest."

"I've heard the same."

"The knight is sure to win," a man blurted from beside them.

"Aye. Neill Waryn," another agreed.

The blonde woman smiled. "I believe you are correct, gentlemen. His reputation precedes him."

Kathryn watched the contest more carefully, attempting to ignore Neill's physique and determine the best answer. She would agree, except . . .

"The older brother," she finally said, garnering looks of surprise.

They continued to watch as Neill and Bryce clashed swords, the afternoon air stifling. The discomfort did nothing to disperse the crowd.

Suddenly, it was over.

Kathryn hadn't seen it happen, but Bryce held his sword to Neill's side. If the weapons had not been blunted, it would have been a disabling blow.

Neill raised his hands, conceding.

Kathryn was about to make a comment to the English-woman, but as quickly as she had appeared, the lady was gone. Likely for the best. Kathryn was supposed to be hiding, after all.

Making a quick retreat, Kathryn returned to her hiding place, the walkway behind the stables that led to the curtain wall, a perfect place to finish her midday meal and bide her time until darkness fell. Until she could go about more easily without being noticed.

"Pardon," she said to one of the stable boys. "Has the Earl of Bothwell's party arrived?"

He startled, obviously caught off guard by the directness of her question.

As was her goal. A lesson she'd learned from her father, who had dealt with sensitive information most of his life.

"I . . . I do not believe so."

She inclined her head and walked away, cutting the conversation short. The longer she spoke with him, the longer he would have to study her face.

Kathryn nearly laughed aloud at her own absurdity as she found the walkway, choosing to sit on the concrete slab rather than the hay bale from earlier. Bits of hay still clung to her dress from earlier.

She wasn't sure what made her look up as she pulled the remainder of the bread from her pouch, but when she did,

Kathryn's heart thudded in her chest—so loud she could hear it in her ears.

"Hello, Kathryn."

Oh dear. His shirt hung loose, sleeves rolled to his elbows.

"Hello, Neill."

She wanted to demand how he'd found her, but from the look on his face, Kathryn reminded herself she was not in a position to make demands.

"Didn't take you long," she said instead.

"'Twas easy enough to find you."

It wasn't possible he'd noticed her in the midst of his fight with his brother. Curiosity overcame her. "How?"

"When MacDuff sought me out to congratulate me on my win—"

"Win? I saw your brother . . ." She stopped talking. For every word she said, Neill took a step toward her.

"Before Bryce." He smiled. "The Scot cared little for a match between two Englishmen. Clearly, you did not see me best the chief of Clan Scott before I fought my brother."

No, she hadn't. But Kathryn assumed he'd been more successful that time.

"I don't know this MacDuff."

He took another step toward her.

Kathryn looked around, not because she needed to be rescued from Neill Waryn, but because she was accustomed to looking for an escape whenever she felt even slightly uncomfortable.

Unfortunately, this spot was private and darkness had just begun to settle in.

They were very much alone.

"But he knows you."

Another step.

Kathryn stood, not wanting to be in such a vulnerable position with Neill towering above her.

"How?"

A final step and he was nearly upon her. If he reached out, he could touch her.

"He saw you at the Anvil Inn. He noticed you near the stables earlier and wondered if his eyes deceived him."

"What did you tell him?"

She really did need to be more careful.

"That I knew not where you'd gone to. I made no mention of escorting you here. I assumed you left to find the man who lured you here?"

His jaw flexed, reminding her this was no soft knight of the realm. She'd seen the power behind every swing of his arm, each flex of his muscles. Tingles washed through her body.

"Would he care that you look at me this way?" he prodded.

Her head snapped up. Kathryn hadn't even realized she'd been staring at his chest.

"Pardon?"

His expression took on a harder edge. "You heard me," he insisted.

Jealousy? Could it be?

"Nay. He would not be pleased."

She should have denied his claim—part of her wished to assure him that he was the only man who'd ever drawn her attention in such a way—but then she would need to share everything with him. She was not ready to do so. Not yet. Kathryn was still unsure who she could trust.

"Who is it?"

Aye, he *was* jealous.

"I cannot say."

His eyes narrowed.

Kathryn's heart raced. Could he tell she was lying? It didn't matter. She was deep into her story now and had no real way out. Aside from the truth.

Which she'd do best not to tell him.

He took one final step toward her, standing so close she could almost feel the heat from his body.

Kathryn wanted him to kiss her.

It wasn't the first time the thought had popped into her head. But as he stood there, scrutinizing her as openly as she'd looked at him earlier, she wanted no more than to span the distance between them.

"What is he to you, then?"

The words dripped from his mouth like liquid honey. Slow and deliberate.

She could not tell him what he wished to know, so instead she described the man standing in front of her.

"A savior, of sorts."

He didn't move. Or even blink.

"Gallant and kind. And not just to his own kin."

"So a gentleman, then?" He ground out every word, not even attempting to hide his displeasure.

"Aye. A knight."

The glimmer in his eyes told her she'd said too much.

"As I'm sure you have a lady?" Kathryn blurted, diverting his attention from her words lest he realize she spoke of *him*.

"I do."

Kathryn bristled. She'd not expected that.

Clearing her throat, pretending they weren't standing closer than two people in a conversation should be standing, she boldly repeated his question.

"What is she to you?"

"A mystery."

A rush of air left her lips. *Oh.* He knew she'd spoken of him, and he'd returned the gesture in kind.

Did that mean . . . was there no other?

Kathryn should not care.

"I have to leave," she whispered.

He'd stopped her before, and she expected him to do so

again. But Neill didn't attempt to reach out to her as she skirted around him. He didn't even turn to look at her. As she rounded the stables, she allowed herself a quick glance back, and he was already walking in the other direction, toward the keep.

She stopped, allowing for her heartbeat to return to normal.

Had she misread his interest?

The sun had set while they were speaking. She could move through the courtyard a bit easier, blending in with the other visitors, avoiding notice until he came.

And then what?

The question she'd been avoiding would not relent. Depending on what the man said, Kathryn would have to decide on her next move. Back to The Wild Boar? Make her way to Edinburgh, where her father had been killed?

It seemed she'd find out sooner rather than later. A new riding party had arrived, and though she'd never met the man before, he fit the descriptions she'd heard precisely.

Flaming red hair. Long beard. A large man, though not muscled like Neill.

The Earl of Bothwell.

Lord Chancellor of Scotland and the king's representative here at the council.

Most importantly, the man with whom her father had last dealt before his body was found along the bank of the Firth of Forth.

CHAPTER 11

*H*ungry, tired, and thoroughly confused, Neill strode toward the great hall with the intention of seeking out his chamber. Bryce had mentioned they were housed in the Armorer's Tower, and by the sounds coming from the hall, he suspected supper was already being served.

Another sound reached his ears from the other end of the courtyard, near the stables. Neill stopped at the entrance to the keep. A riding party had arrived, though he couldn't see their banners from this distance.

Fortunately, he didn't need to see. The whispers around him identified the men just as easily.

"Lord chancellor . . ."

"The king's man . . ."

Neill knew of the Earl of Bothwell, of course, but he'd never met him. According to his brothers, the man was not to be trusted. He changed sides as it suited him. Thankfully, on the matter they were here to discuss, the ousting of Caxton and reinstatement of the Day of Truce, Bothwell appeared to support the Scots king, the wardens, and the select group of

Englishmen, like Neill and his brother, who had been invited to this gathering.

According to Geoffrey's letter, word of Neill's actions had reached the border before he'd even left the south. All of the guests at the council meeting anticipated the renewal of King Alexander's oath of fealty to Edward. Once that occurred, Caxton would be removed.

And I will be wed.

Thoughts of Kathryn intruded, just as they did every time Neill considered his intended.

As though his mind had summoned her from the shadows, he watched as a slip of yellow crossed the courtyard toward the newcomers. He changed course and approached the scene, continuing to watch her. As the newcomers dismounted, Kathryn continued toward them.

At the speed she was walking, Kathryn would practically be on top of Bothwell in moments. The earl didn't seem to notice her yet. But he would. Given his horrible reputation, there was no knowing how he'd react to such an approach. He was known to be a cold, hard man.

Neill began to run.

Reaching her before the earl or his men saw them, Neill grabbed her arm and continued to walk, right back to the same spot where they'd spoken moments before.

"Let go of me." She tried to shrug her arm free.

"Not until you explain why you were poised to accost the Earl of Bothwell."

"Accost?"

She managed to wrest her arm away from him, but she did not flee. They listened as the Scotsmen's horses were led into the nearby stables.

"Do you deny you were walking, quite briskly I might add, toward his riding party?"

She glanced in the general direction of the newcomers, but

with a building separating them from the newcomers, there was nothing to see but a dog barking at the activity.

"I wished to speak with him."

Ignoring the scent of lavender, Neill pressed. "Bothwell? What could you possibly have to speak with him about? The man is a . . ."

No. Not him.

Kathryn's eyes widened. "You don't think? Bothwell and I?"

Her nose wrinkled, and Neill immediately felt like a fool for having considered such a match.

"You insult me, sir." She was jesting, but the comment was not without some annoyance.

"And you have lied to me at every turn, Kathryn. So please, just this once. Tell me the truth. What were you planning to say to Bothwell?"

She crossed her arms and let out an exaggerated breath.

"I have to go."

"To Bothwell? To the man you came here to meet? Kathryn, please, tell me the truth."

She glanced up at him then, meeting his gaze, and said, "It may be too late already." There was a look of regret in her eyes, but damned if she didn't try to walk away again.

He should let her go.

He had no right to detain her.

And yet . . .

He grabbed her hand, just like he'd done at the Boar. This time, though, he made it clear why he'd done it.

Neill wanted to touch her. He wanted to be near her. He wanted to know what she hid from him and who she'd come here to see.

He'd seen the way she'd suffered for breath the other night. The glimmer of fear had danced in her eyes then, and he saw it again now.

"Are you afraid of me?"

She shook her head, still holding his hand.

He'd known the answer already but had needed to be sure.

He took a step toward her, squeezing her hand as he did so. "I would never, ever hurt you."

She blinked.

Kathryn must have known that already.

"Or betray you."

This time her mouth trembled.

So that was it. She did not trust him.

"Please. Tell me the truth." He squeezed her hand again, silently urging her to unburden herself.

"You said you didn't want to know," she said softly. "That you didn't want to involve yourself in my affairs."

He had said that. And regretted it.

"Tell me," he repeated. He licked his lips, his throat suddenly dry.

Her shoulders sagged in defeat, but still she held her head high. "I mean to ask the Earl of Bothwell about my father."

Shocked she'd relented, Neill was nevertheless confused. "You told me your father was dead?"

Her head dropped down, making Neill feel like a complete arse.

"I apologize."

She looked back up at him.

"I did not mean to speak so bluntly," he said.

"My father is dead. And he—" she nodded toward the court-yard, "—was the last man to speak with him before it happened."

If he was expecting an explanation of the circumstances of her father's death, including why a man from a tiny village in England would have been speaking to one of the most powerful men in Scotland . . . it wasn't going to happen.

As sure as he had three siblings, Neill knew Kathryn would say no more.

"Answer me one final question." *For now*, he added silently. "Is Bothwell the reason you wanted me to bring you here?"

She nodded. This time, it was she who squeezed his hand.

Joined as they were, it was not appropriate. Especially not given his agreement to wed Lady Alina. But if the king of England himself had ordered him to release her hand, Neill would not have pulled away.

"There is no other man?"

He held his breath, waiting. Her answer should not matter, but it did.

"Nay. There is none other."

He really should not keep pushing. "Earlier, when you spoke of 'him'?"

He didn't need to finish the sentence. Her silence was his confirmation—as he'd suspected, Kathryn had been speaking of him. "If I am to be your savior, of sorts, you will have to tell me more about the situation."

"It could put you in danger."

"My lady." He took hold of her other hand. "Much of our world is dangerous, but right now, as we stand here in the recesses of Brockburg's courtyard, there is only one imminent danger. And it is not of me knowing too much."

Her brows furrowed. She didn't understand his meaning.

"Right now, the most imminent threat is whatever is growing between us. For I have never wanted to kiss a woman more than I want to kiss you."

Her lips parted as she tipped her head up to him, inviting him to do as he'd suggested.

He shouldn't. They shouldn't.

If she tasted as sweet as she looked, he would be lost in her. And not just for one night. Neill knew it instinctively, as if his training all these years had prepared him for something other than how to best a man on a battlefield.

He thought of the king and queen, sitting side by side,

responding to his request to replace Caxton with one of their own.

He thought of his brothers and sister, who counted on him to keep his agreement.

He thought of Adam and Cora. Their words, their actions, preparing him to be a man of honor.

All of this went through his mind, warning him not to do this. Not to lean down. Not to take what she offered.

For he knew, with every part of himself, if he did this, there would be no turning back.

CHAPTER 12

For a moment, Kathryn thought he would kiss her. But the moment seemed to pass, even though he continued to hold her hands.

She'd forgotten, until now, another lesson her father had taught her.

To trust her instincts.

And though she'd known Neill Waryn less than a sennight, Kathryn knew he would never betray her. She'd told him a partial truth, realizing, even as she said the words aloud, it would only lead to more questions. Ones she couldn't reasonably answer without telling him everything. And if her father's murderer resided in the English court, she had no way of knowing who they might be connected to.

Certainly not the Waryns.

And yet, she held back.

He looked down, stared into her eyes, and swallowed. She was about to comment on the torturous look on his face when he suddenly released her hands.

Before she could object to the loss of his warmth, he stepped even closer.

When he reached up to cup her cheeks, Kathryn forgot to breathe. As he leaned toward her, giving her ample opportunity to stop him, she silently communicated that she wanted him to kiss her.

And he did.

His lips touched hers, warm and soft. She covered his hands with her own, kissing him back. Or so she thought.

"I want to kiss you properly, Kathryn." He pulled away slightly.

"That wasn't a proper kiss?"

It was just like her first two kisses, though much softer. Sweeter. Maybe because his hands still held her as if she were a delicate piece of glass.

In answer, he moved toward her once again. When his lips were just about to touch hers, he murmured, "Open your mouth."

She did.

And this time, his touch was not so gentle. He slanted his mouth over hers, his tongue begging for hers. So she touched it to his, tentatively, but Neill didn't allow for tentative.

He showed her what to do, their tongues tangling. She moved her hands to the back of his head, and he did the same, pulling her even closer. Kathryn met his every touch with one of her own, her chest tightening with the very idea of what they were doing.

She didn't want it to stop.

Apparently, neither did Neill.

The loud bark of a nearby dog shattered the moment, Kathryn pulling back and looking around them.

Nothing.

She forced herself to step back, her hands falling to the sides, and tried to catch her breath.

"I . . . never."

I've never been kissed that way before.

"That . . ." Neill smiled slowly. "Was a proper kiss."

"'Tis a wonder people don't do that more often."

When he laughed, Kathryn wanted him to kiss her again. The happy sound, from deep within his chest, made her forget everything else in the world.

Including her purpose here.

That, she could not allow.

"I must go," she said, although her feet did not move.

"To find Bothwell? Tell me why. Let me help you, Kathryn. Bothwell's reputation is not of an easy man to deal with."

Although, she'd decided to trust Neill earlier, now Kathryn felt a throb of uncertainty. She'd kept her background a secret for so long . . . was she really going to blurt everything out to a man she hardly knew?

A man who she'd just allowed to take more liberties than any man before him.

She could not allow her interest in him to overcome her sense of reason.

"Come to the hall with me," he said softly. Gently. "Allow me to introduce you to Lady Juliette."

"Has Douglas arrived yet?"

Neill seemed taken aback. "The lord warden?"

"Aye."

"I don't believe so. Why?"

"Then I suppose I can dine in the hall just this once."

She knew he didn't understand, and Kathryn also knew she had no choice but to tell him something. But that kiss had muddled her thinking, and really, she just wanted him to do it again.

Or she would if she did not know what would come of it. Although Kathryn had little left, she did still have her virtue.

"And what will you tell Lady Juliette?"

"That you needed escort. That you are on your way to Dunbar and, fearing a delay, I brought you here first."

Her eyes widened. "You would lie for me?"

Neill crossed his arms, and Kathryn's fleeting elation was immediately tempered.

"If you'll tell me why you wish to speak to Bothwell. Why you avoid Douglas." He cleared his throat. "And how a *lady* such as yourself has landed in such a predicament."

A fair trade, she supposed.

"I will tell you after supper."

The bread she'd eaten hadn't quite quelled her hunger.

"You'll tell me everything?"

"Yes," she lied, feeling poorly for doing so.

Neill, for his part, didn't look as if he believed her.

"Then come." He started to walk away, stopped and turned. "One more question."

Kathryn groaned, eliciting another laugh from Neill. But he sobered as soon as she looked up to meet his eyes.

"Do you regret it?"

Aye, she'd pulled away. But no, she did not regret kissing him. Not even a bit.

"No." And then, hesitantly, she added, "Do you?"

He was shaking his head before the question even left her lips.

"I should, Kathryn. I will tell you why later, although you'll think less of me for it. But no, I do not regret it. I'd not let that thief steal this moment."

He said the words as if they meant something more than they did. As if it weighed on him to admit that he did not regret kissing her.

But he began walking again, so she let the comment pass.

For now.

"Tell me," Bryce said as they finished the best meat pie Neill had ever tasted, "how did the king react to your request?"

Surrounded by their own men, Neill and Bryce spoke freely as they ate with the one hundred or so other guests. They had been invited to dine on the dais, as family, but had opted to eat alongside their men instead. Just as Neill had expected, only a few Englishmen were present and the guests consisted of mostly men. With the peace at the border so tenuous, the clan chiefs and wardens had left their wives at home.

Most of the women in the hall belonged at Brockburg, with a few exceptions. Kathryn had agreed to attend the meal, but so far, he did not see her.

"Neill?"

He shifted his attention back to his brother. Though he'd written his brothers and sister straightaway to tell them of the king's agreement to do away with Caxton, he'd told none of them yet of the queen's condition. "He didn't answer right away," he said, "but he also did not appear overly disturbed by it. I do wonder if he'd been planning to remove Caxton anyway."

It was Edward's father who'd favored the crooked warden. The son had returned only recently from abroad to claim his crown.

Bryce shook his head, scowling. "With a war brewing in France, I've no doubt he'd have let the border languish."

Aylmer, who sat across from them, interjected. "Rumors in the south would agree with your sentiment."

"Aye." No denying it. Neill lifted his mug, a fine-looking pewter piece in a hall that was both functional and resplendent. The tapestries on the wall were simple and tasteful, though of fine quality.

Neill had never imagined himself dining in Brockburg Castle. Time had wrought unexpected changes on his family, to be certain.

"Either way, 'tis done. And as much as I wish the plan had been solely mine, it was Sir Adam who first suggested the idea."

"Do you remember *that* day?" his brother asked.

Neill groaned.

"Please, do not speak of it."

Bryce turned to Aylmer, a touch gleeful. "After losing Bristol Manor, Geoffrey, as I'm sure you know, turned to reiving in order to support our aunt and uncle with whom we lived."

"Bryce, do not," Neill protested.

His brother ignored him. Some things had not, apparently, changed.

"After Geoffrey wed Lady Sara, we all moved to Kenshire for a time." Bryce smiled, a slightly fierce smile.

He had missed his siblings, but not Bryce's love of telling stories. Especially not when the stories were about *him*. There was no avoiding it now, though—his friends were listening intently.

"Neill begged to stay at Kenshire, but the situation was tenuous, Bristol still in the hands of Clan Kerr."

All glanced toward the dais where their brother-in-law sat with his wife. Toren obviously knew they were speaking of him, and he raised his mug in response.

Bryce did the same, the former enemies silently toasting each other.

"We thought it best he foster away from the borderlands."

Bryce set down his mug and leaned back on the bench, crossing his arms as he continued with his tale.

Neill would find a way to thank his brother later. With nothing left to do but wait for the worst of the story, he drank. Deeply.

"Sara, of course, suggested Sir Adam." Their connection was a deep one—Adam honored and admired her grandfather, the man who'd granted him Langford Castle, and her father, his dear friend.

"A finer man than most," Aylmer cut in. "All here were fortunate to serve under Sir Adam."

Bryce raised his brows. "Do you hear the wisdom of your man-at-arms, brother? 'Fortunate' he calls himself, and you, for having such a mentor."

Neill tried to cut his brother off. "You'll understand I'd lost my mother and father. My home. I was young—"

"Not that young," Bryce interrupted him.

"I was young and did not wish to be separated from my siblings."

Bryce cleared his throat. "He ran away."

Neill sighed, waiting for it.

"He—" Aylmer nearly choked on his ale, "—ran away?"

"My little brother was quick to anger in his youth," Bryce remarked.

Neill's companions at least had the grace to appear somewhat surprised.

Thankfully.

"When Geoffrey told him, Neill simply . . ." He shrugged. "Disappeared."

When his brother started to laugh, the others joined him. Neill knew there was no defense against such an action, so he didn't even attempt to speak for himself. Besides which, he knew his brother was finally reaching the joke he'd spent the last minutes setting up. Instead, he looked around the hall.

No sign of her.

"Where did you go?" Aylmer asked.

Bryce was all eagerness. "He made it to the village, to the alewife, who was more than happy to make the acquaintance of the new lord's young brother."

Bryce's hearty laugh drew the stares of those around him. His brother was not prone to laughter, and all knew it. By now, even Neill could not help a small grin.

"A widow," he said. "And an amorous one at that."

"By the time she'd finished with him, Neill was a virgin no longer."

This time, the men's laughter was so raucous it caught the attention of their host, who called out from the front of the hall.

"Behold, my English family," Toren called out. "And the savior of the Day of Truce."

Mugs pounded on the trestle tables as they became the center of the hall's attention. Bryce was still laughing at the story he'd so kindly shared with the men. Neill was left shaking his head, enduring both the ribbing and the cheers.

A feeling of heaviness descended on Neill as the noise finally died down.

"I fear they celebrate too soon. Caxton is still warden," he warned.

"But his days as such are coming to an end," Bryce said, "and for that, we are thankful to you, brother."

The look of pride on his face was a far greater reward than any prize he'd won in a tournament.

"And we're thankful you eventually made your way to Langford," Aylmer said. "And that the alewife's thighs did not detain you permanently in their grip." He lifted his mug and drank.

Neill was about to comment when he saw her. Finally.

Kathryn had entered at the very back, against the wall, and claimed a seat at a far table. To others, it might appear as if she belonged there, but Neill knew otherwise.

She should be with me.

He dismissed the thought as quickly as it entered his mind. He had no claim to her. Nor would he ever. But to see her sitting there, where she so clearly did not belong . . .

She spotted him, and their eyes locked.

He stared at her lips and could not help but think of their kiss.

Though they could not repeat it, at least Neill would learn her secrets that night.

But did he really want to know them? Or would it make it more difficult to do as he knew he must and walk away from her?

CHAPTER 13

*S*he couldn't do it.

She just couldn't risk it.

Changing her mind, yet again, about how much to tell Neill, Kathryn stood from the table and fled the hall. She would lose herself for the night, until the meal was over.

Her plan was to sleep in the hall with the other servants, something she'd never done in all of her travels. As royal messenger, her father had been considered a member of the king's retinue, treated as well as any other in his household.

She'd stayed in royal palaces, the finest castles in England, Wales, and France. But she'd also slept on makeshift pallets on the road, where such accommodations were not available. Thankfully, Brockburg Castle was extremely well-kept, the rushes clean.

Kathryn would sleep anywhere to get the answers she sought.

Rounding another corner, exploring the ground floor of the castle as she sought a spot to sleep, Kathryn reached a rather dark stretch of hallway, the last wall torch well behind her.

Compared to the darkness of the woods, this corridor should not give her pause. But it did.

"Kathryn."

She jumped, for she hadn't thought he'd seen her leave.

"Why did you leave?" he asked as she turned to face him.

Why indeed?

She inhaled, the scent of sandalwood telling her what she'd already noticed when she had first spotted him sitting with his brother and their men.

He'd cleaned himself for the meal. But she hadn't noticed his tunic earlier, it's silver-embroidered royal blue marking him a man of wealth and importance. She'd known that, of course, but it was the first time Kathryn had seen him outfitted in such a way.

That he had the power to awe her when she'd been in the presence of kings and queens for most of her life was the reason why she'd left the hall. She was frightened of the power he held over her—and of how much stronger it would likely grow should she take him fully into her confidence.

But she couldn't tell him that.

"I . . . I cannot."

"You cannot tell me why you left? Or you cannot tell me the truth you promised earlier?"

"Both," she ventured.

Though Neill did not look pleased, he didn't press her. But he did grab her hand, a gesture that was becoming something of a habit.

He led her down the darkened corridor, and Kathryn followed mutely.

"Where are we going?"

No answer.

They wound their way up a set of circular stairs and through endless corridors, some better lit than others, finally coming to a hallway with four or five doors.

Opening the second door, still holding her hand, Neill entered and took her with him.

He didn't let her go until he closed the large oak door behind them.

"Is this your chamber?" A silly question, but she couldn't think of anything else to say.

"Aye."

Four wall torches lit the small but well-appointed chamber, boasting a canopied bed, two chairs, a small table, and one very unusual feature.

"A window?"

She walked toward the stone benches that bracketed a much larger window than she was accustomed to seeing in a castle of this size. Kathryn turned back to him, silently asking for permission to open the wooden shutters.

He nodded for her to proceed, and she did.

"Ahhh." She understood now. This particular room faced the training yard, the reason for the large window without bars. An unseasonably cool evening for summer, the air felt good as Kathryn breathed it in.

"A full moon," Neill said.

She hadn't heard him approach, but he now stood next to her, his breath gusting her hair.

"Aye."

Sitting on the stone seat, he looked up at her as if waiting for her to say something.

"Why am I here?" she asked.

Uncomfortable under his careful scrutiny, Kathryn sat down across from her savior of sorts, leaving the shutters open. She could still see the moon from this vantage point, but eventually she was forced to look back at him.

Well, not forced exactly.

Neill was more pleasing to look at than anyone else she'd

ever met. But he also stared at her as if he could see into her very soul.

"A fine question," he said finally.

Kathryn smiled. "I meant here, in your chamber."

She could tell from his expression that Neill knew exactly what she had meant.

"I thought you might find it difficult to avoid me in here."

She looked around the room. "A private chamber when so many will be present for the council."

His wink sent a fluttering feeling from her stomach downward.

"One of the benefits of my brother being married to the sister of our host."

Of course. How could she have forgotten?

"If I'm found here . . ." She couldn't say the words aloud.

"You're worried for your reputation?"

A small shrug was all she could manage. She should be, but it hardly seemed to matter now. After all, she'd traveled with him without a chaperone. Lived at the inn without one too.

Neill leaned forward, his elbows resting on his knees.

"I will not allow you to be discovered here. And you can trust me, Kathryn."

Kathryn believed him.

And in truth, she wanted to share the burden. She wasn't sure she could do this alone, and perhaps it would not be necessary.

"I am certain my father was murdered," she blurted before she lost the courage to tell him even part of her truth. "The Earl of Bothwell found his body, so when I learned he would be here, I thought to make my way to Brockburg. To question him."

If he was surprised by her revelation, Neill didn't show it.

"I believe, my lady, you left out the beginning of your tale."

And the middle, as well as the end.

She looked into the eyes of the man who'd agreed to help her despite knowing next to nothing about her. The man who'd always acted honorably toward her, even as she lied to him. Taking another deep breath, Kathryn made a decision she hoped she'd not later regret.

"My father was the king's royal messenger."

That managed to surprise him.

"I grew up in the English court, my mother the only daughter of a minor baron. She died during my birth."

When his eyes softened, Kathryn rushed to continue lest she dwell too long on the woman she'd never known and whom her father had never stopped loving.

"When I was younger, I stayed at court, eventually becoming a lady-in-waiting to the queen." She laughed at his strained expression. "Is that so difficult to imagine?"

"In fact, it is not. But when I guessed you were a lady . . ." His voice trailed off, so Kathryn resumed her tale. If she did not finish now, she did not trust herself to continue.

"As I grew older, the men became bolder in their attentions, and my father decided it would be less dangerous for me to accompany him than to stay at court. He had trusted the king with his life, but did not trust his regents the same way."

She wouldn't say aloud what her father had thought of them. Or the new king. To do so would be treason.

"Edward had just returned to England when my father was given a missive for the Scottish king. So we left for Edinburgh, only my second visit there."

"Second visit? Kathryn, where else did you travel with your father?"

"Many places. France, Wales, Scotland. Even once to Rome."

Shaking his head, Neill sat back and crossed his legs. He looked as shocked to hear the words as she was to say them. Although she'd intended only to tell him the broad strokes of the situation, she found she could not stop.

"When my father arranged for us to stay at an abbey just

outside the village, I knew something was amiss. Typically we would stay in the castle. He admitted the message he carried was 'particularly sensitive' and urged me to remember my training."

"Training?"

"My father had many friends. He had established a few safe places for me to go, no matter where our location, should something happen to him." Her voice thick, Kathryn stopped. She'd dealt with the grief of her father's loss by focusing on her intention to catch his killer. But when she thought about Edinburgh, about the last time she'd seen him, it felt again as if all the air had left her body . . .

Neill was there, suddenly, next to her. And though she knew that everything about their situation was wrong, Kathryn welcomed his presence. She welcomed his hand, which wrapped around hers in a now-familiar embrace, and also his heat, a respite from the cool night breeze that wafted in from the open shutters.

Still, she couldn't look at him, and so Kathryn stared down at her road-weary kirtle instead. She'd brought only two others, ones Magge had procured for her. Kathryn's own gowns had been discarded, too fine for a serving woman at The Wild Boar.

"I'd chastised him for worrying, convinced I would never be forced to travel alone to find one of his safe havens. Or to make my way south to my mother's relatives."

Her hand sat on his lap, their fingers entwined, and it suddenly occurred to her that she'd never held a man's hand before.

Well, before Neill.

"When he returned from his audience with the lord chancellor that night, he told me . . ." She did look up then. Neill waited patiently, and she realized once these words were said, there would be no going back. "Are you certain you want to hear this?"

"I'm certain."

"He told me that the chancellor had refused to grant him direct access to the king. And since his orders were to ensure the king received his message, my father would not leave Edinburgh. He expressed mistrust of Bothwell and told me we would be staying a bit longer than usual."

His gaze did not waver. The confidence with which Neill carried himself was never more evident than in this moment. He would accept whatever she said as truth, and the fact that he trusted her—she could see in his eyes that he did—emboldened her to finish.

"That was the last time I saw him."

She shivered, remembering. And then Neill's arm circled around her shoulder, and it felt like the most natural thing in the world to lean into him. Kathryn stared straight ahead, watching the light play across the stone wall as the torch flickered in the breeze.

"The next day, I waited, expecting him by the midday meal. By supper, I grew worried, and when darkness fell . . ."

She thought of the night she'd spent pacing the room. She'd thought, at the time, it was the worst night of her life.

Until the next day.

"I'd not ventured far, staying at the abbey as my father had instructed, speaking only with Father Peton. And it was he who found me just before dusk to tell me . . ." She closed her eyes, ignoring the tingling in her cheeks. "My father's body had been found along the bank of the Firth of Forth."

She would not cry.

Opening her eyes, she met Neill's gaze, and the sympathy there was her undoing. The tears began to flow, so fast and thick she barely even noticed the handkerchief Neill had given her or the tightening of his arm around her shoulders. She only knew that the man who had loved her so fiercely was gone, and she'd never even said goodbye. Or confirmed the priest's words.

When she collected herself enough to look at him again, Neill reached out and wiped an errant tear from just under her eye with his thumb. So gentle a gesture for a celebrated knight. "I did not need Father Peton's urging to leave the abbey at once."

"You traveled to England, alone?" Neill asked, incredulous.

"Nay. As I was leaving, Father Peton introduced me to a younger man, one who was both priest and warrior. He escorted me to The Wild Boar, where my father had always urged me to go if I found myself alone in the north."

She swallowed.

"Which is where I've been for the past seven months."

"Seven months? This must have happened just after King Edward finally returned from the East." He tightened his fingers around hers.

"Aye."

"Your father was murdered for the message he carried."

"More like the knowledge. Often his letters were sealed, as this one most assuredly was. But he also knew its contents. 'Twas the reason he'd insisted on a direct audience with the king."

"I am very sorry, Kathryn." His tone, low. His voice, uneven.

She managed a shaky smile, her heart still feeling broken. That was the second time she'd told the tale, and Kathryn vowed it would be the last. Speaking of it felt like squeezing the wound.

"If your father did not trust Bothwell, and he was one of the last men to speak with him, I assume you've considered that he might be quite dangerous?"

She nodded. "I've considered it."

"And yet you planned to march up to the man in the court-yard and demand to know what happened to your father?"

"Aye." She'd hoped the surprise would work in her favor.

"You are a brave woman, Kathryn . . ."

"Wyld."

"From Bondgate-in-Darlington?"

She shook her head. "Nay. Sherborne."

Neill said nothing more, but he did pull her closer. She let herself lean her head against him, nestling closer yet, and they both fell silent.

So much to discuss, but for now, no words were necessary.

CHAPTER 14

*W*hen Neill awoke, it took him a moment to remember where he was.

Then it all came flooding back at once. Kathryn. Her story. Her father.

Kathryn.

He sprung up from his makeshift pallet on the floor and moved toward the bed. He watched her sleep, thankful that no worry lines marred the beautiful face that he ached to lean down and touch.

She'd insisted she'd sleep in the hall, but he'd fought her on it. Although her concerns were valid—what remained of her reputation would be ruined should they be caught—he feared for her safety too much to let her sleep alone. His insistence that he'd afford her the privacy she needed in the morning, paired with a gentle reminder that they had stayed together in tighter quarters, had finally served to convince her.

Last eve, he'd fetched a bowl of rosewater for her himself, then paced the corridors so she could wash and dress in peace. Thankfully, Bryce had been nowhere to be found.

He dressed quietly, unwilling to wake her. Neill rose before the sun most days, and today was no exception. After pausing one last time to glance at her, a surge of protectiveness mixing with a very real stirring that forced him away from the bed, Neill left his chamber as quietly as possible.

A soft knock on the door to his left, and it was opened a moment later.

"Another change," Bryce said. "You were never awake this early in the morn as a lad."

Bryce, on the other hand, had always risen early, something Neill had counted on.

"We need to talk."

Bryce stepped to the side and Neill entered. With the exception of the alcove and window, his brother's chamber was much the same as his own. Clean, well-appointed, fairly small. Having a private chamber was a rarity, so Neill was thankful.

Especially after last night.

Sitting in one of the two chairs at the small table, he didn't waste time exchanging pleasantries with his brother. Instead, he told him everything.

Although Kathryn had not given him leave to share her secret, he did not feel overly guilty for doing so. He needed both advice and assistance, if he were going to help find Kathryn's father's killer.

And Neill planned to do just that. The man deserved justice.

Kathryn deserved peace.

The mere fact that she'd planned to question Bothwell herself, so brazenly, was reason enough for him to assist her. There was a real danger to her, and he'd not have her harmed.

"Neill," Bryce said, sitting on his bed. "Do you realize the delicacy of this situation?"

"I do. But there is more to consider."

He couldn't see his brother's expression clearly from across the chamber, but he could easily imagine it. Years, days . . . it didn't matter how long they'd been apart. Neill had been raised with this man, and he knew his habits well. His eyes, as blue as his own, will have grown dark.

"More than the fact that there's a woman asleep in your chamber, whose father, once the king's royal messenger, was murdered by someone in the Scottish court, potentially a man who will be present at the council we both plan to attend in two days."

"Was that a question?"

Bryce growled, "Aye, more than that."

He stood, grabbing the only light source as the wall torches had gone out in the night, a lone candle, and took it with him as he sat next to his brother on the bed.

"There was a condition to the king's reward. The boon was only granted after some negotiation."

"What condition?"

"King Edward is vexed that King Alexander has hesitated to repledge his loyalty. He wished for it to happen soon after his return to England. He insists that it happen before he removes Caxton from office."

Bryce frowned. "Why didn't you say so?"

"I know I did not mention it in my letters, but I knew of no secure way to tell Geoffrey in writing."

"The Scottish king has pledged to the English crown since the Treaty of Falaise. Why should he refuse to do so now?"

Neill wondered the same. "That's the very question I plan to posit tomorrow. It worries me that he's delayed for so long."

Bryce stood. "Then it is even more important the wardens understand the stakes and communicate them to their king. Douglas will ensure it."

"Brother, you should sit. I've not finished."

Bryce did as he'd asked, the flickering of the candle between them casting an eerie glow on their early morning talk.

"There's more?" he asked tiredly.

"Aye. One more condition."

Bryce swore under his breath.

"I am to marry Lady Alina deBeers, the daughter of Baron deBeers and a personal attendant to the queen."

Bryce whistled. He thought on it a moment, then said, "The queen's condition or the king's?"

Bryce, though a pain in the arse at times, was also quite intelligent.

"The queen's, I believe."

Bryce crossed his arms. "Is she fair?"

"I've been told she is, but that hardly matters."

"It matters some."

"Though I do not believe you understand."

"I understand the king's reward comes with a high price, but you've no choice but to pay it. As long as Alexander renews his pledge of fealty, all will finally be well again. At least as well as the borderlands have ever been." He shrugged.

"Such is the life of a border lord," Neill said, a common refrain they'd both grown up saying. But it was their home, and one worth fighting for.

He'd planned to tell Bryce more. He'd wanted to unburden himself about his feelings for Kathryn and the vow he'd made to help her. But something stopped him.

"What do you plan to do about Bothwell?" Bryce asked, standing once again. "And more importantly, do you care to have a quick session before we break our fast?"

It had been a tradition when they were lads, and Neill looked forward to having another go at his brother. But first he had to speak to Kathryn.

"Aye. I will meet you in the training yard."

As Neill left the room, he felt a certain heaviness bear down on his shoulders. Although he wasn't sure what he'd hoped for, part of him had wanted his brother to solve the problem for him. To convince him, perhaps, that the queen's condition was not as important as he knew it to be. No matter. Surely he could help Kathryn while also ushering in a new initiative of peace at the border.

The only cause he could not afford to advance?

His own.

As he walked back to his chamber, Neill chided himself for the thoughts that had stirred within him.

She is not your lady.

As natural as it seemed to offer her comfort, to touch and hold her, he could not afford to do so again.

Certainly, he must refrain from kissing her.

He opened the door, nearly groaning from the memory of her lips, so very hesitant, pressing against his with raw enthusiasm. Though obviously inexperienced, she'd learned quickly, the touch of her tongue so pleasurable it had infiltrated his dreams.

Neill entered the chamber and froze.

His good intentions evaporated in an instant.

SCRAMBLING OVER TO THE BED, Kathryn grabbed the undertunic and attempted to pull it over her head. She'd never dreamed Neill would return so soon, and so she'd thought nothing of standing around his bedchamber in her shift. When she'd awoken to find him gone, she'd assumed he'd left for the day.

The shift was the only item of clothing she'd kept from her past life, reasoning no one would actually see it. The fine, sheer cotton was the only luxury that she allowed herself.

And now it was on full display, her attempts to hurriedly don the undertunic failing miserably. Of course, she definitely never attempted to clothe herself in front of a man. And certainly not one as compelling as Neill Waryn.

When she did finally manage to get it over her head, she smiled at her gallant knight. His back was now to her.

Clearing her throat, Kathryn reached next for her kirtle. Though at least now she was somewhat properly dressed.

Neill turned. "Pardon, Kathryn."

"'Tis your chamber. I am the intruder here."

They stared at each other, light just beginning to stream in from beyond the shutters she'd opened. Kathryn's chest rose and fell, her heart beating faster than was its custom, driven by an aching awareness of him.

"You're thinking of it too." Kathryn could not believe her own boldness. Something about this man made her not want to hide. Her feelings. Her past.

"I've thought of little else since we met."

The admission, not what she'd been expecting, prompted her to share the thoughts she'd been having as well.

"I swore never to tell anyone my true identity, unsure who to trust. But then I met you . . ." She smiled. "You are a good man, Neill Waryn." She knew the truth of it in her heart.

"If you knew my thoughts at this very moment, you'd take back your words."

A thrill of excitement shot through her. She could not back down now.

"I doubt that I would."

Neill closed the space between them, his breath smelling of the mint she'd found on the table.

His mouth covered hers, and she welcomed it.

This time, she knew what to do. Opening for him, Kathryn grasped the nape of his neck as he pulled her close. This kiss, more frenzied than the first one, held all the promise of his vow to her. Now that she'd shared her secrets, she felt closer to him, their connection sweeter.

"Kathryn," he murmured against her mouth. "I've so much to tell you."

Pulling back just slightly, she looked into his eyes. It struck her that she was nothing more than a serving maid for now. Neill was a third son, aye, but he was also brother to an earl. His extended family, one of the greatest borderland clans in Scotland.

And she didn't know how long it might take, finding her father's murderer. This, between them, could never be. And she knew that. Accepted it, even. But when he looked at her as if no one else in the world mattered . . .

When he cupped her face, Kathryn closed her eyes.

"Nay, open them."

She did.

"Your eyes are beautiful. Like you."

She'd been told as much many, many times. But she'd never paid the words any mind. Not from her father, who was obligated to say such things. Not from her suitors, who said the same about countless other ladies at court.

"I believe you."

He chuckled—a low, rich sound that reverberated through her. "You should. I'm not in the practice of saying things I don't mean."

She smiled.

"I told my brother."

It took her a moment, but when she absorbed his words, Kathryn pushed him away in horror.

"Neill. No."

"Kathryn, listen to me. You trust me. You'd never have told me if you did not. And I trust my brother with my life. He'll not say a word to anyone. I made a vow to you I intend to keep. But to do that, I will need the help of others I can trust. But you have to understand, Bothwell is dangerous." He scowled, his jaw flexing. "Please do not speak to him alone."

"Others? Please, no. Who else have you told?"

She'd made a mistake. Telling him had been a mistake.

"I'd be grateful if you'd stay up here, just for a time. You said yourself that Douglas might recognize you. Bryce and I will speak to Toren, and—"

"You propose to tell the lord of Brockburg my secret?"

"And his wife."

Kathryn spun away, panicked now. This would not do. She was to tell no one but Magge, and now Neill and his brother knew, and it sounded as if he aimed to tell half of Brockburg.

"Nay. I cannot let you do that."

"Kathryn." He grabbed her hand, his manner urgent. "Listen to me. Bothwell is one of the most powerful men in Scotland. One who very likely had your father killed."

Her eyes widened. "You suspect it too?"

She thought it more likely someone from the English court wanted her father dead. But the very man who had seen him last? Aye, he could just as likely be the culprit.

"I don't know, but it's certainly possible. The situation is beyond suspicious. But to learn the truth, we cannot face this alone. If you confront him, do you really believe he will confess all he knows?"

"No," she admitted. "I never thought he would, but I thought his reaction might tell me what I wished to know. My father always said you need only to look into someone's eyes to know if they're being truthful. If I knew . . ."

"Then what?"

Of course she'd thought about that many, many times, but she'd never come to a conclusion. Another sign of her impetuous nature, she knew.

Someday, Kathryn, you will learn patience. Otherwise, I fear you will kiss the hare's foot.

Her father's favorite saying. No doubt it would have horrified him to learn she'd put herself in such a situation without a real plan.

"You cannot go this course alone. You must understand, if Bryce or I were to question him, it would raise suspicions.

Toren, however, has dealt with Bothwell for years, and he and his wife would be ideally suited to questioning him quietly. Delicately. But we must keep you safe in the interim."

"I am safe enough."

He made a face. "And when Douglas recognizes you?"

"I'd planned to stay away from the hall."

"Then where, pray tell, did you plan on confronting Bothwell? Did you think he would simply grant you an audience?"

She crossed her arms. "I could have spoken to him upon his arrival if a certain English knight had not waylaid me in the courtyard."

"And thank the heavens I did," he shot back.

They stared at each other, neither of them speaking, until Neill said, "Bryce awaits me. Shall I bring my brother and our hosts here after they break their fast, so that we may speak to them and devise a plan? Or will you follow me through that door, find Bothwell, and demand justice for your father in front of a hall filled with his loyal subjects? The choice is yours."

He made it difficult to think.

Her very life could be in jeopardy if she made the wrong choice, but like a silly twit, Kathryn could not stop staring at Neill's lips. She'd never imagined a man's lips could bring her such pleasure.

This time, it was she who closed the distance between them. Touching his hand, because she needed to touch him, she gave him the only answer she had. "I simply do not know. If my father were here—"

"Kathryn," he said gently, "he is not."

She was still unsure.

"What do *you* want? What does Kathryn Wyld, and no other, want?"

That was easy.

"I want you to kiss me again."

He groaned and pulled her head toward him, giving her

what she asked for. His lips moved over hers as he tilted her head to the side. It was heaven, his kisses. And she never wanted them to end.

When he pulled away, Kathryn expected to see the same regret in his expression she'd noticed each time, as if he was angry with himself for kissing someone in her station. Instead, he looked at her with a combination of desire and resolve.

He emboldened her.

"Bring them," she said. "If you think it best."

He nodded, stepping back with a formal bow as if she were the queen of England and not a lowly serving girl he'd picked up from an inn.

And then he was gone, leaving Kathryn to contemplate the choices that had led her so far astray from her plans.

Nothing good would come of this, she was sure.

CHAPTER 15

"The timing is all wrong for any sort of confrontation," Toren said.

Neill agreed, but there was no help for it. It was just before the midday meal, and he, Toren, and Bryce were making their way to the solar to meet the mistress of the castle, Lady Juliette, and Kathryn. That morning, he'd pulled the lord and lady aside to explain he needed their help. And although Bryce had scowled throughout his explanation, his brother had at least possessed enough sense to remain quiet.

After they'd arranged where to meet and when, Lady Juliette had left to attend to "that poor woman." Neill had spent the rest of the morning meeting with the other Englishmen in attendance, all of whom were anxious to hear firsthand about his interactions with the king prior to the larger council meeting with the Scottish wardens and border lords.

The whole while, his mind had been fixed on Kathryn. Only now it appeared he might not have the help he'd counted on.

"I can make some inquiries," Toren continued, "but Bothwell is known for his neutrality. If Lady Kathryn had hoped to discern anything from him in a short discussion, I fear she would have been disappointed. None are privy to his thoughts, save the king."

Neill fell in behind Toren as they made their way to the second floor of the great keep. They could not see who might be waiting above them, so they all ceased talking for fear of potentially being overheard.

Bryce fell in step beside him as soon as they reached the landing.

"I told my brother as much, Toren. But it seems he takes his role as knight of the realm quite seriously." Then, to him, he added, "You're not bound to save every maiden in the kingdom, brother."

"Not all," Neill said. "Just Kathryn. And I intend to help her, not save her. She can do quite well by herself."

Bryce stopped, and so Toren and Neill did so as well.

"Kathryn?" Bryce asked.

"Aye."

"Not Lady Kathryn or Mistress Kathryn?"

Neill realized his mistake immediately, but he would not discuss this matter in front of Toren. "They're waiting on us," he prompted, and Toren, at least, took his meaning. After looking back and forth between the brothers, clearly not understanding the problem, the chief pushed open the door.

Neill froze in the entranceway, but it wasn't the large, well-lit chamber or colorful tapestries that caught his attention. Kathryn sat with Lady Juliette on the far side of the room. Moving toward her, he knew he had completely failed at his goal to conceal his feelings for her from Bryce.

But he hadn't expected this—the lady of the house had given her a gown worthy of her station. Pale blue. He'd never loved a color so much before. She truly looked like an angel, her hair tumbling down her back in waves of brown and gold. He knew not where to look—at her hair, her face, or her perfect breasts, which peeked out from the low neckline of the gown. Their eyes met, and she held his gaze for a moment before he managed to look away.

He recovered quickly, but mayhap not quickly enough, judging from Bryce's expression.

"My ladies," he said, sitting across from them in a high-backed wooden chair with royal blue and yellow embroidered cushions. Toren stooped to kiss his wife on the cheek before he and Bryce also took their seats.

"As you know," Neill said to the group, "I escorted Lady Kathryn here, unaware of her true identity."

"And for that," she cut in, "I am sorry. It was never my intention to involve anyone in my plan."

"A plan," Bryce admonished, "that could have gotten you killed."

Without hesitation, she responded. "Aye, but I cannot apologize for seeking the truth. He was my father. And a good man who served his king and country well."

Of that, Neill had no doubt, knowing Kathryn as he did.

"Tell us," Toren said, "everything. Neill is our family, and he has pledged himself to your cause. You can count on us to do the same."

Neill avoided looking at Kathryn as she shared her tale, knowing his brother was watching him closely. Instead, he kept his attention fixed on Toren, the man his family had despised for so long. He had a new understanding of why his siblings thought so highly of this man.

He had a council to host. A country to keep safe. And yet, here was the chief of Clan Kerr, one of the most powerful of the border clans, listening to the tale of a woman he'd never met. And he did not doubt Toren intended to keep his word and pursue the matter.

He was an honorable man.

It was what Emma had told him in a letter some time ago. At the time, he'd struggled to understand how his sister and brothers could set aside their hurt and anger to open their hearts to the Kerr family. But Adam and Cora had helped him understand the truth: his parents had been casualties of a war none of them could control, one that raged even now.

Neill finally gave in to the urge to look at her. He wished more than anything he could take away her pain.

He tried to tell himself he'd feel this protectiveness for any woman in Kathryn's position, but he knew that to be a lie.

"Does anyone," he said when she finished, "believe it's possible her father's death was an accident?"

None spoke up.

"And if he was, indeed, murdered, Bothwell's refusal to give him an audience with the king seems more than suspicious. Aye?"

Again, it seemed all agreed.

"So the question is, why would Bothwell want to have him murdered?"

"And what was the message?" Juliette added.

Everyone turned toward Kathryn, who shrugged. "I do not know. Even when my father was privy to the messages he carried, he never shared them with me."

"The timing is curious," Bryce said, sitting back in his chair. "This happened soon after King Edward returned from his long sojourn in the East."

"Could it have been a request to renew his allegiance?" Neill speculated. "It was one of his conditions of my reward."

"I don't understand why Caxton has not already been removed," Kathryn said. "Everyone I've spoken to says he's awful."

Bryce answered for him. "And yet he lines the king's pockets."

"The reason," Toren interjected, "we refused to treat with Caxton is because he accepts black mal in exchange for setting even the worst criminals free. If Englishmen aren't held accountable for their crimes, why should we submit to the Day of Truce?"

"But the situation has changed," Neill said. "With his attention now on France, the king will need both funds and support. Alexander's fealty has become more important."

Kathryn startled at that news. "Do you believe we will go to war with France?"

Neill exchanged a look with his brother. No one was sure of the answer, but he had a definite opinion on the matter.

"I do."

Toren whistled. "Edward is willing to release his profitable warden if he can retain the loyalty of a king who might provide him with some security."

"Where does Bothwell stand on any of this?" Kathryn asked.

"A question I've been wondering about," he admitted, "since you told me of your suspicions."

Toren frowned. "None know. He never speaks at any of the councils, much to Douglas's annoyance. He attends to report back to the king. No more, no less. 'Tis a role Douglas fills whenever Bothwell is not in attendance."

"Hmmm."

Despite the seriousness of the situation, Neill smiled at Kathryn's expression. She looked so intent, so serious.

"I bet I can guess his leanings," she blurted.

They were all thinking the same thing now. The English king's messenger had disappeared under mysterious circumstances after bringing a message so inflammatory he would only share it directly with the king. The king's chancellor had refused to allow it, and the messenger had been killed that same night.

The Earl of Bothwell had no wish to see the Scottish king allied with King Edward.

Which made Kathryn's revelations akin to the most important information they had currently about the situation along the border.

"How much of this situation do we report to the council?" Toren asked.

They all looked at Kathryn, who, rightly so, appeared panicked. "You cannot tell them."

"Do we agree," Toren said finally, "about what all of this implies?"

"Aye," Neill said, "although we know naught for certain. Naught except Lady Kathryn is not safe here."

"Neill, you need to get her out of here," Juliette said at once.

He'd already thought the same.

"They'll want to hear the king's words directly from my brother," Bryce began. "He needs to be at the meeting."

"And I will be." Neill already knew what he had to do. "Tomorrow morning, I will tell them everything."

"Everything?" Bryce interrupted.

"Aye. And you will watch Bothwell closely when I do."

"Watch him?" Toren snorted. "We will do more than that. When I explain the king's conditions, when Bothwell realizes even now a message is on its way to Edinburgh asking for a renewal of Alexander's vow—"

"You will have him followed," Kathryn said to Toren, catching on.

"Aye."

"But I suppose I'll not be here to see how this plays out?"

"Where will you go after the meeting?" Bryce asked, looking between Neill and Kathryn. "Bristol Manor?"

"Nay," he said. "'Tis too close." Kathryn asked the silent question, and he answered, "Kenshire Castle. We leave on the morrow for Kenshire Castle, my lady. You will be safe there."

CHAPTER 16

$\mathcal{K}$enshire Castle.

Kathryn had heard of it, of course, but seeing one of the most formidable strongholds in the north was a very different experience than being told about it. Before their party even approached the outer curtain wall, she could smell the North Sea. Having traveled on a ship with her father, Kathryn knew the beauty of the sea could be deceiving. She still had a bump on her head from one particularly bad storm. A "testimonial to your travels," her father had called it.

Despite everywhere she'd been, all the people she'd met in the course of her travels, this experience stood out among the others. One of the greatest castles in England loomed above her, and one of its greatest knights rode to her left.

Neill had spoken to the council as planned, recounting his audience with the English king. As expected, Bothwell had not reacted to the news that the English king had set a condition on the reward he'd granted his Tournament of Peace champion.

They'd not stayed long enough to witness the events that came afterward. Neill had excused himself before the midday meal while the council was still in session. They'd left at once.

The plan was for them to remain safely in Kenshire until matters had settled at Brockburg and both royal courts.

She wished to speak to Neill about it, to hold his hand and kiss him, but they'd not found themselves alone for long on this four-day journey. She had an escort now, a young Scottish maid grateful for the opportunity to travel to Kenshire, along with a contingency of men provided by the chief of Clan Kerr.

Even so, she'd caught Neill looking at her plenty of times. The previous day they'd both approached a small stream at the same time on a break from the saddle. Kathryn had hoped they might have the opportunity to speak. It had almost seemed as if he'd sought her out, but Innis, her ever-present companion, had approached them before any words could be exchanged. Innis, who was simply doing her duty.

Kathryn had tried to thank Neill for taking her here. For keeping her safe. For leaving the council. That discussion, which they'd had before embarking from Brockburg, was the only private one they'd had in days. Kathryn very much looked forward to speaking with Neill again.

Kissing Neill, more like.

As many times as she'd chided herself for thinking of him that way, Kathryn simply could not stop thinking of his lips on hers, their tongues tangling greedily. Neill Waryn was in her blood.

"'Tis beautiful," Innis said beside her as the portcullis was raised. The hooves of their mounts clanked across the drawbridge. Kenshire's lower bailey was nearly the same size as Brockburg's main courtyard, the immensity of the castle a testament to its preeminence along the northeastern coast.

"Aye," she agreed, watching as Neill spoke with a rider who'd come to greet them. Nay, not any rider.

His brother.

He had the same raven-black hair as Neill and Bryce, the same wide shoulders. Kathryn rode closer and both men turned to her. Almost as quickly as he'd ridden out toward them, Geoffrey Waryn turned back to the castle and their riding party followed. Neill glanced her way, which was when she noticed his broad smile.

Neill obviously cared deeply for his siblings, and not for the first time, Kathryn wished she'd had brothers and sisters. But her father had fulfilled his promise never to remarry, her mother, he'd said repeatedly, "a woman who could not be replaced."

They rode through the inner bailey and a passageway that climbed steeply upward, the main keep high above them. When the ground finally leveled again, Kathryn found herself in the most magnificent of courtyards, one that could rival that of any royal palace. It was unusual to see grass in an area so heavily traveled, but patches of it grew in various places, flowers even sprouting up here and there. When they had all dismounted, Neill gave Kathryn's reins to a stable boy, who bowed his head to her, a reaction to one of the two gowns Lady Juliette had insisted she take with her.

When she looked up at the main keep, Kathryn blinked. The woman walking toward them did not look as if she could be real. Lady Juliette was lovely, but this woman, who could only be the Countess of Kenshire, was striking.

Her dark hair and exotic beauty looked almost out of place here in this cool climate, but her face was not the most noticeable thing about her. The lady wore what appeared to be an altered version of men's breeches paired with a tunic, not unlike the ones Neill wore, and no overtunic. She looked as if she were heading to the training yard.

In all of her travels, Kathryn had never seen anything like it.

The lady rushed forward and swept Neill into a hug before pulling away to look him over from head to toe as a mother or a sister might.

"You are a boy no longer," she exclaimed, her voice as bright as her visage.

And then the lady's eyes fell on *her*. It felt as if she'd walked into the sun, an awareness of her own shortcomings nearly choking her. How could this woman in men's breeches exude more grace than the finest of ladies at court?

"Geoffrey, Sara," Neill said, smiling back at her, "may I present Lady Kathryn Wyld, daughter of the late Sir Richard Wyld. She is to be my guest at Kenshire."

Sara took her hand, apparently a common gesture for this family.

"Richard," Lady Sara beamed. "That was my father's name as well."

Instead of asking how she'd come to be his guest or inquiring about the circumstances that had led to their visit, Sara winked at Kathryn. "We will leave you to your reunion," she said to her husband. "Come—" she tugged Kathryn's hand, "—I've something to show you."

"Show me?" she asked in bewilderment.

The countess did not know her at all, let alone why she was here, but none of that seemed to matter to her. With a final backward glance at Neill, who met her eyes and smiled encouragingly, she followed Lady Sara around the great keep, past tower after tower. The castle was bustling, with knights and servants milling around every corner.

Lady Sara had released her hand and was now climbing a set of stairs built into the side of the inner curtain wall closest to what appeared to be a guardroom. When they arrived at the top, Kathryn, beyond curious now, looked out and immediately knew why Lady Sara had taken her here.

They stood above a most spectacular view of the North Sea. Below them, a steep drop of grass and rock gave way to taller blades of grass waving in the breeze, and then sand. Beyond it, the sea. The sound of its waves did not reach them here, but Kathryn could easily imagine its song.

Kathryn spun in all directions, taking in the view. To their left, nothing but fields, farmlands most like. Behind her, beyond the retaining walls, she could even see the village they'd passed on their way to the castle. Her eyes finally came to rest again on the ocean.

"'Tis breathtaking, Lady Sara."

"Sara. And aye, it is that."

Kathryn looked at the other woman in surprise. "My lady?"

"I am not one for formality." She nodded down, toward her attire. "As you can see. Most especially with a woman who has captured the heart of my brother-in-law."

This woman was full of surprises.

"Oh, no, my lady, 'tis not that way at all."

She wished to ask the other woman why she'd formed such an impression, but the Countess of Kenshire made her uncharacteristically shy.

"Sara."

Kathryn relented. "Sara."

"And if I may have leave to call you by your given name?" Sara prodded.

"Of course!"

"Then I would be so bold to ask, Kathryn . . . how *is* it between you and Neill?"

"I . . . that is . . . we . . ." In truth, it was a good question, one she was wholly unprepared to answer, especially to a stranger. Even if she was Neill's sister-in-law.

"I see. Well, luckily, this will not be my very first foray into a complicated relationship. It seems this family has no shortage of them."

"There is . . . we are not together, my . . . Sara."

Kathryn didn't understand her own impulse, but under the warm summer sun, along the ramparts of what was one of the loveliest places she'd seen in her life, she found herself sharing her story with the countess.

She began at The Wild Boar. She told Sara of her plan, one that seemed rather foolish now that she'd shared it aloud, twice. She told her of her father too, although the recounting was no easier than it had been when she'd told Neill about his death.

"I am very sorry for the loss of your father," Sara said when she finally finished. "I understand how painful it is to lose your only parent. Your mother?"

"Died in childbirth."

In that moment, something passed between them. The hairs on Kathryn's arms stood straight up. She knew without asking the countess's mother had passed under the same circumstances.

"It seems we are kindred spirits, you and I. Daughters of great men—" Sara smiled, "—two Richards who lost their loves too early."

It was remarkable, really, when she put it that way.

"Though you are a countess . . ."

"And you, the daughter of a man who might, even after his death, alter the course of history."

Kathryn held her shoulders back, a vision of her father flashing before her. He'd been a handsome man with dark hair speckled with grey. Articulate. An expert horseman, and one who knew the land above all others.

A great man indeed.

When she saw the glint of tears in Sara's eyes, Kathryn could no longer maintain her composure. She'd thought the countess too strong to succumb to tears, and the sight called forth her own emotion.

Sara closed the space between them, her arms wrapping around her as if she were a sister and not a stranger. They cried together for all they'd lost. Great men. Mothers they'd never known.

Kathryn had never allowed herself to cry like this, as if her father were truly gone forever. Though she had not questioned the truth of the cleric's words, some tiny part of her, never having seen his body . . .

But he was gone, and Kathryn would never, ever see him again. She was alone in the world.

Sara pulled away.

"I do not normally greet new guests with tears," she said, a sad smile forming on her lips, "but neither am I embarrassed to have done so. I thought to press you on the bits of the story you left out. But perhaps I can do that later this eve."

Kathryn's eyes widened. How had she known? The only aspect of the story she had kept to herself related to Neill.

"We are very much alike, you and I," Sara said, as if reading her thoughts. "We will speak more later. Now let us go and join the men."

CHAPTER 17

"*H*ayden and Hugh."

Neill watched from the dais as his nephews were led away from the hall by Faye, his aunt by marriage. Faye had fussed over him quite a bit, for they'd not seen each other since soon after she had wed Uncle Hugh. It was clear Hugh had acclimated to life at Kenshire quite as well as Geoffrey—he was the namesake of Neill's youngest nephew, the newborn babe who had kept Geoffrey from the council. Hayden held on to Faye's leg as they left the hall. He had just started walking recently, according to Geoffrey.

It had been a good, satisfying day, which Neill and Geoffrey had spent talking and training. Kathryn had been absent from the midday meal, although Sara had assured them she was well. He'd pressed her, wondering why she had not joined them, but the countess had put him off, explaining only that she'd needed some time to herself.

Thankfully, she'd arrived moments ago looking more than well. Once again, her lovely hair hung down her back, drawing his gaze and making his hand itch to touch it. He was not sure if he should bless or curse whatever fate had seated him next to her. It would have been customary for him to sit beside his brother, but instead he'd been positioned to Kathryn's left. So far, she had spent most of the meal speaking to Sara, leaving Neill to observe the activity in the hall. Luckily, they weren't forced to share a trencher, courtesy of the individual bowls of stew that had been served.

His brother's words from earlier echoed in his ear as he struggled not to stare at her.

"You understand your duty, brother?" Geoffrey had said.

Neill had told his brother everything. Though he was very close to his sister, Emma, and had always admired Bryce, it was Geoffrey with whom he shared the closest bond. After their parents had been killed, it was Geoffrey who had kept the family together. Geoffrey reminded him most of their father, and he'd always striven to make him proud.

His brother had said exactly what he'd expected—and feared —he would say. From the moment the king had set that second condition, he'd known his life was no longer his own. He would share it with Lady Alina. A small sacrifice for what he'd gained, or so he'd thought.

"Aye," he'd told Geoffrey, "but I'll not lie and say I like it."

"You've not told her," his brother had admonished. With those words, every excuse he'd conjured up for his reticence had been laid to waste. He told himself he'd not had the opportunity. On their journey to Kenshire, he'd even approached her once, intending to apologize for his behavior and explain the conditions of King Edward's boon. But the maid had joined them, and he'd used her intrusion as a reason to put off his explanation.

He chanced a glance at Kathryn.

And damned if she wasn't peering at him over her wine goblet.

She seemed very at ease here, sitting with his family on the dais. Geoffrey had mentioned Sara had convinced Kathryn to continue to dress as befit her status. To sit with the family who hosted her. The men who had come with him from the start already knew, as of earlier that day, the maid was, in actuality, a lady. Though her true identity remained a secret. But one thing had been bothering him.

"Your very diligent chaperone," he said, before she looked away. "Does she not wonder about your transformation?"

He looked down, meaning to glance at her gown, but his gaze settled on her deep neckline. Trimmed in gold thread, it glimmered in a way that had caught his attention.

Recognizing that he lied, unsuccessfully, to himself, Neill attempted to ignore his body's reaction.

"Sara has other ideas for how to keep the maid occupied while she remains here at Kenshire and is thankfully no longer my personal maid."

"I see."

Lifting his mug for a drink, he tried to keep his mind from remembering the times she'd melted into his arms, her lips a perfect fit for his.

Neill shrugged away the thought.

So . . . Sara and Kathryn had become fast friends. It warmed him to think of the two women getting on so well.

Wresting him back to the present moment, Kathryn frowned and said, "You do not believe I put myself in danger?"

"By dressing for your station?" Neill shook his head. "I trust my men. If they are confused by the situation, they'll keep their thoughts to themselves."

Kathryn placed her goblet onto the table, folding her hands quite prettily on her lap.

"I've been hearing tales of your childhood, you know."

Geoffrey was watching them as Sara spoke to him. He understood his brother's discomfort. But there was no law preventing him from speaking to a guest. They were simply conversing. Nothing more.

"And you still wish to speak to me?" he asked with a small smile. "I am a lucky man indeed."

Kathryn's laugh was like the sound of some mischievous wood-sprite. He wished he could listen to it all day.

"I've heard naught but good stories, which is suspicious now that I think on it."

"Mmmm." He knew what she was going to say next.

"I've heard you were the quickest. The smartest. The most gallant."

"And that was all before I left for Langford."

"In fact . . ." Kathryn peered around him at his brother and lowered her voice. "It's said the only tournament you have lost since becoming a knight was after you wrote to your sister saying, 'None could possibly best me.'"

"Lady Sara has much to say about me, then?"

"Aye."

"If I recall, by the time Emma received that very missive, Lord Blackburn of Anglewood had already bested me."

"Aye, so Sara said."

"But he was the last."

"Until Bryce, of course."

"My dastardly brother-in-law," Sara said beside her.

"Aye, he is that." Neill picked up his mug. "As Kathryn has so kindly reminded me, Bryce somehow managed to best me in training at Brockburg."

"Somehow, eh?" Geoffrey interjected, addressing Kathryn. "A boy left for Langford, a man returned north. But—" he cleared his throat, "—I fear my brother still has much to learn. I suspect he forgot the lesson Blackburn taught him."

"I left a pain in the arse," he explained to Kathryn, "and returned to a pain in the arse. Aside from my brother's beautiful wife and two strapping youngins, it seems all remains the same here at Kenshire."

If Kathryn smiled that way every time he spoke, Neill would never stop talking.

"Does Lord—"

"Geoffrey," Sara interrupted. The two women exchanged a look, and Kathryn nodded and corrected herself. "Does Geoffrey have the right of it, then? Did your brother best you because he took advantage of your over-confidence?"

His brother burst out laughing, and Neill could admit, it was somewhat amusing how keenly Kathryn had assessed Geoffrey's hidden meaning. Though he was not surprised.

"We shall see tomorrow in the training yard."

"Aye," his brother replied. "Aye, we shall."

He relaxed then, knowing he needn't fear for Kathryn's well-being while they waited for word from Brockburg. In the meantime, he would do well to heed Geoffrey's warning.

As Neill's gaze strayed to her again, he reminded himself of what was at stake. Once King Alexander renewed his oath of fealty, King Edward would no doubt expect his other condition to be fulfilled. Neill would be required to submit to a formal betrothal. He was all but wed, which meant his delightful and very beautiful companion should be avoided at all costs.

Though he would have thought himself more disciplined, it seemed he had more weaknesses than the one Bryce had exploited. But succumbing to this weakness would be disastrous for his family and the borderlands, and that was if he kept his head for disobeying the king and queen.

And then she looked at him.

CHAPTER 18

"*I* must speak to you," she whispered.

Kathryn had wanted to say as much all evening, but only now, just before the meal ended, did she finally get the words out. She had to make sure Neill knew she had not encouraged Sara's matchmaking efforts. Because no matter what she'd said to the countess that day, she would not be waylaid. Sara was convinced she and Neill had feelings for one another.

Which was not entirely untrue.

Kathryn and Sara had enjoyed a pleasant afternoon together. So enjoyable, Kathryn could almost forget what was even now unfolding in Scotland. They had goaded the Earl of Bothwell, her father's potential murderer, and in so doing, they might succeed in uncovering a larger plot.

Of course, Sara thought it wildly romantic. If, she argued, Bothwell was the murderer and had been secretly undermining peace along the borderlands, it was wildly fortuitous for Kathryn to have come across Neill, who had been on his way to the council meeting.

It was, indeed, fated.

Although speaking openly about Lady Sara's scheme would mortify her, Kathryn knew it had to be done. Lady Sara did not appear to be the kind of woman who would give up easily. Geoffrey would likely soon know of her plan, and the count might well decide to share the news with his brother.

Before that happened, Kathryn had to be sure Neill understood it was not her doing.

Neill watched her so intently, without answering, that Kathryn thought he must not have heard her. She was about to repeat the question when he said, "I'll find you."

What did that mean? When would he find her? After the meal?

She had assumed he might simply pull her aside here in the hall. Her chaperone, after all, was no longer watching them. Surely they could speak privately for a moment?

When Geoffrey and Sara stood, they did the same, as was custom.

"I will see you to your chamber," Sara said, smiling at her husband and taking Kathryn's hand. The gesture was highly unusual, much like everything about this remarkable family. Though Sara wore a gown now, she certainly acted like no countess Kathryn had ever met. It was to her credit.

With a final glance back at Neill, who stepped off the dais with his brother, Kathryn followed Sara to the same comfortable chamber where she'd been installed earlier in the day. It was in a separate building from the main keep, one obviously reserved for the guests of Kenshire. On their way, Sara stopped a serving maid and whispered something to her, although Kathryn didn't overhear enough to guess at her latest kindness.

The chamber itself was a kindness. Stone walls encircled the room, a large burgundy tapestry covering one entire wall. A canopied bed sat in the center with a wooden chest on one side of it, a hearth on the other. The maid Sara had whispered to entered the room behind them with a pitcher and two wine goblets. Another maid followed with a bowl of rosewater and a cloth, which she placed on a stone step near the sole window in the room. Although it was currently shuttered, Kathryn knew the view from the small opening was spectacular. They were at the rear of the castle, and when she'd looked out earlier, sand and sea lay beyond.

"I hope you do not mind," Sara said, "I had the hearth prepared. Even in summer months, it can get quite cool here."

"Thank you. You are too kind."

The maids left the room, and Sara poured them each a goblet of wine.

"A toast," she said. "To your future."

Kathryn eyed the woman suspiciously. Was she always so tenacious?

Taking a sip, she blurted, "Neill and I . . . cannot be."

"Whatever do you mean?" Sara's eyes widened, a play of innocence somewhat undermined by the laughter she burst into moments later.

Once she recovered, she looked into Kathryn's eyes and said, "'Tis quite simple. You like him."

It was not a question, so she did not answer.

"And he likes you."

Kathryn resisted the urge to ask why Sara thought that to be true. Although it was undeniable that Neill had kissed her, more than once, that only meant he desired her. If Kathryn had learned one lesson from The Wild Boar, it was that desire could exist without affection. Two people could be together, in that way, without any prospect of marriage.

She'd even considered the possibility of giving in to desire with Neill, although she'd quickly dismissed it.

"I believe," Sara said, placing her goblet on the small wooden table in front of them, "this family was destined to find love through tribulation, and most unusual circumstances."

Kathryn had no idea what she meant by that.

Sara smiled. "I'll explain more on the morrow. For now, I bid you goodnight, Lady Kathryn."

Staring down at her wine, Kathryn didn't move at first. Why had her companion left without taking a sip of the wine she'd poured? Why had the lady of Kenshire, a countess in her own right, personally escorted her to her chamber?

She'd told Sara earlier she did not need a lady's maid. The fine gown Sara had lent her, along with the ones from Brockburg, were nonetheless simple enough for her to manage on her own. Embarrassed to have borrowed them at all, Kathryn placed her goblet back on the table and moved to the bowl of rosewater.

How easily I've slipped back into my former life. Foolish Kathryn.

She had fine gowns again, fine food too, and no hands to grab at her as she walked by. Her chamber, one which five of her rooms at the inn could fit inside.

And yet she would trade it all for a chance to say goodbye to her father, to know what had truly happened that day she was forced from Edinburgh.

When a knock sounded at the door, Kathryn's shoulders sagged. She'd prefer not to be fussed over, her mind at war with itself.

"I told Lady Sara . . ."

It was no maid. Neill filled the entranceway, his expression dark.

"You seem surprised. I told you that I would come."

She peered around the chamber. "Surely not here? Your brother, Lady Sara . . ."

She swallowed. Her heart raced as he waited for her acquiescence. The old Kathryn would never have considered it. But she was not the same woman who'd blushed to her very core after allowing a baron's son to sneak a quick kiss at court.

"I need to speak with you as well," he said. "There's something I've been meaning to tell you, and it would be better done in private."

Kathryn stepped aside, closing the door behind him. When she turned, Kathryn saw him looking at the two wine goblets.

"Sara," she started, and then stopped.

They'd toasted, but Sara had never sipped the wine. And not because Kathryn had interrupted her.

It was not intended for Sara.

"Did you tell anyone you were coming here?" she asked.

"Nay, I would not do that."

For the sake of your reputation.

He didn't say it, but the words were there.

So that meant . . .

Kathryn stared at the goblets in bafflement. How could she possibly have known?

I believe this family was destined to find love through tribulation.

Kathryn still did not understand what that meant, but she did know that Sara had suspected Neill would come. Somehow, she had guessed it. More than that, she'd encouraged it.

Which was exactly what she needed to speak to Neill about.

CHAPTER 19

"**S**ara?"

When he'd seen the two goblets, he'd imagined for a brief moment that another man had been here, in Kathryn's chamber. Though he'd immediately dismissed the thought, the burning sensation it had spread through his chest remained. The idea couldn't be set aside so easily.

Perhaps because she *would* be with another man. Someday, someone other than him would slip off that gown, discard the shift under it . . .

Nay.

Never.

"Sara brought them here." She frowned. "In fact, that is precisely why I wanted to speak with you."

Neill sauntered over to the table, picked up the goblets, and extended both to her. She took the one that was apparently hers and he took a sip of Sara's wine, though it appeared untouched. Nodding to the velvet-covered chairs by the hearth, he sat in one and watched as Kathryn lowered herself into the seat across from him.

She sat with as much grace as any highborn lady. Hair

streaming around her shoulders in glorious waves, her chin held high. Though he'd known from the start she was very much a lady, Neill chastised himself for harboring even a moment of doubt.

"You are not the same woman who left The Wild Boar with me," he said, unable to keep the thought to himself.

"I am." She took a sip of wine, her lips wrapping around the rim of the cup.

"Nay, you are the daughter of a royal messenger now."

"Just as I was that day."

"But you were also a serving maid, and there's no sign of that woman left in you now. The transformation is . . . remarkable."

He didn't voice the other thoughts that whirled around his head. Ones he should not be having, lest he forget his role in this dangerous game played by the border lords.

"'Tis the problem, I suppose," she said with another sip from her goblet. "I know not who I am."

The red wine slipped down his throat, a welcome companion in an impossible situation.

"I am so grateful for Magge and what she has done for me. She allowed me to remain close to the border, kept me safe. And yet . . ."

"And yet, here you are."

"I've no choice but to accept this may be my new life for some time."

Neill stood and made his way to the pitcher of wine. Filling both of their goblets, though hers was not yet empty, he thought about her words. The decision was easy, and immediate. As sure as he knew he was the son of Sir Thomas Waryn, Lord of Bristol Manor, he would not bring Kathryn back to that place. She was meant to be here.

"You could stay here."

"Here?"

"At Kenshire. My brother would protect you. And you would still be close to the border."

I would protect you. God, this woman was in his blood.

"Nay, I could not," Kathryn said, dismissing the possibility at once. "Neill, I wanted to tell you . . . Sara seems to have some odd notions of our relationship."

"Odd?"

"For some reason, it appears she's taken it upon herself to—" She coughed. Kathryn was nervous. "To believe there is a reason for us. That is, for the two of us . . ."

He suddenly knew precisely what she was about to say, which was why he lifted his full goblet and downed the contents.

Sara did not know the truth about their situation.

But she would, as soon as Geoffrey told her, and then her attempts to throw him and Kathryn together would end.

He didn't wish them to.

"'Tis silly, I know. But I did not want you to believe I'd encouraged it."

"Why silly?" he asked, despite himself.

He took his empty goblet back to the table, returning empty-handed. About to sit down again, he changed his mind and stood instead at the foot of Kathryn's chair. She looked up at him, unsure of what to do.

The way he felt for her . . . it was madness.

If only he were a stronger man. Neill had faced down opponents twice his size. Men hardened by a lifetime of battle. Men who should have bested him . . . but didn't.

And yet, he was still the impetuous young lad his brothers had failed to tame.

He extended a hand to her instead. She hesitated, as she should, but only for a moment. When she lowered her goblet onto the floor and took his hand, it felt like the embers from the fire flitted toward them in protest.

Neill did not, could not, heed the warning.

"She saw what has been between us from the first time I took your hand in mine."

He took her other hand, completing their connection.

"She saw my admiration for a woman who would travel across the dangerous border, intent on confronting the second most powerful man in Scotland." His throat thick, Neill forced himself to continue. "What she did not see, because she could not know, was how deeply I offended you without intending to do so."

"Offend me? Neill, you have done so much to help me, from the very start. You've caused me no offense."

He hated the words he was about to speak. Hated what it would do to them.

"There was another condition to the king's reward," he forced out. "He will remove Caxton with a renewed pledge from Alexander, but I am also to wed Lady Alina deBeers, as decreed by King Edward."

He didn't have to wait long for her reaction.

CHAPTER 20

*K*athryn pulled away so quickly she nearly stumbled backward. Her stomach hardened, a feeling of sickness welling inside her. Perhaps she had no reason to react so fiercely to his news. She had no claim on this man. Except . . .

"You *kissed* me."

Kathryn was aware she sounded like one of those silly ladies she and her friends had giggled about at court, the ones who spoke of nothing except the handsome, well-positioned men in their circle.

But she didn't care.

"More than once."

She took another step back, which was when Neill's hand reached out. Trying to avoid his grasp, Kathryn only realized at the last moment he was trying to save her from stepping too close to the hearth.

"Kathryn, I am so sorry. I never intended . . . I never intended for this to happen. Any of it."

"You did not intend to kiss me?"

She was finding it difficult to breathe.

"No. I did not."

"Then why?" She squared her shoulders. "Why did you?"

He closed his eyes, his jaw flexing as it had done the day they'd left for Brockburg. As it did whenever he was deep in contemplation.

"I have nothing but the truth to offer you."

"A fine time for that," she spat, aware her voice was raised.

"I deserve your anger. And although I doubt it will comfort you, I can assure you that you are no more angry with me than I am with myself."

She waited, though surely he could say nothing to improve the situation. They were beyond hope. "You are betrothed—"

"Nay." He shook his head. "Not betrothed. I am to return to court when the Scottish king's pledge has been given. A formal ceremony for our betrothal will occur alongside the king's decree to appoint a new warden. I've never even met the lady."

"It matters not. You are to be married."

"I am."

Shoulders sagging, her stomach no longer in knots, Kathryn simply stared at him. Like a simpleton.

"But you deserve the full truth. I care for you, Kathryn, so very much, and desire you as I've desired no other woman. Nay, I did not intend to kiss you, but neither could I resist the urge. I crave the taste of you, even now, when I know I should not. That night when you lay so close I could have reached for you . . . I thought over and over again of how to break the agreement without incurring the king's wrath. Because if I could ensure Caxton's removal any other way, I would do it. I would trade every accolade I've earned for the chance to pull you into my arms without holding back. To make you mine, in truth."

She would not be swayed by his words, no matter how pretty they were.

"You would make love to me," she finished, wishing the thought did not make her near dizzy.

"Nay, Kathryn. I would make you mine, for life. I would wake up to your smile, tell tales of my wife's bravery. I would cherish you above all others. I would love you until the end of my days."

She froze. Had he said . . .

"Love me?"

"Aye," he said, meeting her gaze and holding it. "And mayhap I am a fool. I've not been in love before and know nothing of it beyond what I've heard from my brothers and sister. I only know that whenever I look at you, I'm full of long-ing. I ache to touch your hair, your face, to worship your body, which will never be mine. To hear your thoughts and offer you comfort."

He stopped.

And Kathryn understood his reluctance to keep speaking. There was no use for it. A hundred, a thousand declarations of love would not be enough.

He was to be wed.

Or his reward would be taken from him.

"The king would risk unrest at the border just to marry you to this woman?"

A woman she did not know but would never like.

"Edward, like his father, is occupied with France. If his coffers are being lined by Caxton above all others . . ." He shrugged. "Scotland is a nuisance to him. The borders, even more so. Had I not asked for the boon, I do believe Caxton would have remained as warden. And everyone along the border would continue to suffer."

"Save he and the others who benefit from its unrest."

"Aye. And likely Bothwell among them."

"You should have told me."

"Aye, I should have."

They stared at each other, Kathryn still angry but also . . . something else. Her face flushed, her heart beating wildly in her chest. She had to open and close her hands to keep them from shaking.

The reason for her strong reaction to his revelation was simple. She felt the same way he did. The idea that she would never know his lips on hers again . . .

She'd wanted him to know Sara's scheme was not hers. For him to understand she'd never presume to believe the disgraced daughter of a murdered man could ever wed the brother of an earl.

"You told me once to stop looking at you the very same way you are looking at me now," he said.

What in the name of Saint Christopher was she doing?

"I cannot stop looking at you that way. Because despite what you've told me, despite my very real anger toward you at this moment, the thought of you leaving this chamber, of never kissing you again . . ."

He reached her in two strides.

THAT ONE LOOK, the desire he had no right to see in her expression after what he'd told her, had done him in.

His mouth crashed onto hers. When she responded with the hesitant touch of her tongue, Neill relinquished every rational thought for the flood of heat that shot between them.

His mouth slanted over hers, giving and taking alternatively. When his hand crept along the nape of her neck, gently closing on the soft, welcoming tresses that tickled his fingertips, Neill had no other choice but to pull her closer.

Kathryn's moans mingled with his, and he knew this time there would be nothing to interrupt them. No horse neighing nearby, drawing attention to them. No young chaperone.

It was up to him to stop this madness, and he couldn't bring himself to do it. That moment of jealousy earlier, when he'd imagined her with another man, had gotten to him. His gut told him he could no sooner let that happen than he could refuse his king.

Shoving the thought aside, he decided something then. He might not be able to offer himself to her the way he wished he could, but he could at least make her feel good.

"Kathryn," he whispered in her ear, pulling away for long enough to explain. "Let me show you how sorry I am for hurting you."

She turned her head, her lips so achingly close to his own. "Show me?"

"Let me pleasure you." Before she could ask what he meant, he rushed to say, "You will remain a virgin."

She blinked, the innocent gaze of a woman who'd never received such pleasure. And suddenly, he needed to be the one to show it to her first. Even if he would not be the last.

Nay. Never another.

At war with himself, one thought prevailed. He kissed the spot just below her ear and then tailed a line of kisses down her neck.

"Allow me this." He kissed her again. "An apology, of sorts."

He kept kissing. Waiting.

Lower and lower still.

As he pressed his lips to the top of her chest, Neill loosened the ties at each side of her gown. Still, she said nothing. When he turned his attention to the other side of her kirtle, she remained silent.

He stepped back then, lifted the offending garment over her head in one swift movement, and waited.

"I am still angry." The comment was teasing, yet he saw the truth of it in her eyes.

"As you should be."

When he pulled her back to him and kissed her again, the loose shift hardly presented a barrier. Without giving her time to think about the intimacy of what he was about to do, Neill slipped his hand under the fine material and pushed away the undergarments that covered his goal.

Despite her murmur of surprise, he continued, determined now. The fire crackled beside them as his fingers found the curls he would give his sword arm to see. When Kathryn instinctively pulled back, very likely embarrassed, he tore his mouth from hers and watched for a sign that he should stop.

"This is . . . wrong."

But that was not his sign.

"Aye, very much so. For you are not mine." The thought tore at him even as his fingers continued their exploration.

"And I am still very much angry with you."

Her lips, swollen from his kiss, glistened, demanding his attention. Already hard, Neill attempted to ignore those lips. He had a mission to accomplish, and his personal release was not part of it.

"And I am still very much sorry for hurting you."

He slipped a finger inside her.

Kathryn gasped.

"I am sorry for not telling you at the inn."

He slipped in another.

"Or on the road to Brockburg."

Neill moved both fingers, slowly, deliberately.

"Or when I kissed you behind the stables."

He pressed his palm against her, waiting. Watching.

"I'm sorry for not telling you on our way here."

He pressed harder.

"Or before Sara could see how taken I am with the most beautiful woman in the world." He circled his hand and moved his fingers in and out.

Her lips parted and Neill resisted the urge to take a taste. He was enjoying watching her face as she took her first real pleasure.

At his hands.

"I'm sorry to be crippled at the behest of a king I do not like."

Her eyes widened at the heresy.

He increased the pace.

"I'm sorry for the violent thoughts I had when I first came into your chamber and saw two goblets."

Faster and faster he moved his hand, knowing by her expression she was close. The hem of her shift teased his arm as it lay limp, the opposite of him. Neill would do well not to think of it. The feel of her under his hands, the sight of his hand under her shift in such an intimate position . . . he had to look away for a moment.

The knowledge that Kathryn felt for him what he did for her nearly tore him in two.

Neill looked back up, this time into her wide, surprised eyes, and held her gaze as he brought her to climax. She clenched around him, her nails digging into his undertunic.

"Neill," she breathed.

And then she shattered.

Kathryn's eyes slammed shut as she came apart in his hand. A victory as sure as any, Kathryn calling his name so much sweeter than a herald declaring him champion.

Though he slowed his movement, Kathryn did not yet relax around him. He watched, waited, and then smiled when her eyes flew open.

Reluctantly, he pulled away his hand, letting her dictate the next move.

In answer, she stepped away from him, letting her shift fall back into place.

"I've heard, but never imagined."

The moment was perfect, until an ugly thought intruded. If he did as he should and left her, another man's hand would be pleasuring his Kathryn someday.

No. As God was his witness, no.

He could not allow Caxton to remain in power, but neither could he allow the sun to rise and set each day without seeing Kathryn's face.

"What is it?" she asked, her shoulders rising up and down as her breathing returned to normal.

How could he put into words that everything, his world and hers, would never be the same?

He simply couldn't.

"Nothing," he lied. When he reached for her, Neill was relieved she didn't pull away. "All is well."

In fact, the very opposite was true. Neill wasn't sure anything, after tonight, would be well again.

CHAPTER 21

S *he knows.*

    One look at Sara, who sat alone on the dais, and Kathryn realized her husband must have told her Neill was a promised man. There was only one way to describe her expression.

Troubled.

There was no sign of the boys. Likely they were with Faye and Hugh as they tended to eat earlier than the others.

As she made her way toward the dais to break her fast, Kathryn was sure her own expression looked the same. She'd not slept much the night before, with good reason. After Neill had left her chamber, she'd stared into the darkness, her mind turning over the events of the evening again and again.

His revelation.

His parting kiss.

But mostly, she'd thought of his ministrations—and her response to them. Never had she felt more out of control, and happy to be that way.

"Come, sit next to me," Sara said, pointing to the ornate

chair next to her. "Geoffrey is already with Neill in the training yard."

She did as she was bid, her curiosity over Neill's whereabouts satisfied.

Not that it should matter.

But it did.

Though it was still early, the sun having risen not long ago, the hall was already abuzz with activity. Servants refilled pitchers as Kenshire came alive.

"How was your evening?"

Kathryn could feel she was blushing.

"So the second goblet was needed after all."

Sara took a bite of bread and lifted her hand in greeting to a woman who had just walked into the hall. Kathryn believed her name was Faye, and she seemed to be Sara's favored lady.

"Sara," she started, unsure of where to begin. Surely the countess was disappointed that her matchmaking efforts were for naught. "Neill told me about Lady Alina last eve."

Just as she'd expected, the countess had been told.

"As did Geoffrey. I will admit to being quite surprised, but —" she shrugged, "—no matter."

She cocked her head to the side, ignoring the meal, and simply looked at Lady Sara. She couldn't possibly mean . . .

"We will find a way—" Sara smiled, "—for you to be together."

Kathryn stared. Did Sara know all? If she did, how could she possibly hold out hope for a love match between Kathryn and Neill?

"I will admit to having feelings for your brother-in-law," she said, for there was no use denying it, "but that hardly means we could, or should, be together."

Sara laughed, the sound eliciting glances from below.

Picking up a piece of cheese, Kathryn nibbled on it, not really hungry but knowing she should eat. When she worried, as she'd done often of late, her stomach turned and turned inside until she couldn't breathe.

Her current situation? Most definitely worrisome.

"I apologize for laughing. But I'm certain most everyone who sees the two of you together already knows you have feelings for each other."

She groaned. "He's promised to another." Although she hated saying the words aloud, she needed to remind herself of them. And often.

"Not yet."

Kathryn made a face that had Sara laughing again.

"Without a formal betrothal, or even with one, there is always still hope."

She did not agree. If the situation was as Neill had presented it to her, quite a lot hinged on his marriage to Lady Alina.

"If you'll permit," Sara said, "I'd like to tell you a story."

Relaxing slightly, Kathryn picked up a piece of bread. "Of course."

"When Geoffrey and I met, I was betrothed," she said, smiling. "You've heard of Lord Lyonsford, Earl of Archbald, I presume?"

"Of course." The earl of Archbald had been a favorite of Edward's father, and the new king seemed to value him as much as the old.

"A powerful man whom I was to wed. My father had recently died unexpectedly, and a distant kin of mine with no real claim to Kenshire tried to take it away. My marriage to Lyonsford would have ensured that could not happen."

Kathryn had heard rumblings of this but did not know the full story.

"The marriage had been sanctioned by King Henry, so when a reiver came to Kenshire at my late father's bequest to help protect me . . ." She shrugged. "The situation seemed impossible when I fell in love with that very same reiver."

A mother who'd died in childbirth. A father who died too soon. An unwanted betrothal.

Despite their different circumstances, she and Sara did indeed have much in common.

"I don't know what to say."

Sara sat back, contemplating the situation. "Do you believe in fate?"

The question took her aback.

"I . . . I am not sure," she admitted.

"*Rota Fortunae*." Sara smiled. "I believe Fortuna can be influenced, but I do believe in her power. I'm convinced she brought you here. To Kenshire."

Kathryn was not as sure. "I agree the similarities between us are striking."

"As our outcomes will be."

If only that were possible. "If Neill does not marry her, the king will not remove Caxton. And if Caxton is not removed as warden—"

"No Day of Truce. No peace. Increased violence. Possible war with Scotland. Aye. I know it all well."

Kathryn stared at her. "That cannot be."

"Nor will it be."

The countess's certainty was such that it made her hope.

"Even without his obligation," she forced herself to say, "I am not in a position to marry."

That she was even speaking about such a thing with the Countess of Kenshire, Neill's sister-in-law, seemed preposterous. Kathryn shook her head.

"This is a setback, to be sure. But mark my words, Kathryn. Only a fool could not see what is between you and Neill. And I've learned much these past years. Love, my dear, is more powerful than hate."

"We are not . . ." She swallowed. "We are not in love."

Sara looked pointedly at her.

"Are you certain of that?"

No, she was not certain at all, but she didn't dare contemplate such a thing, not when the prospects were so dim for a happy outcome.

"Describe my brother-in-law to me?"

"Pardon?"

"Describe him. As you'd do if he were a stranger to me."

Kathryn could not help but smile as she imagined him standing before them now.

"He is handsome, to be sure."

"He is a Waryn." Sara finished her meal as Kathryn continued to consider the words she'd use to describe the man who'd come into her life a few weeks ago.

"And loyal. The night we met he'd come to my defense against a Scotsman at the inn." A king, she added silently, he had no love for. "And kind, of course. Not many men would have escorted me north without knowing why I needed to go there, but he didn't require much convincing. I didn't even have my own mount . . . I kept pushing him away, and yet he was always there when I needed him. Offering me support."

She thought of every time he'd grabbed her hand. Of that first kiss. Of last night.

"And . . ." She couldn't find the words. Or wasn't willing to share them.

"You can keep those thoughts to yourself." Sara smiled. "For now."

"You think Neill and I can find a way to be together despite the king's decree?"

"Aye."

It was foolish. Absurd. The very idea.

And yet, if Sara believed it with such conviction, maybe she could too?

"This," a familiar voice boomed, "looks dangerous."

Kathryn spun toward the sound, not having seen him enter.

Her heartbeat thudded in her ears at the sight of him striding toward her, all confidence and determination. She couldn't help but wonder at his purpose this morn.

And how she had not realized earlier that Sara's assessment were true.

She had done the most foolish thing a woman in her circumstances could do—she'd fallen in love with Neill Waryn.

NEILL EXCHANGED GLANCES WITH GEOFFREY, who knew what he was about to do. His brother did not agree with his decision, but neither would he stop him.

"This is the impetuous boy of our youth," he'd said. "You would undo all you'd fought for. Jeopardize everything."

While Geoffrey was still dressed from training, Neill had changed before coming to the hall. But his brother had insisted on going down to the hall with him. Likely to give him angry looks in the hopes he'd desist from "his folly."

He hadn't hesitated to remind Geoffrey of the unique circumstances of his own marriage to Sara. Indeed, each of their siblings had wed under strained circumstances.

Geoffrey had merely harrumphed at that, but as they walked toward the dais, Neill knew he was making the right decision. He'd thought of little else since leaving Kathryn's chamber.

He'd thought of little else since the day she'd begged him to take her away from The Wild Boar.

"Good morn, gentlemen."

When his brother placed a kiss on Sara's hand, Neill looked at him pointedly as if to remind him of the reason for his own resolve.

Geoffrey merely scowled at him—a fit of pique Neill ignored as he stepped up to the woman who had kept him from sleep.

She looked lovely that morning in a pale yellow gown. Simple but beautiful, like the woman who wore it.

"Good morn, my lady."

"And to you."

He offered a hand. "I thought perhaps you might enjoy a tour of the castle?"

Kathryn hesitated, glancing back at Sara. An interesting development. Yesterday, they'd been friendly with each other, exceedingly so. Today there was something . . . conspiratorial . . . about their exchange.

"I would very much enjoy that."

She stood, and Neill backed away to allow her to step down from the dais.

"Be sure to show her the Sea Gate."

If such a thing were possible, Geoffrey's scowl deepened at Sara's words. The countess still supported their cause, knowing, as she did, about Lady Alina.

"A fine idea, thank you, Sara."

They left the hall together. Although he *had* planned to take Kathryn on a tour—his invitation not merely an excuse to get her alone—Sara's idea gave him pause. Aye, they would go to the Sea Gate straightaway.

"Shall we start with Sara's suggestion?"

"If it pleases you."

He tried not to smile at her unexpected shyness. Kathryn was as bold a maid as ever he'd met, yet this morning she looked away.

Neill had only stayed at Kenshire a short time before being sent to Langford, but he knew it well enough to navigate them through the hall to a door tucked away at the end of a long corridor. Opening it, he gestured for Kathryn to step ahead.

They navigated the dark and increasingly damp passageway to another door that looked as if it had not been often used.

"Mind your step," he said, the stone stairs descending downward in a spiral. Darkness enveloped them. Feeling their way down, they finally came to yet another door, which Neill pushed open with one of the keys he'd retrieved from Peter, Kenshire's steward, for their tour.

Immediately, the scent of sand and sea assaulted them.

A final path, one covered with saw grass that required them to walk single file. When they finally emerged, the reward was immediate.

"Oh my!"

Waves crashed on the shore in front of them as they made their way toward the water.

"Wait," he said, leaning down to remove his boots. Unsurprisingly, Kathryn took one look at him and did the same.

He laughed as they both tossed their boots aside, feeling the same giddy eagerness. Thankfully, all signs of the pain he'd caused with his confession were gone.

Although life would no doubt bring them highs and lows, as it did for everyone, Neill intended never to wound her again.

With that thought in mind, he grabbed her waist from behind. Pulling her toward him, he claimed her lips. She opened for him, giving him what he asked for.

Grasping her head and ensuring he had full access to her mouth, he greedily tasted and teased, his tongue tangling with hers. Her moans made him hard in an instant.

When she held back, this woman was irresistible. But when she acted with abandon?

He groaned, taking her more deeply. His hand moved to her breast, and he squeezed it gently, wishing away the barrier between them.

Not caring about the guards that could surely see them from above, Neill drank from the sweetness that was Kathryn Wyld until he knew a kiss would no longer suffice.

He pulled back, and then nearly reached for her again when

he saw her heaving shoulders, her swollen lips. Kathryn no longer shied away. Unapologetic, she stared back at him.

"We must talk," she said.

"Aye," he agreed. "'Twas my aim."

Taking her hand, Neill led them, barefoot, toward the sea. Inhaling deeply, he allowed the serenity of the peaceful place to envelop them both. When they were so close to the water that a few more steps would see their feet wet, he stopped.

And turned, bringing her with him.

Neill watched her face as Kathryn took in the view above them.

Kenshire Castle.

"Magnificent."

"Aye, as beautiful as any I've ever seen. And not just beautiful. But strong. And courageous."

She gasped and turned to look at him.

"Passionate. Kind. Resourceful. A woman to make a man forget his obligations."

"Neill—"

"Nay, let me finish."

Putting Geoffrey's admonitions out of his mind, he forged ahead.

"I am sorry for keeping the king's condition from you. For hurting you, even for a short while."

As his toes dug into the sand, so too did he bind himself to this decision.

"Until we came to Kenshire, I thought little of accepting his request. For years I've trained, and fought, for a single purpose. To make my brothers proud. To make Adam and Cora proud. To achieve enough to rid myself of the moniker I so hated as a lad, 'the young Waryn.' And I did all of that. Every win led to that final tournament, when I was presented with the opportunity to aid my king, my country. My family."

He took her hands in his.

"But then I learned of your plight. And with God as my witness, I promised then and do so now, the man who killed your father will see justice served. The rage I felt at the thought of you making your way to The Wild Boar alone as you mourned your father . . . I felt that again, last eve."

Kathryn's brows drew together in question.

"I could not bear the thought of you marrying another man." He shook his head. "I cannot allow that to happen."

"What are you saying?"

"You will be with one man in this lifetime, Kathryn Wyld, and that man is me."

He did not mean for the words to come out so forcefully, but he was as convinced of this as he was that, somehow, they could find a way to pacify the king.

"Do I have a say in the matter?"

Nay. She didn't. Not if she loved him the same way he loved her. But Neill knew that was not the answer for which she waited.

"Aye," he lied.

"The implications are vast."

"Indeed."

"You are risking everything."

"I am."

"For me."

"For love."

He'd never said those words to a woman before, and he was determined she'd be the only woman to ever hear them from him.

"I love you," he repeated, "more than my own life."

She didn't hesitate. "And I love you."

They stood there, hand in hand, declarations made and accepted.

But the moment was tainted by Geoffrey's words running through his head.

Do not do this, brother. At least consider it more carefully. Once you declare for her, there is no way to take the words back.

But it was done.

Neill was now pledged to two women.

One he'd never met.

The other he loved.

And though Adam had always told him confidence was almost as imperative as the skill required to be crowned champion, for the first time in a long while, he was unsure if this was a contest he could win.

CHAPTER 22

*I*t had been the most glorious week of his life.

Neill had spent the mornings avoiding his brother's lectures, if not the man himself. The afternoons, with Kathryn. He learned more about her unusual upbringing, which had forged her into the woman that he now adored. It was no wonder that she had been so unconvincing as a serving maid.

She told him of the times she'd been kissed. And of the time one of the king's men had attempted to take that which she had no interest in giving. Her father had arrived just in time to protect her, but he'd insisted that she be trained to use the dagger as skillfully as any man. He knew the claim was an honest one, for he'd put her skills to test in the training yard.

Her aim was true.

Her resolve, even truer.

They spoke of ways to pacify the king, one idea being replaced by another. They had an ally in Lady Sara, who disagreed with her husband, who maintained that Neill had made a terrible mistake. But even she admitted the king's ire would be unavoidable.

After years of relentless training, competing, proving

himself . . . he now faced the most important battle of his life, and it would not take place on any training field.

"Deep in thought, brother?"

He and Geoffrey had ridden out to inspect a new building, a granary that had been commissioned some time ago. As they approached the barbican, returning to Kenshire Castle, his brother slowed and Neill knew his respite from Geoffrey's lectures had come to an end.

"Aye," he answered, waiting for it.

"You play a dangerous game with Lady Kathryn."

As he'd expected. "'Tis no game, brother. As well you know."

"What, then, is your plan?"

Neill's silence was his answer.

"You have no plan. The king is unpredictable."

"Aye."

"His temper, more legendary than your tournament reputation."

"Aye." He knew it well. Once, at court, though he'd not seen it for himself, the king had received unwelcome news from his French emissary smashing a Roman flask dating back to 100 AD.

"What then?"

They rode through the entrance, the guards raising their sword arms to his brother. His brother made a fine earl. Everywhere they went the people of Kenshire welcomed him, offering him the same respect and deference Neill had given Geoffrey their whole lives.

Thankfully, riders from behind interrupted Geoffrey's interrogation. Two of them, neither bearing colors that would identify them. Both he and his brother dismounted, having reached the inner courtyard, and the riders did the same.

One of them, Neill recognized at once.

"Reid Kerr," he said, approaching the man.

Toren's brother extended his hand, and Neill took it. When last the two had met, they'd been enemies. No longer.

"There are few my brother trusted with the message we bring. One best told in private."

"Come," Geoffrey said at once, gesturing to the keep. Neill felt the same tingle of anticipation he always experienced before a tourney. The Kerr brother had news of Bothwell. He must.

"I will meet you in the hall," Reid said to his companion, who left them.

Following Geoffrey and Reid into the great keep, he realized his brother was taking them to the room he'd spied near the entranceway, a rare private space on the same floor as the great hall. No windows graced the circular stone chamber, though two wall torches lit the space. It was empty but for a bench, two chairs, and what appeared to be an abandoned altar.

"That door . . . ," he said, spying what seemed like one of many secret passageways hidden inside the ancient castle.

"Leads to the chapel. The priest uses this space, but none other." Geoffrey stopped and added, "You may speak freely here."

"Bothwell was followed," Reid said, offering no preliminaries, "and it went as expected. Though he stayed at Brockburg for the remainder of the day, one of his men left immediately after you did."

"For Edinburgh," Neill offered.

"Aye. And Bothwell himself followed the next day. He was questioned about his early departure, of course, but he only said he had enough information for the king."

Geoffrey grunted. "He panicked."

"He did."

Reid paced the length of the small chamber.

"Luckily, the person who went after him has enough connections to gain access to court, though how close he'll get to Bothwell and the king remains to be seen."

"Who went after him?" Neill asked.

"My brother Alex. We arrived at Brockburg just after you left for Kenshire. We both agree with Toren—if Bothwell is guilty of what we suspect, he could stand in the way of all we seek to achieve. Including the deal with your king."

"I'm going to Edinburgh." Neill had been considering it for the past few days, but now it would seem he had no choice. Although they did not have much evidence as of yet, it seemed likely Bothwell had indeed turned on Kathryn's father. He was likely aligned with those attempting to take advantage of the instability along the border.

"I will go with you," Reid said. "Restoring the peace is of the utmost importance."

"You will stay, to protect Kathryn?" Neill asked his brother.

Geoffrey looked at him as their father once had, as if he was not sure whether or not he could be trusted. This rift between him and his brother, Neill had not expected it. And he hated it. But until Geoffrey relented on the matter of Kathryn and his obligation to the king, there was nothing that could be done about it.

"I will," he said finally as Reid glanced back and forth between them.

Reid whistled. "You can tell me about it on the way," he said, likely realizing Kathryn was a source of tension between the brothers. "We should leave now."

"Faye will want to feed you first." Geoffrey opened the door, its creak a testament to how little it was used.

"I would be most grateful to take a bit of bread and cheese with us."

Geoffrey's bark of laughter took Neill aback.

"Most grateful? Lady Allie has been good for you, Reid."

Neill did not know the Kerr brothers as well as Geoffrey, but even he knew of the youngest's reputation. It appeared his wife had gone a long way toward taming the wild Kerr.

"I would like to know how Lady Allie managed such a thing," he said, looking around the hall. Kathryn was nowhere to be found. Neill needed to find her before he left.

"You'll have plenty of time to hear the tale," Reid said, following Geoffrey toward the kitchens.

"I'll meet you in the stables," he said, ignoring his brother's frown.

He spotted Peter in the distance and was prepared to inquire after Kathryn when the very lady he sought addressed him from behind.

"Looking for someone?"

He wasted no time escorting them back into the chamber. Pulling her toward him, Neill found her lips, claiming them. Claiming her. Her murmurs of pleasure made it difficult to stop, so he didn't. Instead, Neill tightened his arms around her.

He groaned when her hand tugged on the nape of his neck. She wanted more, and he wanted to give it to her. But now was not the time.

Reluctantly, he pulled away. And without a word, kissed the tip of her nose, smiled, and led them back to the hall.

KATHRYN WOULD HAVE CLOSED her eyes were she not astride a fine-looking mount, following Sara away from the loveliest of places. The countess had taken her to what she'd described as her "favorite place in the world," a small lake surrounded by forest and framed by willow trees.

She'd enjoyed it, really she had, but her mind kept returning to the feel of Neill's lips on hers before he had ridden off to Edinburgh. She'd not been pleased, of course, to learn he was leaving, especially given what had happened on her last visit to Edinburgh. Kathryn would forever be leery of that place. Neill had insisted he and Reid would be safe.

But would she?

Geoffrey did not seem to think so. He had not been pleased about their ride, but Sara had refused to allow Kathryn to be a prisoner in the castle. The guards they'd been forced to take rode both in front and behind them.

Those guards must have heard something, because all four of them closed ranks, cinching in around Kathryn and Sara. And then Kathryn heard it too—the sound of horses' hooves riding quickly toward them. The woods were too thick for them to see much beyond the small clearing ahead, so their small riding party stopped.

And waited.

Suddenly, four riders thundered around the corner. They reined in abruptly when they spotted them.

Kenshire men.

"Gerald!" Sara exclaimed. Breaking free of the guards around them, the countess rode ahead to meet the man in the lead.

"You're hurt."

Indeed, Kathryn saw the blood on his upper thigh, and then something else caught her eye. One of the horses was riderless. From the way Sara leaned sideways in her saddle for a better look, she knew Sara had noticed it too.

"Who?" she said, her voice throbbing with command. This was the Countess of Kenshire, not her spirited hostess, and she was very much in charge.

"Charles, my lady."

"What happened?"

The man named Gerald spoke just loudly enough for all to hear.

"Scottish reivers. We were returning from Dunburg Abbey when they struck. There were ten men, my lady."

"And they attacked without cause?"

"We were close enough to the abbey. They seemed to know that we trade in gold."

"And Charles?"

"Fought bravely, my lady. Two of my men retrieved his body but were separated from us afterward."

He looked as if he wanted to say more but changed his mind.

Violence along the border.

She'd heard the phrase so many times. Had seen fights break out between Englishmen and Scots at the inn. But this . . . this was entirely different. To see the evidence of the unrest before her . . .

As if remembering Kathryn was there, bearing witness to what had happened, Sara rode back toward her. "We are on Kenshire land now and quite safe."

"You return for more men?" she asked Gerald.

"Aye, my lady."

With that, they followed the newcomers on the path they'd been traveling toward the main road. They set a quicker pace, and no one spoke on the ride back to the castle. All seemed to feel the same miasma of dread and horror.

By the time they entered the courtyard, Geoffrey was waiting for them. He must have received word of the attack.

Sara dismounted, and although Kathryn was too far away to hear anything, she could tell the countess was quite upset. No wonder. Her people had been attacked most viciously, without provocation.

This had happened because of Caxton. Because of what he'd done to the Day of Truce.

Not wanting to interrupt, Kathryn dismounted and handed her reins to a stable boy. She hung back until Sara waved her over.

"It is getting worse every day," Sara said to her, pulling her aside as Geoffrey spoke to Gerald. "Before, this would not have stood. Without the Day of Truce, our warden is powerless."

The words hit Kathryn like a knife to the stomach. "I'm sorry to hear of the man you lost," she said, following Sara through the courtyard toward the main keep. "Sorry, also, for his family."

"I will visit them this evening." Sara made her way up the steps as Peter opened the door to the front entrance of the keep. "Thank you, Peter."

"And the other two men who haven't yet returned?"

"Will hopefully make their way back or be found by Gerald and the others."

She stopped when the portly maid, Faye, walked toward them with a bundle in her arms. Sara held out her hands and Kathryn stepped closer. The newborn babe was a sight to behold. She marveled at his tiny features, his mouth a little rose-bud, and caught Sara looking at her.

"Would you like to hold him?"

She hesitated for the briefest moment. She would, but Kathryn did not have much experience with babies. Or children at all, for that matter. She'd been raised mostly at court, where children were discussed but rarely seen.

"Aye," she said, watching precisely how Sara held him. When she took him into her arms, she attempted to do it the same way.

He smelled clean, as if freshly washed.

"Can you tend to him while I find the other wee one?" Faye asked.

"Find?" Sara laughed. "Is Hayden lost, then?"

"Nay, my lady. Hugh has been trainin' him again."

"HUGH BELIEVES 'tis never too early to learn the sword," she explained. "Go," she said to Faye, while Kathryn tried desperately to appear as if she were not terrified.

"He is heartier than you would imagine," Sara said with a small smile.

Apparently she hadn't been hiding her discomfort overly well.

Kathryn stared at the babe, wondering how she'd not given any thought to having children of her own. For the last year, such a thing had seemed impossible, but now . . .

The thought faded as she remembered what had happened today. An innocent man was dead. Others had been hurt.

Sara herself had admitted it was because the Day of Truce had fallen apart.

"The man who died today—" she looked up at Sara, "—does he have children?"

Sara's shoulders sank, her answer plain enough.

"We cannot do this."

She said it more to herself than Sara, but her new friend heard, and understood.

"Do not say that," she admonished. "We shall see what happens in Edinburgh. We'll devise a plan when Neill and Reid return, and not before."

Sara's tone did not invite an argument from her, and so she didn't give one. Even so, Kathryn could no longer dismiss her doubts or pretend they didn't matter. She suspected whatever happened with Bothwell might not improve their situation.

Where is he now? Is he thinking of me?

Does it matter?

Kathryn wanted to believe it did.

But she could not dismiss the image of the blood on Gerald's armor and the riderless mount that accompanied him south.

CHAPTER 23

"*W*hat did you discover?"

Neill and Reid had been at the Fiddler's Inn in Edinburgh for nearly a sennight. They'd stayed away from court, knowing their presence would raise suspicion. Even Alex, who was in town as a guest of Emma's husband, Garrick, had not known they were in Edinburgh those first few nights. Garrick, the Earl of Clave, was housed in the King's Tower with his sister, and while the king did not actually reside there, it was within the walls of Edinburgh Castle. Too close to Bothwell for comfort.

They had since been in touch with both Alex and Clave, although they had not yet met them in person. That would change tonight. They were meeting to share knowledge and decide on a path forward.

Last eve, Reid had spoken to the owner of another inn who'd claimed to know a man who'd seen Richard Wyld's body carried from the Firth of Forth. Neill had found the man and questioned him.

"It was as you said." Neill paced the room, waiting for the others to join them. "He was reluctant to speak, but aye, the body was definitely that of Richard Wyld. Which means only that Kathryn's father is, indeed, dead. It does not explain who killed him. He said nothing of seeing Bothwell or any of the king's men."

A knock at the door quieted both men. Reid opened it, revealing the remainder of their party.

"Brother." Reid opened the door wider to let them in. "Emma, Garrick."

She rushed to him, and Neill engulfed his twin in a hug. Somehow, she managed to grow even lovelier since he'd been away.

"You are a man," she said, shoving him back. "I don't remember you being so thick around the shoulders."

He smiled. "I do remember you being so quick with your opinion though."

"'Tis good to see you, brother."

"And you. Though I wish you'd not have come here."

But he knew his sister well, the most stubborn of all the Waryns. He looked at Clave as if in sympathy. He'd not met his sister's husband yet. Their wedding had been arranged rather quickly, and Neill had been in France at the time, participating in a tournament.

"Well met," Clave said, stepping forward and shaking his hand. "I was sorry to have missed you at the council."

The stranger had a firm grip and a warm smile. He felt as if he already knew the man, for Emma had told him quite a bit about her husband, including details of their unconventional courtship.

He was about to say as much when Alex cleared his throat. "Shall we get started?" he asked, his voice low but firm.

"Richard Wyld is indeed dead," Neill began. "I spoke to a witness who saw his body being removed from the river."

"Aye, and it was Bothwell who killed him."

They all looked at Clave, who'd spoken the words so softly it took Neill a moment to realize what he'd said.

"My other title, Linkirk, holds more importance here than Clave, and with it, I gained access to the inner sanctum."

"The inner sanctum?" Neill asked.

"The inner sanctum is another name for the king's small circle of advisors, which counts Bothwell as one of its members," Clave explained. "Bothwell is sly, of that there is no doubt. But I asked some pointed questions and learned the king had indeed received a message from Edward prior to Bothwell's arrival."

"The contents of the message?" Reid asked.

"Unknown."

They exchanged a look. If the fact that Edward had requested a renewal of Alexander's oath of fealty had not yet been shared with the masses, it meant the king was still considering the request.

"Do you believe Bothwell is attempting to influence him again?" Alex asked Clave.

"Aye, and I believe the delay can be laid at Bothwell's door. I spoke to some who believe Bothwell aligns with those calling for a Scotland independent of Edward. It cannot be proven, but I am convinced it's so. And I strongly suspect he had Kathryn's father killed to prevent the renewed allegiance."

The men were silent.

"We have no proof," Reid said. "Nothing but supposition."

"Wyld's dead body counts for nothing?" Neill was furious on Kathryn's behalf. He was as convinced as Garrick that Bothwell had done the deed, and he aimed to prove it.

"We would agree with you," Emma said, "and yet it proves nothing."

"I need an audience with the king."

Everyone in the room protested at once, but Neill would not be swayed. Bothwell would never admit to his misdeed, and only the king knew if his chancellor was attempting to dissuade him from repledging Scotland's allegiance to the English king. If he was, the information about Kathryn's father was vital. And he trusted none to convey it to him.

"Can you arrange it?" he asked Clave. Emma's husband ground his jaw, apparently displeased by the request. He obviously thought it a poor idea to take such a direct approach, but Neill suspected it may be the only way to expose Bothwell. The man was too wily by half.

"If he does not listen to you—" Reid crossed his arms, "— you'll have made some powerful enemies. Word will reach Bothwell. And it could even put Kathryn in danger."

Indeed, and he would have enemies in England as well, the king and queen among them. Even so, he thought it the best way to proceed.

"She is already in danger," he argued.

None disagreed with that statement.

"But she is under my protection. And I *will* protect her."

"Aye," Reid said, "but at what cost?"

Neill silently wondered the same.

NEILL ROSE FROM HIS KNEES, remembering the last time he'd stood before a king. Even now that man awaited word from the one in front of him. The fate of their two countries, of the borderlands, was in their hands. The great kings were brothers-in-law, though the relationship had not seemed to endear them to each other.

"Sir Neill Waryn," he was presented, "son of the late Sir Thomas Waryn, Lord of Bristol Manor."

He waited and watched from the corner of his eye, and when the king nodded, Neill did the same.

"Alexander, by the grace of God, king of the Scots, I thank you for your audience."

It had taken three days. Three long days for him to garner an audience with the king of Scotland. Neill was not sure how Clave managed to arrange it, but he was thankful.

Neill looked the king straight in the eye, trying to see the man behind the preeminence. Alexander was a king, aye, but he was also a servant of his country, a husband and warrior. He was capable of being moved by reason.

"Sir Neill Waryn," the king boomed. His voice, as was legendary, reverberated throughout the opulent hall. "You are the man who inspired *L'Histoire de Guillaume le Maréchal*, are you not?"

A poem of his exploits in France. Neill nodded. There was little point in denying the truth, and perhaps his reputation would recommend him. "The same," he said.

"Hmmm."

Neill knew this next request would likely get him thrown from King Alexander's presence. But he had made his decision, and he would follow through as he must.

"The information I bring you, Your Grace, can be shared with you alone."

As he had suspected, dissent erupted around him. Thankfully, the Earl of Bothwell was not in attendance, just as Reid had discerned from his scouting earlier in the day, but the royal steward and the twenty or so other men in the room all voiced their displeasure.

Neill did not flinch.

The king watched him carefully. And just when Neill was sure he was about to relent, a voice from behind them broke the lengthening silence.

"Unacceptable, Your Grace."

Somehow, Neill knew who'd spoken those words even before he saw his face.

He didn't turn but waited until the Earl of Bothwell emerged from his right side.

Bothwell's red beard preceded him, and a long, elaborate surcoat trailed him as he made his way to Alexander's side.

Although the earl could not know what message Neill carried, he had certainly learned of his presence here and was threatened by it.

This man was guilty.

Of that, Neill had no doubt.

Of his own ability to leave the court alive, he was less certain.

"No one is leaving this hall," the earl said with authority, as if his king were not sitting beside him.

"I will determine that," the king said, still watching Neill carefully. "Are you quite certain this is necessary, Sir Neill?"

"Aye," he said, his voice strong. "It is, Your Grace."

"Leave us," the king called out to the gathered courtiers. Just when he thought victory was upon him, the king turned to Bothwell. "Stay."

Dammit.

The hall cleared out at once, and he was left alone with the king of Scotland and the man he had intended to accuse of murder.

The idea Alexander might believe him, an unknown English knight, over his own chancellor, the man he clearly trusted above most others . . .

Perhaps the others had been right. This audience might have gone better were Garrick or Reid to bring him the news. Garrick, after all, was the Earl of Linkirk in addition to the Earl of Clave, and Reid was the second to Toren, the chief of Clan Kerr. Neill was English, through and through. But damned if he would trust Kathryn's fate to anyone else, a decision he could admit now had been a little rash.

He thought again of that letter Kathryn had teased him

about—the one he'd written to Emma crowing about his invulnerability, only for it to arrive on the eve of a great loss.

"Go on," the king said, putting a hand up as Bothwell attempted to protest his audience.

He turned to the chancellor, knowing he had only one opportunity to convince the king of what he knew to be true. He would make an enemy today, but so be it. Without hesitation, he spoke.

"Some months ago, Richard Wyld, royal messenger to King Edward, was murdered before he could deliver the same request Your Grace received more recently, to renew your oath of fealty to King Edward and be recognized as the prince of Scotland."

Bothwell immediately began to protest but was silenced by the king, so Neill continued without even glancing at the accused.

"The Earl of Bothwell fled the council at Brockburg when he learned of this message. I suspect he had something to do with Wyld's fate. As evidence, I respectfully ask if the earl has tried to convince Your Grace not to renew this vow even though such an action would provoke an erosion of the peace our countries have enjoyed—"

"Until the eradication of the Day of Truce," Bothwell bellowed.

Neill remained calm and continued to make eye contact with the king. "A decision made by the Scottish border lords—"

"Who will not treat with a man like Caxton."

"Aye," Neill said, addressing the king and doing his best to ignore the man who stood beside him, "and Caxton will be replaced upon word of your renewed oath."

"So says you," Bothwell spat.

"My king granted this as a reward," he said, his eyes still on the king.

"For winning the Tournament of Peace," Alexander finished. "Without such a boon, Caxton would remain in his position.

Edward's lack of resolve to keep peace in his northern borders concerns me, Sir Neill Waryn."

He'd been prepared for this.

"I do believe, Your Grace, his father and Caxton were great allies. My king and the warden are not. He granted me the concession as a reward, aye, but it would have happened eventually if not for King Edward's preoccupation with France."

It was the best, and only, answer he could give.

Would it be enough?

Neill wanted to say more, but he remained silent. Alexander was known to favor silence over speech, and so he waited.

He glanced briefly at Bothwell and did not like what he saw there. The man was *smirking* at him. He did not appear overly concerned for a man who'd just been accused of murder.

At worst, Neill would be tossed in the dungeon of Edinburgh Castle for making false claims against the chancellor of Scotland.

At best, he would obtain King Alexander's agreement to renew his fealty—only for him to have to return to England for a more challenging encounter with a less patient and forgiving king. A man who could easily retaliate for Neill's broken pledge.

Perhaps the choice he faced was between a Scottish prison and an English one.

Finally, King Alexander spoke. "Escort this man from the hall," he bellowed.

A Scottish prison, then.

CHAPTER 24

*K*athryn stood in the muddy road, rain having arrived unexpectedly, waiting for Lady Sara to emerge from the ferrier's shop. They'd come to Kenshire's village for the day, Sara walking from home to home, shop to shop, speaking with her people. She wore her boy's attire, and none seemed troubled by her odd choice of dress.

In fact, the people loved her. Clearly, Sara and Geoffrey knew how to make their people happy. There was a sense of belonging here, one she'd not felt for a long time.

Maybe ever.

Despite the rain, which had diminished to a not unpleasant mist, Kathryn had chosen to wait outside the shop, preferring to watch the comings and goings of the townspeople.

Kathryn thought, as she did most often, of Neill. He'd been gone for more than a fortnight now, and with each day that passed, Kathryn was more convinced their fanciful musings about being together were just that.

She and Sara still spoke of it, at times. Neill's reward, his arrangement, and the various ways he might pacify the king without marrying Lady Alina. They'd not arrived at any acceptable solution, although she suspected Sara would never admit defeat.

Kathryn also thought, as she did every day, of Bothwell and her father, and she wondered what the latter would make of her current predicament.

He would be proud of her resourcefulness, she'd concluded, but not of her relationship with Neill. Her father had always been a king's man, one who had served Edward's father faithfully for years. Still, there was no denying he'd trusted the father more than the son. He had insisted she not return to court if he should fall ill, after all. His reluctance had seemed curious to her, and she wished he'd given more indication of the reason. It may have helped her to learn if someone in the English court could have wished him dead.

"Pardon, my lady."

Kathryn recognized the woman who stood before her. The miller's wife. The mill was the first place she and Sara had visited earlier.

"Good day, Mistress Greta."

The woman startled.

"You are named as my mother was," she explained.

Greta smiled. "Many blessings to her."

She was about to tell the woman her mother had died many years ago when Greta's smile fled from her face. "She's no' with this world, my lady."

Kathryn's eyes widened. "How . . ."

"You've met Greta," Sara said, approaching. "Have you shared your special ability with Lady Kathryn yet?"

Greta smiled broadly.

Ah. Mistress Greta was a seer. Kathryn had met such men and women before, though most did not tout their abilities out of fear. It was not surprising that this woman would share her gift openly with Lady Sara, however.

"I sensed a sadness in her," Greta said. "But nay, my lady, I've not done so yet."

Sara looked at her expectantly, and it struck her that this was one of the reasons the countess had brought her here today. Although Kathryn feared what the future might bring, she was also eager for knowledge of it. She nodded eagerly to the miller's wife. "If you would be so kind as to share any knowledge you have," she said. "I'd be most grateful to hear it."

Stepping off to the side of the road, Mistress Greta took Kathryn's hands in her own. She nearly laughed at the expression on Sara's face, all eager expectation.

Staring at the wisps of red hair peeking out of the woman's cap, Kathryn wondered at the wisdom of what she had so impulsively agreed to. What if Greta foretold something she was not prepared to hear? Neill's face flashed before her, and Kathryn nearly pulled away.

She must have appeared worried because Greta squeezed her hands.

"Three lions, a dragon, and a castle. In a sea of red."

Alarmed, she attempted to pull away then.

"Nay, 'tis not blood. There is . . . resolve. And joy. Though I still can sense a great sorrow in you."

Kathryn glanced at Sara and waited for more, but Greta dropped her hands abruptly as a wagon full of satchels creaked by. "It has finally arrived." The woman offered them a quick curtsy, then ran off before Kathryn could ask her any of the dozens of questions on her lips.

"Grain," Sara said. "Shall we?"

They walked toward the stables, Sara's guards not far behind them.

"Three lions, a dragon, and a castle. In a sea of red." Sara stood at the entrance of the stables, a boy no older than ten and two running inside with excitement to fetch their horses.

"Robbie," Sara explained. "His father is the stable master."

Kathryn looked down at the mud on the hem of her gown. Sara's gown, to be precise.

"These—" Sara pointed to her legs, "—have many uses. You would find them quite freeing."

Kathryn tried to imagine herself in the breeches and laughed aloud at the thought of the looks she'd get were she to ever wear them in court. "Perhaps . . ."

She and Sara mounted and rode along in companionable silence—the only sound that of the horses' hooves sinking into the mud. They didn't speak again until they were on the road back to Kenshire Castle.

"Any thoughts on what Greta said to you?" Sara asked at last.

"Nay, none at all. I confess—I'm troubled by it."

"Her mother had a similar gift." Sara looked up as a bird squawked loudly overhead. "My father often consulted her, although many cautioned against it. I've found her quite believable myself."

"If only she'd given me a hint of how to proceed with Neill. I can't make sense of what she said."

Sara slowed as the guards in front of them did the same. It took Kathryn a moment to see what the men were looking at, but when she did, her heart leapt in her chest.

A party of Kenshire men riding toward the castle from the north. But it was the one who lacked the Kenshire coat of arms that interested her most.

More precisely, the black-haired one without a helmet.

Neill had returned at last.

Had Kathryn harbored any doubts about her feelings for the English knight, the sight of him confirmed what she already knew.

She'd fallen in love with the most skilled tourney knight in all of England. And although she had little hope for their future together, her spirits soared at the sight of him. Nothing mattered at the moment other than the fact that Neill was safe.

She and Sara spurred their horses to move faster, both of them eager to learn what had transpired at Edinburgh Castle.

At least he had not been imprisoned by the Scottish king.

Or worse.

GEOFFREY WHISTLED. "You could have been killed."

They sat in the lord and lady's solar, Neill having just explained all that had transpired at Edinburgh. More precisely, Geoffrey sat while Neill paced the room, wanting to finish as quickly as possible so he could see his lady. His brother, who had been waiting for him at the entrance to the main keep, had brought him here straightaway.

"Aye. And I suspected I would be when Bothwell arrived."

He stopped in front of the door long enough for Geoffrey to guess his intention.

"Go, find her," he said. "Though nothing has changed, brother."

He knew it well.

"I spoke with Clave," he said. Geoffrey frowned, knowing the direction of his thoughts. Neill had already known, in broad strokes, the circumstances of his sister's marriage, but he had not realized their situation was so similar to the one he and Kathryn faced. The matter had worked out to their advantage. Was he a fool to hope?

"You, Bryce, and Emma all married for love, and I aim to do the same."

"I wish it for you, Neill. I truly do," Geoffrey said, and he could see in his eyes it was true. "Indeed, Sara has ensured we've spoken of the matter quite a bit while you were away. But I fear King Edward . . ."

"Is an inflexible man, aye. I know it well."

"Are you willing to incur his wrath? The possibility that he will retaliate by keeping Caxton in his position?"

Neill had thought of little else and knew there was little he could say to appease his brother. Because he knew the stakes were high indeed. He'd nearly gotten himself tossed into a dungeon in Edinburgh. This time he would, perforce, need to be more careful. "Now we wait. 'Tis Edward's move—"

"And when you receive an invitation to court? To your own betrothal ceremony?"

He didn't answer. He couldn't.

When the door swung open, his heart leapt at the thought of seeing Kathryn on the other side. Instead, Sara entered. Alone.

"She's in the hall," she said, in answer to his silent question. "And you can stop scowling," she chastised her husband, which earned a grin from Neill. At least he and Kathryn had one staunch supporter.

Without hesitation, he left his brother and his wife alone and made his way to the great hall. When he entered, Neill spotted Kathryn immediately. She stood by the hearth, the two of them speaking quietly. She appeared, somehow, even lovelier than when he'd left.

Content to watch her, for now, as her hands moved from side to side in conversation, Neill thought of the first night he'd spotted her at The Wild Boar. Though she'd seemed comfortable enough among the patrons, she'd stood out immediately. She had never belonged there, the truth obvious to anyone with a discerning eye.

She belonged *here*.

As if sensing his scrutiny, Kathryn turned toward him. Her broad smile was exactly as he remembered it.

And then it happened.

He recognized the expression on her face and fairly ran toward her. She was breathing heavily, Faye looking on in confusion.

"My lady!" Faye put her hand on Kathryn's back.

"She will be well," he insisted, taking his lady's hand. "This has happened before."

Eyes wide, Kathryn continued to struggle for breath. Ushering her toward the hall's entrance, he reassured his aunt by marriage as best he could.

Neill led Kathryn down a familiar but private path. Stopping at the top of the stairwell that led down to the Sea Gate, he wondered what had provoked her latest attack.

"I'm feeling better." She took a long, deep breath, held it, and smiled. "I don't know what . . . I saw you on our way back from the village, so I knew you were well. 'Twas so hard to wait for you."

He kissed her.

Hard.

She'd insisted she was well, and Neill had thought of little else on his journey but the feel of her lips, the sound of her release.

It was like that first time, their mouths melding together so perfectly that Neill knew this woman was meant to be his. Groaning, he pulled away while he still had the strength to do so.

They stood in the darkened corridor, the only light from the crack beneath the door they'd used to enter the passageway.

"I don't believe anyone but Faye noticed," he said, still wondering what exactly had happened. "Does this occur often?"

She nodded. "The first time was the day after I arrived at the inn. Finally safe after days on the road, I sat alone in my room and began to feel as if I could not take a breath."

"How do you feel now?"

"Much better. Though very curious to learn what happened in Edinburgh, I'll admit."

"Shall we go back to the hall, or down to the sea?"

"Nay, tell me here. Please."

"Bothwell has been imprisoned for killing your father."

He'd not imagined telling her precisely like this, but Neill did not want to hold her in suspense any longer. He wanted her to rest easy with the knowledge her father's murderer had been caught.

He told her then of all that had transpired, including his audience with the king. Her eyes widened when he spoke of Bothwell's sudden appearance.

"When the king called for a guard to escort me from the hall, I thought I would be visiting Edinburgh's dungeon next. I was taken to a chamber as a 'guest of the king's,' where I waited for hours. It wasn't until late that evening that I was escorted back to the king, this time in his solar. He informed me that Bothwell had denied all charges, of course, but one of his men had buckled under the king's questioning."

He hesitated, unsure whether or not he should share the details.

She deserved to know all that had transpired.

"The man who actually killed your father . . ."

She sucked in a breath.

Neill reached for Kathryn, pulling her against him.

"He confessed quite easily, I'm told. Alexander assured me Bothwell would receive 'a king's justice' and that he would renew his oath to Edward, which he'd intended to do before learning about Bothwell. I expect the message has already been delivered."

He pulled back, watching for her reaction.

"Bothwell has been imprisoned?"

"Aye. As has the man who carried out his orders."

"The oath of fealty. King Alexander will give it."

"Aye."

She shivered in his arms. Neill cradled her against his chest, soaking in her presence, the warm, soft feel of her. The smell of sea air wafted up to them.

"This changes nothing between us," she said.

"It serves only to hasten Edward's reward. One I was most grateful to have been given, but no longer."

She pulled away to look up at him.

"You can bring peace to the border."

"Nay, not I. The borderlands alone can do that."

"But you can provide the conditions to make it happen."

"Aye."

"By marrying Lady Alina."

"Never."

He said it emphatically, for he felt emphatic. They *would* find another way. He could live with no other conclusion.

"Thank you."

He barely heard the whisper that sent shivers through him. Her gratitude was more valuable to him than any tournament he'd ever won. It had sent him to Edinburgh, to the Scottish royal court. He'd go anywhere to defend her.

He closed his eyes and breathed in the scent of her, a scent he'd come to love more than any other.

She belonged here, he thought again.

She belonged with him.

CHAPTER 25

"*I*'m going to London."

Neill made the announcement at supper, waiting for his brother's censure. Two days had passed since his return from Edinburgh. Two days of keeping himself from Kathryn, knowing they were a heartbeat away from the kind of encounter that could not be undone.

For as much as they belonged together, he would not take her virginity until he had freed himself from his obligation. His brother's words continued to haunt him.

Kenshire. Bristol. Brockburg. Clave. We will all be affected by your choice.

Neill had been taught to be loyal, a king's man, and yet it infuriated him that Edward had not removed Caxton long ago, without his intervention. As always, the north was treated as a distant concern when compared with the south. The monarch had more interest in France than he did in the top half of his country.

"To court?" Sara asked.

"Aye."

He chanced a look at Kathryn, who sat beside Sara. He

hadn't protested at the revised seating arrangements, which bore his brother's stamp—he, next to his brother and achingly far from Kathryn. Being close to her reminded Neill the discipline he'd worked for so long to cultivate was a mere illusion.

"For all that we've discussed the alternatives," Neill said, "there is only one way to change course, one person who can stay this marriage but also remove Caxton."

"What will you say to Edward?" Kathryn and Sara exchanged glances as Sara asked that question. The two women had become even closer in recent weeks, as she had with Neill's young nephews, so much so that the idea of Kathryn leaving Kenshire had become absurd. He'd asked Geoffrey that very question the night before. Would he have Neill take her back to The Wild Boar on his way to court to marry a woman he'd never met?

Even Geoffrey had reluctantly agreed that Kenshire suited her—and that his wife and sons would likely murder him if he sent her away.

"I will ask him to reconsider the conditions of his reward."

Geoffrey made a sound that could be interpreted only one way. And though Neill tended to agree—the king would hardly lend him a sympathetic ear—he had no other choice. He'd confronted one monarch, and now he must face the other.

"I will offer to compensate her family for their troubles."

None spoke for some time.

The somber mood did not improve all night, each of them contemplating Edward's response. They all knew the king was unlikely to grant his request.

And what would happen then?

He asked himself that question over and over again over the course of a mostly sleepless night. Neill hadn't told his brother or Kathryn he planned to leave right away. He knew she would want to come, but it was much too dangerous. So when he strode into the hall, prepared to do just that, he was surprised to see Kathryn.

She stood with Faye at the hall's entrance as those who had attended mass walked by them, ready to break their fast. "I am coming with you," she said as he approached her.

"No."

He pulled her to the side, not liking the resolve he saw on her face.

"Even if there is no murderer there, at court, it would serve only to instigate the king. And the traveling. Kathryn, you cannot. 'Tis not safe."

Head held high, Kathryn stared him straight in the eyes but did not say a word. This was not the same maid who had served him at The Wild Boar, and Neill knew even as he spoke his argument was lost.

Even so, he tried.

"He could suspect you are the reason for my request. If we travel together—"

"I will not go to court but will stay in London, with an escort."

"No."

"I did not ask a question."

Faye had moved away, but he could see the small smile on the older woman's lips. If Faye thought the battle lost, then surely Sara also knew what Kathryn intended. He knew both women well enough to know this would not end as he wished. And so, though he had many more arguments for Kathryn to stay at Kenshire, he kept them to himself.

He looked down at her riding gown and serviceable leather boots. "How did you know I planned to leave this morn?"

"There is no reason to delay."

Indeed, there was not.

CHAPTER 26

*N*eill had arrived in London three days ago, but he had still been unable to gain an audience with the king. The king, he had been told, was indisposed. So he spent his days speaking with court officials at the royal palace, his nights at the inn with his men. And Kathryn, although they feigned a lack of intimacy.

They'd agreed she would not come to court, and although Neill had many contacts throughout the city, Kathryn had insisted on remaining at The Fox and Goose. It was one of the more respectable inns, and he was there with her each night, though in his own room. Still, Neill despised leaving her each morning.

Unlike in Scotland, he and Kathryn were never without a chaperone. Here, in London, there would be repercussions if an unmarried woman were seen alone with a man—even more so if *this* unmarried woman were seen alone with *this* man.

And yet, he longed to hold her. It had been too long since they'd had time alone, which was why Neill stood outside her door in the thick of night. Thankfully, she slept alone, without her chaperone. So as not to be discovered, he knocked softly, praying none of the other doors in the dark hallway opened.

When she opened the door, he lost no time stepping inside.

Kathryn was prepared for sleep, her shift covered with a robe that he guessed was borrowed from Sara. Deep crimson, edged with lace, it gave Kathryn a very regal appearance. And a seductive one as well.

"What are you doing here?" she whispered. "If you're caught in my room—"

"There will be questions, aye."

He took a step toward her. "Which is why I don't plan to be caught."

"We agreed . . ." She stopped. They'd danced around each other all the way to London. Although they were staying at the same inn, they'd avoided interacting any more than need be. At night, Kathryn and her chaperone would sit with Aylmer and another of his men, who did not wear the distinctive colors of Kenshire. The other guests hopefully thought Neill and Kathryn were strangers.

"Do you remember the story you told me," he said, taking another step toward her, "of how your father chastised you for running through the halls of the French court?"

"Aye." Kathryn blinked, her hands moving to close the robe that he fully planned to reopen.

"Then, the next day, he caught you doing the same thing?"

"With good cause," she said, the candle sitting next to the small bed flickering against the wall. Her face was clearly outlined by the dim light, but Neill did not need it to see her. He knew her appearance more and more each day. Could recount every aspect of her face in enough detail for a master to paint her sight unseen.

"I was being chased."

"By a girl whose ribbon you'd stolen." He took the last step.

"In jest, after she hid my shoes, making me miss morning mass. For which Father was none too pleased."

Neill reached out, cupping her neck with one hand, and waited for her response.

"And you said . . ."

"I said if I should be punished for a bit of fun, then I await your punishment."

His fingers tangled into the hair at the nape of her neck as he prepared for her objection.

"This is different," she whispered, her voice low. "If you and I are connected . . ."

He pulled her toward him, capturing whatever words she would speak in his mouth. His tongue slashed at her, demanding. Desperate. And she gave back in kind.

Neill slipped her robe from her shoulders, exposing the thin shift beneath. His hands moved quickly, covering each breast, squeezing ever so gently.

When she let out a soft sigh, Neill stopped just long enough to remove his own tunic and shirt. Eyes wide, Kathryn moved her hands to his chest, as he'd done to her. He closed his eyes, the feel of her hands on his bare flesh making him hard in an instant.

"Though we should wait," he said stupidly.

She moved one hand toward his stomach, and as it lowered . . .

Oh God, no.

He grasped it just before her fingers reached a place from which there would be no return.

"Aye, we should," she said with a sigh. "I've preserved my maidenhood for this long, and we don't know what the king will say."

Neill moved the hand he'd grasped around to his back. Even there, the flesh shivered in anticipation beneath her warm, soft ministrations.

"It does not matter."

And to him, it didn't. He would take no other woman as his wife.

He briefly glimpsed her look of surprise before he captured her lips once again. When he pulled away, it was only to lift her shift and wrap her legs around his waist. He moved them to the outside wall, knowing the inside ones were thin. There, with her back propped against the wall, Neill continued to ensure she was ready for him.

Because Kathryn would become his in truth that night.

He circled his hips against her, Kathryn mimicking his movements, kissing him back passionately.

This was reckless. Completely mad.

Her first time could not be like this. Really, it should not be here, now. He should wait until they had leave to marry. But Neill tightened his hold on her and carried her to the bed. Kneeling over her, he ran his hand up toward her inner thigh but did not stop.

She did not stop him.

He felt her readiness for him. This time, he'd not make her come with his hands. Trying to decide if he would undress himself or the beautiful woman beneath him, Neill froze.

Kathryn looked at him in confusion, obviously not having heard the sound.

Another knock landed on the door.

She heard it this time and scrambled off the bed. Neill found his shirt and, tossing it on, made his way to the door.

"Neill," came the hushed voice.

Aylmer.

He whipped open the door, pulled his friend inside, and closed the door behind him. His long-time friend raised his brows as he watched him put on his shirt, but he did not so much as glance in Kathryn's direction.

Good Aylmer.

"There are men below looking for you."

"Men?"

"The king's men."

"At this hour?"

"Aye." He made a face that some would say was borderline treasonous. "'Tis the king. And you're being reminded that you serve the king's whims."

He knew the truth of it better than most.

"How did you know to find him here?" Kathryn asked, standing beside him.

"Only Aylmer knew where I would be," he answered. Neill pulled his surcoat over his head and turned to Kathryn. "I will be back as soon as I can."

She nodded, clearly worried. He left with Aylmer, praying none would see them leave the room, but thankfully, the hallway was empty. They made their way belowstairs, and sure enough, two men bearing the king's colors stood waiting for him.

"Twice within a fortnight," he murmured as they stepped forward.

If only this meeting went so well as the last.

NEILL NEVER RETURNED.

Kathryn was surprised she slept at all, but as the sun streamed into the small window, she yawned and tossed her legs over the side of the bed. What did it mean? Had he spoken to the king?

Had Edward denied his request?

Dressing quickly, she made her way belowstairs, looking for Neill's men. Aylmer had gone with him, she was sure, but she spotted the others in the corner breaking their fast. About to join them, Kathryn lifted up her skirts and stepped onto the landing. Which was when she spotted him at the entrance.

They exchanged a look, and he nodded toward the stairs. In silent understanding, she turned around and nearly fled back to her room.

Kathryn couldn't sit, so instead she paced back and forth, waiting. What was taking him so long?

The door opened.

She knew the moment he entered that the audience had not gone well. Running to him, Kathryn threw her arms around his neck as he embraced her. They stood that way for some time, Kathryn unwilling to let go.

She worried the embrace may be their last.

"What did he say?" she finally murmured against his chest. Her head drifted up, and down, as he took a deep breath.

Before he even answered, Kathryn could feel a pinch in her cheeks, her eyes beginning to well.

I will not cry.

But when he pulled away, he kept hold of her. She had a moment of hope. Perhaps it was not as bad as that? If anyone could find a way around the king's request, surely it was Neill.

"The king, apparently, does not sleep. He brought us to the palace, and we waited, Aylmer with me, just outside the throne room. Others entered and left as the night grew later and later."

"That seems unusual."

"Not for Edward. I've heard rumors of his preference for such nighttime conferences, but always imagined they were exaggerated."

Neill loosened his hold so she could see his face fully now.

"I made my appeal, and as expected, Edward was not pleased."

"What did he say?"

"He said Alexander renewed his pledge of fealty, as expected.

And that his counselors have chosen a new warden to replace Caxton."

That managed to surprise her. "They did?"

"Aye. But he insisted that I fulfill my end of the bargain. He proposed a betrothal ceremony in three days' time."

Nay. She shook her head.

"I told him of Bothwell. About my visit to the Scottish court, though I did not mention your involvement. The king's lord high chamberlain attempted to aid my cause, insisting our intervention exposed a treachery in the Scottish court which had undermined the peace process."

"Alexandar's oath was delayed because of Bothwell. Surely he realizes the man would have remained in power were it not for you—"

"Nay, Kathryn. It was not I who uncovered Bothwell's treachery. 'Twas you."

She accepted his words but could focus only on the other information he relayed.

"Three days . . ."

"I will not do it."

"Neill, you must. You have no choice." The words felt like poison coming from her mouth, but they needed to be said.

His jaw was set. His expression, so serious.

"I cannot be the cause of Caxton remaining in power. Think on it, Neill."

"I already have and would have denied him already, but he ordered me from the room before I could do so. But mark my words, Kathryn, I'll not be swayed from my purpose so easily. I will not marry any woman but you."

Kathryn sank to the bed, defeated.

She had to make him understand.

"I have to go," he said abruptly. "Lord Lyndwood learned I was in London and wishes to speak with me."

She'd heard the name before. "Lyndwood?"

"You met Reid Kerr. Lyndwood is his father-in-law. Lady Sara knows him well, though I've never met the man. Besides, it would not do for me to be caught here. Especially now. I don't want you connected to me in any way."

He moved to her, but Kathryn shook her head. His touch always made her forget the obstacles between them, and right now she'd do best to remember them. She could not let herself be swayed by him now. She needed to think.

He cannot do this. I cannot let him do it.

CHAPTER 27

"*T*his way, Sir Neill."

He knew little of the man he was about to meet other than what he'd learned from his friends and siblings. The man's elder daughter, Gillian, was a close friend of Sara's. Lyndwood Castle was less than a two-day ride from Kenshire, and the women had practically grown up together. Now married to the chief of Clan Scott, Gillian resided with her husband in Scotland. Her sister, Allie, had wed Reid Kerr, who had told Neill much of what he knew of the man before him.

Neither Reid nor Graeme deSowlis, Gillian's husband, cared for their father-in-law. They did count him as shrewd, however, and admitted he'd done much to repair his relationship with his daughters after attempting to marry both of them off to an old, though very wealthy, man.

As the castle steward led him into a bedchamber in the East Tower of the royal court, far from the throne room where he'd spoken with the king earlier, Neill caught his first glimpse of the man he'd come to meet. Tall. Well-built for his age. Likely no more than sixty. Stern.

"Lyndwood."

The man stood to greet Neill as he approached.

"The great tournament champion." Shaking Lyndwood's hand, he took in their surroundings. From the size of the chamber the man had been given, Neill could determine his connections at court.

The space was small though well-appointed. Still, Lyndwood was here as Edward's guest, no small feat. Neill could only assume that his past troubles with the crown, something to do with a rival claim to his title and home, were no longer of consequence.

"Well met," he said, taking Lyndwood's cue to sit. Two goblets waited for them on the small wooden table adorned with a red and gold cloth, the same colors that could be found throughout the royal castle.

"I heard of your meeting with the king," Lyndwood said, pouring them both wine from a well-used pitcher.

"Did you?" he asked, cautious. Lyndwood's purpose was still unclear.

"Aye. And asked you here to warn you."

Neill took a sip of wine. Red. French.

"We're bound together, you and I."

Neill disagreed, but remained silent.

"You might have heard of some of my past decisions . . ."

He paused, giving Neill an opportunity to refute him, which he did not do.

"But all that I've done was to preserve my home, my land. One that has been in our family since William."

"We all make difficult decisions," he said to be polite. Privately, he thought no piece of property was worth more than family.

Lyndwood drank deeply, his cheeks already reddening. This was not his first wine of the day. But still, Neill held his tongue, giving the borderer the opportunity to speak his mind. Though he was not inclined to like this man, Lyndwood was a borderer still, and that afforded him some respect.

"And you've one still to make. But I wonder, do you know Lady Alina's father?"

That gave Neill pause. He did not, in fact, know anything of deBeers other than that he was a baron whose daughter was a favorite of the queen's.

"His wife is cousin to Joan of Navarre," Lyndwood continued, after pausing long enough for effect.

"The French queen?" It was not possible. He'd have learned of the connection after the tournament. Adam or Cora would have told him.

"Very few know of it."

"Yet you are privy to this information?"

Lyndwood smiled, and Neill decided he rather agreed with Reid and Graeme—he didn't much like this man. He was the sort who thrived on power. Who cared little for the consequences of his actions if he directly benefited from them.

Are you acting any differently with Kathryn?

But he didn't have any time to devote to that thought, for Lyndwood had already launched into his explanation. "DeBeers and I fostered together many, many years ago."

"Ahhh."

That, he could understand. The ties between boys who were trained together were as strong as those of family, much like he and Aylmer.

"Which means . . ."

He considered the import of what he'd learned as Lyndwood watched him, likely knowing the exact direction of his thoughts. If deBeers was a relative to the French queen, he could be dangerous to Edward, whose father's policies had brought the two countries to the precipice of war. If this man, the one whose daughter Neill was supposed to wed, had any influence over the French king . . .

He was an important man to Edward.

Too important to disappoint. Much more important than the long-running, exhausting situation on the England-Scotland border.

Hadn't he always said this king was more interested in France than he was in Scotland?

"If I do not wed his daughter," he said aloud, "Edward risks falling out with a man who has the potential to tip the scales of war."

"Some say 'tis an inevitability. But certainly Edward attempts to avoid it. You cannot renounce your betrothal."

"We are not betrothed," he said, knowing the argument was weak.

Lyndwood finished his drink and poured another, filling Neill's goblet without being asked.

"A minor detail."

Of course, he knew as much.

Kathryn's face flashed before him. He could feel her head nestled against his chest even now. Reaching up to rub the back of his neck, Neill sat back against his chair's velvet cushion, even Lyndwood's small chamber not without the luxuries of the royal court.

"If you do, Caxton will remain as warden. The Day of Truce will not resume."

Angry at Lyndwood, at himself, and the king, Neill slammed his goblet on the table, splatters of red wine flying out. "That he would risk so much for a woman . . ." He cut himself off, shaken. He'd been thinking of the king's commitment to Lady Alina, although his words could just as easily be applied to himself.

"You've more to consider than just the borderlands," Lyndwood said, his expression dark. But Neill already knew what the man was going to say.

"If you spurn the Lady Alina, you risk not only Edward's wrath but that of her father, who will not take kindly to a broken promise. Though how he would retaliate, I cannot say." Lyndwood drank deeply of his wine.

DeBeers would see it as an affront both from and to Edward. But would he really use his connection to the French crown to retaliate?

Could Neill's decision cause not one but two wars?

Clearly Lyndwood thought so.

"You cannot do it," the man repeated.

His chest tight, Neill stood. He'd heard enough.

"Thank you for your counsel, my lord."

With that, he turned and left. And for the first time in a long while, Neill felt utterly and completely defeated.

He cared not for the feeling at all.

KATHRYN RUBBED the cloth across her face, down to her neck and over her arms. She should not have spent her precious gold on such a trifle as dried rose, but had indulged herself. The men, of course, had questioned her about their visit to the floristry and tailor, but she'd remained sufficiently elusive. They'd accepted her explanation, or lack thereof, and followed her about the city, making sure to leave for the inn before the most dangerous part of the day.

Vespers, otherwise known as the murdering hour here in London.

Her mind kept straying to Neill. Wondering what he was doing. She knew it didn't matter—she couldn't allow him to sway her from her purpose. And though she should be terrified, Kathryn felt at peace with her decision.

A knock at the door interrupted her musings. Opening it, she let out a breath of relief, realizing she'd not inquired to the identity of her visitor.

"You should be more careful," Neill said, not unexpectedly, as he walked in past her.

She said nothing. The awkwardness between them from earlier lingered. Dressed only in her shift, Kathryn noticed that Neill had recently bathed. His hair, still wet, curled at the ends, and she had the overwhelming desire to touch it. To feel the tendrils beneath her fingers.

Which, of course, made her think of the only time she had allowed herself to explore him with her touch, his stomach as hard and unyielding as an iron sword. Without a word, he drew her to him, and this time she did not protest. Kissing him felt as natural now as breathing.

His tongue delved inside her mouth, and she met it with her own. Desperation, knowing what was to come, made her cling to him more tightly than usual. When he pulled away, Kathryn felt . . . lost.

"I would make you mine this night if I could."

She knew and wished it too.

"Come."

Kathryn tugged on his hand and led him to her bed. Though he seemed surprised, Neill did not argue. Instead, he lay down as she silently suggested he do. And then she climbed up against him, burrowing her head into his chest.

He put his arms around her, one under her head, the other holding her hand, and they lay like that for some time.

"You smell like roses," he finally said. She repositioned her head to look at him.

"Aye."

Unwilling to tell him where she'd gotten the fragrance, worried he may make further inquiries, she tried to guide the conversation away from what was to come.

What tomorrow would bring.

"Tell me another story about your childhood," she said instead. "Something I do not yet know."

He was silent for some time. Kathryn watched his face as his expression turned from thoughtful to pleased. His lips curled up ever so slightly, faint lines appearing around the corners of his eyes.

The light from a single candle showed her what she already knew. They were clear blue, just like his brothers'. Sometimes, when he was angry, they appeared darker. But they were as light as a summer sky tonight, and it seemed Kathryn could peer through them into his very soul.

"Emma could be willful at times. One day, when I was given my first training sword, she asked our father for the same. He refused her request, saying only boys could become knights. I remember Bryce saying that Emma had gotten too quiet. We'd expected her to argue with our father, but she did not."

Kathryn was glad her own father had understood the value of her own training, even if it was with a dagger and not a sword.

"What did she do?"

"Nothing. Or at least, she did nothing *that* day."

He adjusted himself on the bed and then pulled her even tighter against him.

"Or the next. Or the day after that. It was a sennight later when she was discovered missing by Geoffrey, who raised the alarm."

"Where had she gone?"

"Into the village. Which, of course, she'd not been given leave to do on her own. She'd hidden herself among sacks of grain, and so the miller's son had unknowingly brought her to town. From there, she visited the blacksmith—" his grin widened, "—to commission a sword, of course."

"Of course," she said, laughing. "He did not make her one, did he?"

"Nay. He sent his assistant back to the manor to inform us that she was there. She spent the next hour watching him work."

"And what did your father do?"

"Father? He did nothing. But Bryce, admiring her bravery, fashioned a dagger suited for a young girl and showed her how to wield it."

Her eyes widened in surprise.

"Aye, much like your father taught you."

"I would like to meet Emma someday." She said it without thinking and immediately wished she could take back the words. Sighing, she laid her head back down. "I'm sorry. I should not have said that."

"There is nothing to be sorry for, Kathryn."

His voice sounded sad to her ears, but there was nothing she could say to him. Knowing what she had planned . . . she'd do better to remain silent. They should enjoy this time together while they still could.

Neill must have been thinking much the same. He rubbed her back as she lay there, her head still nestled firmly against his chest. The last thought Kathryn remembered having was that she loved him and wanted to tell him as much.

But it was not the time for such words.

And then she slept.

CHAPTER 28

*W*hen Neill walked into the royal training yard the next morn, the reaction was as he expected. One by one, heads turned toward him as he strode to the captain-at-arms.

"Sir Neill Waryn," he declared himself.

"Well met, and welcome, Sir Neill," the man said, handing him a red and yellow surcoat to be worn over the light armor Aylmer had helped him with earlier. He'd left his squire at Langford, knowing the boy wanted to stay in the south. Aylmer had accompanied him to the royal training yard instead.

Neill had awoken before dawn, although he couldn't bring himself to rise for some time. Despite the diminutive bed, which had barely held them both, Neill could not remember a more pleasant night's sleep. The only difficulty had been ignoring his body's response to the beautiful woman in his arms.

She was not his, as much as he willed it otherwise. The thought that he'd almost taken her virginity disturbed him now. The choice he'd thought so clear was anything but.

Two days until the king received him again. Until he would be forced to make a choice no man should be asked to make.

Before meeting Lyndwood, he'd made his decision. It would be ludicrous for the sovereign to decline to remove the only barrier to peace along the border, but it was his decision, and his alone. Aye, he could aid the cause by marrying Lady Alina, but Neill could no sooner forsake Kathryn for his unknown bride than he could lose a joust.

Count victory before you've achieved it, and you are lost.

He could hear Adam's words in his ears, cautioning him, teaching him humility. Geoffrey had urged him to rethink his choice time and again, despite knowing the happiness of being loved. Despite the similarity between his situation with Sara and the difficulties Neill and Kathryn now faced.

So much hung in the balance:

The Day of Truce.

Caxton.

His family's safety.

Lyndwood.

DeBeers.

War with France.

His mind had been awash with uncertainty, and so he'd done what he always did in times of trouble—he'd fetched Aylmer and the two of them gained entry to the very place he now stood. The training yard was the only place he could find peace, and Neill desperately needed to calm his mind this day.

"Quintain?" he asked. The captain pointed, and he and Aylmer made their way to the far end of the field. Once, grass may have grown beneath their feet, but no longer. Men's feet and horses' hooves had turned the ground beneath them to dirt. A wall of stone surrounded them, encircling one of the largest training yards Neill had ever encountered.

"Do you remember the first time we were here?" he asked Aylmer, who rolled his eyes in response. "What is it?"

"We're being watched," Aylmer said. "Word spreads as the mighty Neill Waryn makes his way through the yard."

Neill pretended not to notice. "Yet another reason to return north."

"You'll not lack competitors if it's a fight you want this morn."

Sounds of clanging swords and the grunts of men practicing their skills rang in the air all around them. A comforting sound that brought Neill as much peace as he was likely to feel under the circumstances.

"*Need*," he clarified.

Aylmer knew most of Neill's situation, but he'd not yet told him about his meeting with Lyndwood. He knew why he'd kept the details to himself, which troubled him nearly as much as the decision he would be forced to make.

He knew in his heart Aylmer would agree with Geoffrey.

With Lyndwood.

Even with Kathryn, who'd seemed horrified by Lyndwood's revelations about Lady Alina. "We cannot do this," she'd said. He knew she worried about her role in the breakdown of peace, but as he'd told her, the decision was not theirs but Edward's.

Still, she was not wrong to think everyone would cast blame on him. On Kathryn.

He could endure it, but could she?

"Neill?"

"Aye," he said, reaching the quintain. Three were erected far enough apart to allow them to be used simultaneously. One held a shield, another a sack of grain, and a suit of armor waited in the third. The areas were used for training, each serving a distinct purpose.

In the joust, some men excelled by the strength of their hit, for which the armor would help them practice. Others, speed, the force of their lance coming from the quickness of the mount beneath them. Still others, for precision. The swinging bag of grain was more often missed than hit and provided practice to hone that particular skill.

Neill was known for all three.

"Will you progress?" Aylmer asked.

Neill nodded, approaching the area reserved for those who awaited their turn. They'd not been permitted to bring their own mounts, as was customary in the royal training yard. When it was Neill's turn, he would borrow one of the king's crusaders, another name for the destriers bred expressly for this purpose.

"Aye," he said as he was summoned to the first quintain.

Nodding to the stable master, who handed him the reins of a black destrier, Neill grabbed his helm from Aylmer. Donning it, he then took the practice lance from an eager young squire.

Moving into position, he focused on the very spot that would remove the armor with one blow. The hit needed to be strong and sure, and if he wished to progress to the next of the practice areas, he had just one chance. Patting his mount with his free hand, Neill then wrapped the reins around his wrist and readied his lance. He saw nothing but the armor at the end of the field. He heard nothing but the breathing of his horse, save his own breath, which he steadied in preparation for their lunge.

With a word, and a kick, he charged toward his opponent. Not a suit of armor, in his mind, but a man intent on dismounting him. Which Neill would never allow.

When he hit his mark, Neill knew before turning back he'd accomplished his task. He'd done the same hundreds of times. Thousands. In training and in tournaments. And he could always tell if his mark was true.

He heard the shouts as he rode back, but he ignored them.

"Another run?"

The captain was present now, along with another man Neill remembered as the master-at-arms. A growing crowd encircled them. Murmurs of "Waryn" and "champion" reached his ears, but Neill blocked them out as surely as he did his troubles.

This time, the shield. His goal, to break the lance into pieces, attesting to the speed with which he could hit his mark.

"Remember Anjou," he heard Aylmer cry out in the crowd, a reminder of the time he'd nearly lost to a much younger, quite agile French knight. He'd angled the lance just slightly too high from top to bottom, but Neill had no intention of making that mistake again.

Still, this maneuver could be tricky—even more so on a borrowed mount. Neill would have to rely on subtle movements to bring the charger to full speed. But judging from his first run, the horse was capable if he could steady him and strike at just the right time.

When he struck the shield and shattered his lance, Neill was unsurprised at the outcome. He'd trained long and hard, and he was rightly confident in his skills.

By now, none were left to their own training. The crowd had swelled around him. To progress was a feat few mastered, and Neill knew it well. But he ignored the cheers as he prepared for his final run.

The most difficult of them all.

The sack was small, and a squire would swing it from side to side just as Neill brought his horse to a gallop. Hitting the tiny moving target would require him to reposition the heavy training lace he'd just been handed.

He heard Aylmer's shouts above the others and smiled. None cheered louder than his friend. Aylmer still hadn't told him if he intended to stay in the north with him, at Kenshire, but he hoped so.

Would Kathryn be there too?

He'd been able to block her from his thoughts until now. But as he prepared for his final run, her sleeping face, so peaceful and lovely, appeared before him.

If I can be victorious here, I can do the same with Kathryn. I will win. And I will not denounce the woman I love.

It was no way to make a decision, especially such an important one. But the thought came unbidden, and so Neill embraced it. He would not lose. Had not failed a quintain progress in years. And when he succeeded here, he would tell the king of his intent.

Kathryn was his.

For a final time, Neill spurred his mount toward the target. He never took his eyes from it, watching as it swung from side to side, learning its precise path to time his strike perfectly. Moving his lance into position, he determined just where it would be when he approached. Horse steady, arm steady, he aimed.

And missed.

CHAPTER 29

*K*athryn had not told Neill.

And she could not tell his men.

So as much as she despised traveling even the short distance from the inn to court alone, she saw no help for it. It had been easy enough to convince the men to escort her back to the tailor earlier that morn, but now, she was on her own.

The tailor's work had cost her much of the gold she had remaining on her person from her father, but he had nevertheless adjusted her gown as she'd requested. Kathryn looked as if she belonged back at court.

Though she wore no gems, a fact that would be immediately evident to a courtier, her gown, at least, looked appropriate. Trimmed in fur, it also boasted a gold-trimmed cotehardie top layer, which the tailor had fitted perfectly to her height.

Most inns had less-used entrances, and this one was no exception. Kathryn made her way to the stables without being noticed. She was not a prisoner here, but she knew Neill would disapprove mightily of what she was about to do. Secrecy was vital.

"Good day," she said to the stable boy, also the innkeeper's son. "Will you ready my horse, and quickly?" Kathryn handed him a coin, hoping it would stop him from asking the question in his eyes.

And it worked.

"If anyone should ask for me, please tell him . . . them . . . I am safe."

"Aye, my lady."

Thankfully, they were situated in the northeast quarter of the city, the Tower a short ride away. As Kathryn passed a water mill and rode along a small stream, she felt a familiar tightening of her chest. So very many things could go wrong. But instead of allowing panic to overtake her, she thought of waking up during the night in Neill's arms. He'd fallen asleep, or had she done so first? It had felt so natural. So comfortable. She'd spent much of the morning dreaming about what it would be like to wake up thusly every day.

Ignoring a few odd looks as she rode down the narrow road, a chapel to her right and monastery to her left, Kathryn spotted her destination ahead. The journey to the Tower was only one of many challenges she would need to overcome that day.

Gaining entry would be the next.

She had been here many, many times, even when the king was not in residence. Kathryn approached the Coldharbour Gate at the southwest corner of the Tower, preparing for the questions she would inevitably face. A lady riding up to the king's castle, alone, on horseback was hardly a normal occurrence.

"Good day," she said to one of the guards, who gave her a dubious look. Kathryn could see the inner ward through the raised gate—which looked like, but was not, an invitation to enter.

"Lady Kathryn Wyld, daughter of Richard Wyld—"

"The missing messenger to the king," he finished for her.

Kathryn was not sure if his immediate recognition of her

father should please or worry her, but she'd hoped for it regardless. It would be easier to gain an audience this way.

She shivered at the thought.

Still, he eyed her suspiciously as other visitors rode past.

"Not missing," she clarified. "Dead."

He and another guard exchanged glances, both of them obviously leery of her claim.

"My father served King Henry loyally for more than twenty years. It was he who carried the message to King Louis that confirmed our king as the legitimate ruler of Gascony and avoided war with France. I am well known to the queen, whom I served once, if you will allow me entry to gain an audience."

And that easily, she was nodded onward. Whether they believed her or, more likely, did not see a lone woman on horseback as a threat, Kathryn could not be sure.

She was inside. The bustle reminded her of the years she'd spent here, and also of Kenshire. Knights passed her as they made their way to the training yard. Mothers chased after their children. Servants scurried from one building to the next.

She knew whom she needed to find in order to gain the audience she desired. Her name was Rosalind, and she'd served as Mistress of the Robes to two queens. An imposing figure with white hair piled atop her head always, Rosalind was known as a hard woman. Unkind, some would say, Kathryn had seen many girls run from her chamber in tears, though, oddly, she never had trouble with the woman.

Making her way to St. Thomas's Tower, Kathryn gained entrance easily. No one so much as glanced her way, a feat accomplished by the modifications she'd so hastily made to her gown. Kathryn could fit in here, and she did.

"Pardon me," she said to a serving girl when she entered the great hall, "I am looking for Mistress Rosalind . . ." Before she even finished the question, the girl was pointing toward the Presence Chamber, a guarded space.

"Many thanks," she said loudly. The hall was as noisy as she remembered it.

Just as she'd done at the gatehouse, Kathryn announced herself to the guard who stood at the entrance to the Presence Chamber. Within minutes, a familiar wrinkled face stood before her.

Eyes wide, Rosalind blinked in surprise and then did something quite rare for her.

She smiled.

"You are alive."

"Aye," she said, moving to the stone wall at the side of the hall as the guard watched them. Rosalind walked with her.

"Your father?"

Kathryn shook her head.

"I am sorry, my lady. He was a good man." She cocked her head to the side. "Who simply disappeared?"

It was stated as a question. For a moment, Kathryn's stomach felt as if it were made of metal. Had she made a mistake coming here? Her father had told her not to return to court, but now that Rosalind knew she was here, Kathryn could not reverse her decision.

I have no other choice.

"I've much to explain," she said, knowing the words were hardly adequate.

Then, as she was wont to do, Rosalind looked down at her gown, which may have passed the scrutiny of the guards but could not fool the Mistress of the Robes.

"You have come in difficult times." She stated it as fact, not a question. "Why did you not come back sooner?"

It was the question she'd dreaded for fear of causing offense.

"As you say, Mistress Rosalind, I've much to explain. But there is little time to do it . . ."

Looking as if she'd suggested pairing a blue kirtle and purple surcoat, Rosalind's face contorted into a look that would have scared another woman.

But Kathryn was afraid of only one thing. And it was not Rosalind.

"I must ask a favor of you and then," she promised, "I will tell you everything."

And she would. For once Kathryn was finished with her audience, nothing else mattered. Her fate, whether she believed the work of Fortuna would be in the hands of the most powerful woman in England.

"What is your favor?"

Whether because of her desperate tone or the strength of their past relationship—and a bond created by the fact that neither had known her mother—Rosalind could prove to be the godsend Kathryn needed.

"My Lady Eleanor. I must speak with her immediately."

"You wish to gain an audience with the queen?"

"Aye, if it pleases you."

Rosalind, thank every saint in heaven, looked back toward the private chamber behind her. Eleanor was in there!

"It pleases me well to have you safe back at court, my lady. Your request is easily granted. I'm sure Her Grace will be eager to see you."

Rosalind turned, expecting her to follow.

She'd come for this very reason. Had met with fewer troubles than she'd expected. And now that she was on the cusp of getting what she wanted, she felt horribly unprepared. It didn't matter—she needed to do this.

Kathryn took a step forward. And then another.

The door opened, and there she sat.

The queen of England.

CHAPTER 30

"What do you mean, you don't know where she is?" Neill stood next to his men, who had apparently just sat down to a fresh pitcher of ale. Despite the late hour, the inn's hall was crowded.

"She is not with you?" one of the men asked.

Neill was not amused.

"When did you see her last?"

The men, who'd now turned on the bench and were finally looking sufficiently concerned, looked up at him. "We escorted her to the tailor and then back here."

He and Aylmer exchanged a glance.

"The tailor?"

"Aye, my lord. The tailor."

"What need did she have of a tailor?"

"I know not. But have you checked the stables?"

He turned to Aylmer, asking the silent question. Aylmer shrugged. "Let's go."

He left the inn so abruptly, Neill garnered looks from the other patrons, but their opinions little mattered. He was in a foul mood from the yard, from his ongoing predicament and his inability to solve it, and this was not what he'd expected.

He craved Kathryn's touch. Her lips. Her warmth. Her conversation. Neill wanted nothing more than to have her with him now, unharmed.

"The stable master," he asked a young boy who was just emerging from the stables as he and Aylmer approached. "Where is he?"

The boy, no older than ten and two, looked from him to Aylmer, his eyes wide and wary, and Neill immediately regretted his harsh tone. "I'm looking for my companion's horse," he said more gently. "And wish to speak to the stable master."

Most inns had, at best, one stable boy, but this was larger and fancier than most. The boy squinted his eyes at him. "Yer the lord with my lady who left this morn?"

"Who left?"

Nodding, the boy swallowed hard, no doubt believing he was in trouble.

"I, she . . . she gave me extra coin and bade me to ready her horse. I thought it unusual," he stammered.

Neill put up a hand to silence him. "You did nothing wrong, lad. Just tell me, when did she leave?"

"Earlier today, my lord."

"Earlier today." Neill clenched and unclenched his hands. "Did she say where she was going?"

He would gather the men. Look for her. Scour the city.

"Nay, my lord. Though she told me to tell anyone who came looking . . ." He frowned. "Mayhap she meant you, lord. She said to tell you she was safe."

He waited, but the lad did not elaborate.

"Go on," he prompted.

"That is all, my lord. And then she left. A good rider she be too."

"Thank you, lad," Neill said finally, realizing the boy had no further information to share.

"Gone. Where?" he asked Aylmer, turning to him in shock. "Will we look for her?"

Aylmer shrugged at his stricken expression. "A fair question, Neill, as she appears to have left of her own will."

"A woman. Alone. In London. Of course we look for her."

Aylmer wisely remained silent and did not say what he himself was thinking. Kathryn was a resourceful woman. If she'd told the lad she was safe, he had no reason to believe otherwise. She might not *want* to be found.

But why?

As Aylmer had their horses readied, he thought of the night before. They had not discussed his answer to the king, the one he'd be forced to give in the morn. More fool him. He should have asked what she was thinking.

Neill had spent the day in contemplation, knowing he'd lost that morn for the same weakness Bryce had taken advantage of in Brockburg. He'd been too sure of his own victory. He'd allowed himself to become distracted.

And although he'd vowed to act based on his success or failure in the training yard, he'd decided he could not allow such an important decision to rest on a silently spoken vow during training. Instead, he'd concluded he must consider what his brothers would do in his situation. What Adam would do. The answer, he and Aylmer had agreed, was to speak with the woman who'd been named in the king's damnable request, Lady Alina. In doing so, he hoped he might free himself without causing an uproar.

Except Kathryn was gone.

On the eve before she knew he would be forced to answer the king.

Which meant . . .

Which meant she had made the decision for him. They

would look for her, but Neill had little hope she would be found.

Without Kathryn, there was only one answer he could give the king.

He would have to marry Lady Alina.

ELEANOR OF CASTILE.

Daughter of Ferdinand III, king of Castile, and Joan, the Countess of Ponthieu, whom Kathryn had met on two separate occasions while Edward was in Acre.

Some said, secretly of course, the queen had nearly as much power as her husband.

The queen had received her earlier, briefly, before a young page burst into the chamber begging the queen to attend her husband, who'd requested her presence. Before Kathryn could say a word, Eleanor had been escorted away. She'd never had a chance to ask the question she'd come to ask.

Kathryn fretted that she'd not have another opportunity to speak with her despite Rosalind's assurances otherwise. At least the queen had appeared pleased to see her. Whatever reservations her father had felt about Kathryn returning to court, she did not believe they extended to this woman who had always been so kind to her.

"I've word from Your Grace," Rosalind had finally said some time later. "She will receive you in the morn. The king, it seems, has taken ill."

She left the rest unsaid. While their marriage had, of course, been arranged, everyone at court knew it was nonetheless a love match. If Edward was sick, his queen would remain by his side, of that she had no doubt.

When Rosalind had Kathryn escorted to a private bedchamber, Kathryn began to panic. Neill would return to the inn soon, and even though she'd left a cryptic message for him, he would no doubt worry. She could ask Rosalind to have a message brought to the inn, but Kathryn didn't know what to say.

Should she tell Neill she was here, at court? Her worry, of course, had been that he would prevent her from coming. But now that she was already here, could she tell him so? Surely he could not force her to leave before she spoke with the queen?

In the end, she decided to say nothing other than to assure him, once again, that she was safe and not to worry. After giving Rosalind the parchment, she'd returned to the bedchamber, one of a few reserved for the queen's attendants. It was smaller than the one she'd lived in at the castle, yet no less opulent. The bed covering gleamed in the candlelight, the gold thread a testament to the wealth that the English monarch enjoyed.

A lone window with a seat below looked down on a garden, one of many. More importantly, a wooden tub filled with hot water sat in the center of the room. Silently thanking Rosalind both for the bath and for the gown, which lay on her bed, Kathryn cleaned herself. She was in the bath when the door flew open, startling her.

"Pardon, my lady," a young chambermaid said as she scurried into the room. "Mistress Rosalind bid me assist you to supper."

Feeling very much like the queen herself, Kathryn dressed in the deep purple velvet gown, smiling at Rosalind's accurate assessment of her measurements. If not for her worry about Neill and her audience with the queen, Kathryn could almost feel as if she'd returned home. This was, at least, as close to a home as she'd ever had.

Except for Kenshire.

Pushing the thought aside, Kathryn allowed the maid to style her hair and then followed her down to the hall where supper was already underway. More than one hundred men and women were crowded inside, and yet this was only one of three great halls within the Tower serving a meal now. The queen's ladies, the king's officers, and their children could be found here, while the other retainers, including the royal men-at-arms, would dine separately. The king and queen often ate privately, in their own chamber, but occasionally graced one of the three halls with their presence.

Though not this eve.

The dais remained empty as Kathryn made her way to the table where Rosalind sat with the other ladies-in-waiting. Some were new, while others Kathryn knew well.

"Good eve," she said as she came close.

"Lady Kathryn," said Lysa, a tall blonde-haired daughter of an earl whom Kathryn had always found most endearing. Sweet and conversable, Lysa was the oldest of Eleanor's ladies. Widowed young, Lysa claimed she had no need of another husband again, and true to her word, she remained unwed.

"I'm so pleased you can join us."

She sat next to Lysa, aware the others watched them carefully.

"'Tis nice to be back." She arranged her gown under her, her back straight, chin held high. Kathryn was being judged, and she knew it well.

There was a time she had cared very much about the opinions of the other women, when the court was her home. These ladies, her family. But she was no longer that same person.

"You've met the others," Lysa said as conversation ceased around them. "Although I do not believe Lady Alina was present earlier . . ."

Kathryn froze.

While Lysa continued the introduction, Kathryn's heart thudded in her ears.

Lady Alina.

This was *the* Lady Alina. The one Neill was promised to marry.

When the young woman smiled, a kind and seemingly

genuine smile—a rarity here at court—Kathryn managed to mumble out an acceptable greeting.

Sneaking glances at the pretty young woman, she couldn't help but compare herself to the striking beauty. Everything about her was pleasing, from her long, dark hair to her deep brown eyes.

Just when she'd thought herself above the petty comparisons and competitions of the ladies of the court, Kathryn had taken the first opportunity to emulate them.

But this is different. This is the woman who is to marry the man I love.

Nay!

A ferocity Kathryn hadn't known she possessed took hold of her then, rebelling against the thought.

"Where have you been these past months?"

It took a moment for Lysa's question to penetrate.

"I have been making my way back from Edinburgh."

A servant poured wine into her goblet at exactly that moment, and she was able to avoid further questions by taking a long draught from it.

Lady Alina was watching her.

Kathryn half-heartedly listened as her companions chatted excitedly about their brief respite. With Eleanor at the king's bedside, they were not required to attend to her. Which meant the night would be spent dancing and flirting. Musicians even now began to play in the far corner of the hall.

Just as she was prepared to excuse herself to her chamber, the conversation took a turn Kathryn had dreaded.

They started discussing Neill Waryn.

The others clasped their hands in excitement as Lady Alina answered questions about the knight who would be coming to court the very next day.

"The queen says we will be formally betrothed any day now that he has returned."

"Minstrels will sing of it. The favored knight and his reward," Lysa said.

Kathryn could stay no longer. She had to shake the mental image of Lady Alina holding Neill's hand as they were bound together in a ceremony that was as binding as marriage.

"Pardon," she said, not waiting for the women to bid her a good-den. Neither did she stop to ask for the maid's assistance. She would manage her gown somehow.

Most importantly, Kathryn needed to get away from the hall at once.

Away from Lady Alina.

CHAPTER 31

*H*e was a fool.

Kathryn had not come back, and he still felt unsure of the path he would take that day. Aylmer was unsurprisingly frustrated with him, enough so that he'd let Neill ride ahead of him to the royal stables, although not as frustrated as Neill was with himself.

You must accept Lady Alina. Kathryn wishes for you to do so.

Neill dismounted and handed his reins to a stable boy.

"Pardon, my lord."

He turned, knowing that voice.

"Morley!"

He grasped arms with the only man who had beaten him in the joust in the King's Tournament, the annual event held during summer solstice attended by the best knights in England and beyond. Neill had been named champion the following year, but still remembered the hit this man had given him.

Sir Kenton Morley was also a borderer, so Neill had a fondness for the earl's son.

"Are you lost?" he asked, knowing Morley's aversion to the south.

Morley laughed. "Of sorts. My father sent my brother and me here to petition the king, once again."

"I can likely guess. This is over Derrickson land, is it not?"

"Aye."

The Morleys and Derricksons had been fighting for years over property, something that should have been decided by the border line drawn in the Treaty of York.

Morley lowered his voice. "My father attended the council and told us of your intervention. I've also heard the Scottish king has renewed his pledge of fealty."

Neill watched as Aylmer followed the boy into the stables. His friend would bring his horse into the hall if he could and trusted few with his keeping. The boy was about to get an earful.

Smiling, he gave his attention back to Morley.

"He has."

Neill knew what Morley's next question would be, and he dreaded having to answer it.

"So it is done? Caxton will be removed?"

He was prepared to say aye but stopped and spoke the truth instead.

"The king granted my request with a condition, one I did not share with the council."

If Morley was confused by the confidence, Neill was no less so. Why was he sharing his story with a relative stranger? He had no true answer for that, and yet it felt good to be honest.

"My marriage to Lady Alina deBeers."

Morley cleared his throat. "I don't know a deBeers."

Neill continued. "Since that time, I have fallen in love with another woman. The king was not pleased—"

"You told him?" Morley tsked and shook his head.

"Aye. And he gave me three days to set a date for my betrothal to Lady Alina, or Caxton will remain as warden."

"He would risk the continuance of our upheaval? I understand why his father was pledged to Caxton," Morley said, lowering his voice, "but surely Edward is not so indebted."

"Lord Caxton's bribes bring him coin when it's needed most."

"So what do you plan to do?"

Aylmer made his way toward them.

"There is only one choice," Neill said, knowing he did not quite speak the truth. One obvious choice, aye, and a choice Kathryn seemed determined to foist upon him. He imagined she had left because she wanted him to give the king what he had demanded. And yet . . . "Caxton must be removed."

He waited for Morley's affirmation, but the man cocked his head to the side.

"Indeed. But perhaps there is another way," he said, giving him a knowing look.

Neill must have seemed surprised. And not slightly confused.

"Love is love," Morley said as Aylmer approached. "I bid you well, Sir Neill."

"And I you, Morley."

The earl's son nodded in greeting to Aylmer and walked away. Neill watched him go.

"Recalling your tumble at his hands?" Aylmer said, laughing at his own joke.

"Aye," he lied. "Would you like to bring him in the hall with you?"

Aylmer's only answer was to scowl at him, a look that was becoming all too familiar, as they made their way through the courtyard. His audience with Edward was just past midday, but as was his custom, Neill had arrived early.

Love is love.

He stepped through the double doors and into the castle.

And so it began.

SHE'D WAITED for this audience for the better part of two days. Finally, Kathryn was ushered into the queen's solar, a room two floors above the bedchamber she'd been given. Silently thanking Rosalind for the second gown—everyone at court would notice had she donned the one she'd worn to dinner—she made her way to Eleanor's high-backed chair and curtsied as deeply as she'd done the day before.

Normally surrounded by her ladies, the queen was quite alone this morn. Though unusual, the circumstance was cause for celebration. She'd dreaded the possibility that Lady Alina might be present.

"You are a lovely sight, Lady Kathryn. Mistress Rosalind?"

Kathryn nodded. The deep blue velvet gown fit her perfectly. Its wide-hanging sleeves, though fashionable, hid her hands when lowered, so Kathryn clasped them in front of her as she prepared to speak.

"My thanks, Your Grace," she said. "May I inquire after the king's health this morn?"

"You may," she said. "He is feeling much better this morn."

All knew the queen loved her husband, and it was that love she would appeal to now. It was her only hope.

Knowing Neill's audience was arranged for that day, Kathryn launched into her request. She was running out of time and could not afford to be waylaid again.

"I have a request for Your Grace, if she would be kind to allow for a story first."

Eleanor indicated she should continue.

"I believe Sir Neill Waryn met with our king and told him about the Earl of Bothwell's interference with the message my father brought to King Alexander."

"Aye, Lady Kathryn. He did so."

"Sir Neill told him that my father was murdered to prevent his delivery of the message."

As expected, the queen began to look suspicious.

"Go on."

"He did not tell him that we met at The Wild Boar, where I worked as a serving maid these many months. Once he learned my true identity, he pledged himself to my father's cause, which was, as we learned later, also his own."

Eleanor's shrewd eyes narrowed.

"He did not tell him, Your Grace, that we fell in love."

She allowed those words to settle before continuing.

"It is for this reason Sir Neill, the most loyal and honorable knight in England, asked our king to grant him the reward given as the Tournament of Peace champion without provision."

"A provision," the queen said, her voice firm, "which I myself added."

Neill had suspected as much. It was a favor to one of her ladies, likely at the request of Lady Alina herself. She was hardly the only woman in England to have taken an interest in the tournament champion, Kathryn suspected, and her father was likely eager for the chance to align himself with one of the most powerful families in England.

"Today Sir Neill is asked to choose between peace along the borderlands, where his family resides, and a love forged by circumstance but no less powerful for it."

She'd said it. Hands trembling, Kathryn was thankful now for the fabric that hid what she hoped was the only indication she was terrified of what she'd just done.

Eleanor did not speak at first. In fact, she hardly moved at all.

"Why did you not return to court?" her lady asked her.

Kathryn had no answer but the truth.

"I worried his murderer could reside here, at court, Your Grace."

Eleanor breathed so loudly through her nose, Kathryn could hear it from where she stood.

She thought to continue explaining herself, her desire to find the man who'd murdered her father and inability to know whom to trust. Instead, she remained silent.

"Hmmm."

She wasn't sure if anything she'd said had moved the queen, but her expression was uncharacteristically flat. Was she angry that Kathryn had stayed away? Did she consider it a mark of disrespect?

"Men and women do not marry for love," the queen said. "You know this, Lady Kathryn."

"And yet, some find it."

Had she gone too far? The suggestion that the king and queen were in love, even though it was obvious to all, was risky. It was not something openly discussed at court.

Kathryn looked away, and her eyes pinned on the banner hanging above the queen. Three lions, a dragon, and a castle on a field of red. She had to hold back a gasp as she thought of the seer's vision at Kenshire.

The queen startled her out of her reverie.

"Indeed."

The queen sat up then, waved her hand, and said, "That will be all. I will send for you this afternoon, my lady."

Stunned, Kathryn did not move at first. When she realized she'd been dismissed, by the queen of England, there was nothing left for her to do but bow.

And leave.

She'd expected an answer. Or at least some indication of the queen's thoughts. She'd received neither.

Defeated, she listened to the swishing of her grand gown with each step she took back to her chamber. Not even glancing up at the guards who stood outside the queen's solar, Kathryn tried to be thankful she'd had the audience at all. Thankful the queen even listened to her plea.

But all she could think of was her frown of displeasure when Kathryn had admitted she'd stayed intentionally away from the court.

Without warning, her cheeks began to tingle as tears streamed down her face.

She wanted her father.

CHAPTER 32

*W*hen he entered the throne room, the first thing Neill noticed was the queen sat beside the king. He'd not expected to see her today. He also noticed that, aside from two guards that stood on each side of the door he'd entered, no others were present.

Typically, the king was surrounded by his retainers.

Neill bowed before his sovereign and his wife, then stood tall and awaited Edward's direction. The king's word was absolute, and only he could guide their conversation.

"You've come to claim your reward," Edward said, nodding to a nearby table. A piece of parchment sat upon it, rolled and sealed. "An order for Lord Caxton to be removed as Lord Warden of the Middle Marche, to be replaced, forthwith, by the Earl of Morley."

Neill took a small step back. Morley? Did Kenton know of this appointment? He hadn't made mention of it, though he had seemed to have knowledge that Neill did not.

Another reason to accept the king's reward. He liked the Morleys and would be pleased to have their father as the replacement warden. Did that mean Edward would support their claim against the Derricksons as well?

"I have come to discuss your reward," he hedged. "Aye."

"Discuss?"

The king was not a stupid man. "Aye, Your Grace. As I said the other day—"

"Bring her in," Edward bellowed, interrupting him.

Neill turned when the door opened behind him, and gasped. It could not be.

Kathryn walked toward them with all of the grace of a gentled courtly lady. She was dressed the part. So beautiful.

Kathryn was at court. But what the hell was she doing here?

"You are surprised?" the queen asked him as Kathryn curtsied perfectly beside him.

"I am," he admitted, realizing he could not elaborate.

Chancing a glance at Kathryn, he saw a similar look of surprise on her face. So she hadn't known he was here either.

"Lady Kathryn came to see me earlier this morn after our discussion was interrupted yesterday . . ." She stopped, looked at her husband, and then continued. "And had a curious request."

Neill suspected he knew exactly what Kathryn had requested. Had he known earlier, he would have warned her away. But now that she was here, pride welled in his chest. Of all the places she could have gone, this possibility had not occurred to him.

"I was not aware," he said, "that Lady Kathryn was here, at court."

"Oh, she is very much here," the queen said, "despite having been warned away by her father."

Neill did look over at her then, surprised she'd told Eleanor everything. But he should not have been. Kathryn was as fearless standing here across from the king and queen as she'd been striding up to the Earl of Bothwell in Brockburg's courtyard, prepared to demand answers about her father.

And now they both awaited Edward and Eleanor's judgment.

"Your request, Lady Kathryn, is granted."

Neill stared at the queen, wondering if he'd misheard her words.

"Go," the king added. "Take the message with you and deliver it to the Hedford. The lord warden will know how to execute it."

"If you need assistance," the queen added, "Lady Kathryn is well-equipped on how to deliver royal messages." She smiled for the first time since Neill had entered the chamber. "She's had much practice in doing so with a man whom this court misses deeply."

Neill looked from Eleanor to his king.

"It is as the queen wishes," he said. "Lady Alina was her request, and 'twill be her duty to see Lord deBeers mollified when he learns his daughter will not be betrothed. At least not yet."

Neill could not believe their luck, but he did as his king bid him and took the missive from its position at the center of the table.

"That will be all."

The king had dismissed them.

"Fare thee well, my lady," the queen said to Kathryn. "I am sorry about your father."

"Many thanks," Kathryn said, curtsying. Neill bowed as well, and then they both turned to leave together. Just before they reached the door, the king spoke one last time.

"Discuss," he boomed. "You said, 'I have come to discuss your reward.'"

Neill turned.

"When I see you next in my hall, I would ask you consider a swift agreement in lieu of a discussion."

Edward knew Neill had planned to refuse him once again. And was ordering him to repledge his allegiance as a subject of the king. And to understand his position.

"With pleasure, Your Grace."

With a final bow, he joined Kathryn in the corridor, glad to have given such a pledge. Now that he'd been given leave to be with the royal messenger's daughter, no other request mattered.

THEY HADN'T MADE it far from the throne room when Neill grabbed Kathryn's hand, pulling her into a corridor.

He said nothing but pulled her into his arms, kissing her as if they might not be caught at any moment. Having thought she might never feel his lips on hers again, Kathryn kissed him back with all of the longing and anxiety she'd felt these past days. Grabbing the cloth of his tunic under her hands, she held on as if she might not let go.

But the not-so-distant sounds of footfalls and voices finally penetrated, and so she pulled away.

"It would not do to be caught like this." Kathryn searched his clear blue eyes for an agreement, but found none. He leaned down, his breath smelling of the mint he chewed each morning, and bypassed her mouth, nuzzling her neck instead.

"'Twas reckless, coming here," he murmured.

"Aye," Kathryn agreed. "It was."

"You could have been—"

"Turned away. Aye. And you, married. Instead, I will marry you."

He'd not asked her yet, of course. But since nothing about their courtship had been conventional, she saw no reason to start now.

"Aye, my lady. You will."

His slow, seductive smile reminded Kathryn of the first time he'd taken her hand, when he'd questioned her beside the inn.

"Tell me, what precisely did you say to the queen?"

"I told her naught but the truth. All know of Eleanor's great love for her husband. I thought perhaps if I appealed to her, as a woman . . ." She shrugged. "I decided it was a risk worth taking."

"And one I'm glad you took, though you were right to keep it from me. I'd never have agreed to such a thing."

"Agreed?"

He didn't appear to understand her meaning, but she quickly educated him.

"If you think me some simpering maid who will bow and curtsy at your command, I fear you do not know me well at all."

Again, that smile. Joy flooded her at the thought that she would be able to see his smile every day, for the rest of her life.

"I know you better than you think, my lady."

His fingers brushed up the side of her neck, ran along her cheek, and then his thumb touched her lower lip.

"I know you are headstrong, aye. And that you will get on with all of the women in my family quite well because of it."

He tugged on her lip, forcing her mouth open.

"I know you will marry me the moment we return to Kenshire, and as we've waited this long, I suppose I can wait to make you my wife in truth on our wedding night."

Kathryn shivered as his thumb continued its exploration.

"I know that when we do make love for the first time, it will be glorious."

Somehow, she knew to touch her tongue to his thumb, and when she did, Neill's eyes hooded ever so slightly. A fluttering raced from her stomach to her very core as she imagined them coming together in that way.

"I know, Lady Kathryn, that I love you now as surely as I did the day you sat in the solar at Brockburg, defiant and full of ideas. Ready to take on the second most powerful man in Scotland, alone if need be."

When he groaned, Kathryn was lost.

"And I love you, Neill Waryn. If we are to have that wedding night you speak of," she said as his hand dropped, "perhaps we should be on our way with all haste."

"Perhaps you are right."

Kathryn murmured "always" and caught his smile just before he turned to leave.

CHAPTER 33

*I*t had been the worst torture Neill had ever experienced.

On their return journey, he'd been alone with Kathryn on only a few occasions, and the moment he'd attempted to seduce his betrothed, her chaperone, who they had retrieved from the inn, reminded them they were not yet married.

The only reason he'd acquiesced had been to please Kathryn.

She had taken him at his word—they were to wait until their wedding night to become husband and wife in truth. He had meant the words when he'd said them, but he dearly wished he could take them back. For even though they'd finally made it through the gates of Kenshire Castle, the banns would still have to be posted, arrangements made . . . Besides which, he would need to take care of the matter of his reward.

He would take back the foul words if he could.

Looking at her now as she ran to Sara and the babe in her arms, Neill groaned.

"For a man who returns victorious, once again, your mood is foul, brother."

Geoffrey clasped him on the back and nodded up toward the

wall-walk. He caught Kathryn's eyes and told her silently where he was going. Then he followed his brother up the stone stairs and to the far end of the wall, where the view opened to the sea below. Neill tilted his head back, enjoying the final moments of sunshine for the day.

"From the pleased look on your face, I can assume London treated you kindly?"

"London? You mean the king?"

"Aye, he as well."

"Kindly? I suppose so."

He smiled, knowing his brother well. Geoffrey waited patiently for him to recall the events at court, because patience was what his brother did best. Neill would do well to learn some forbearance from him, even if they had disagreed about Kathryn.

Neill reached into the pouch hanging at his side and pulled out the missive. The king's seal stared back at them as Geoffrey took the rolled parchment from him.

"What is it?"

"An order for the lord warden."

Geoffrey's eyes widened.

"Lord Caxton is to be removed as the warden of the Middle Marches, replaced by the Earl of Morley."

His brother continued to stare at the missive.

"I will be leaving at once to take it to him myself."

"I will go with you."

Neill had thought his brother might say that.

"How did it happen?" Geoffrey finally asked.

Neill explained everything that had happened at court, from his initial audience with the king to Kathryn's appeal to the queen.

"I believe you left something out, brother."

He had, of course. His brother raised his eyebrows, waiting.

"I was not going to do it."

Geoffrey shook his head. "As stubborn as Bryce. Always have been. You truly planned to disobey your king? Perhaps cause a war?"

"Unlikely."

"And Caxton?"

"I believe Edward would have replaced him anyway."

Geoffrey, rightly so, looked skeptical.

"After Alexander renewed his vow, it would not have made sense for the king to provoke him again by refusing to remove the one barrier to peace at the border."

"Perhaps you are right. But perhaps not."

Neill turned away from the view in front of him to the even lovelier one in the castle courtyard.

Hayden ran around his mother in circles as Sara spoke with Kathryn, who now held the babe in her arms. He didn't need to explain himself to his brother, but he felt he owed it to him.

"When I first arrived at Langford, Aylmer was one of the first men I met."

He and his brother continued to watch the scene below.

"We got along from the start, I think because he reminded me of you. And still does."

"Handsome," Geoffrey said. "Skilled—"

"Nay," he laughed. "Serious, but humorous. Intelligent. Patient. A quality I admired in him, and in you. Mostly for my lack of it."

"You've other good qualities."

Neill looked at his brother. "I missed you, Bryce, and Emma. Our parents. Our home. You are everything to me, and I'd not jeopardize that."

Geoffrey turned serious. "A choice between the woman you love and your family is no choice at all." His gaze shifted to Sara. "Perhaps I should have counseled you differently. But it seemed you did quite well on your own."

"Kathryn did quite well for us both."

Which reminded him. "I want to hold the wedding the moment I return. Three days, at most."

He didn't like the look on his brother's face.

"Our priest . . . cannot marry you."

Had he heard his brother correctly?

"If he were here, I should say, he could do so in three days' time. But just yesterday he left for the Holy Island near Clave Castle. A pilgrimage of sorts."

"And who, prithee, will serve the good people of Kenshire while he's away?"

Geoffrey frowned.

"No. I will not have *that man* say the vows that bind Kathryn and I together for life."

That man was the village priest. Geoffrey tolerated him and his rather extreme views about the church and its people only because Sara insisted. He'd been here at Kenshire since she was a girl, and so their compromise had been to find a new priest for the castle. One who had apparently taken an untimely leave of absence.

"I will take her with me."

"And marry among strangers?"

"We will find another priest."

Geoffrey cocked his head to the side. "Why are you in such a hurry?"

Neill cleared his throat.

A smirk spread across Geoffrey's face. "Ahhh. Well, little brother, it seems you have no other choice."

"We always have a choice."

He thought for a moment.

"Father Simon."

"Brockburg's priest?"

"He's practically family to Clan Kerr. We will invite everyone, provided they can be here in less than a fortnight. Emma, I know, can make it here quickly."

Geoffrey chuckled. "'Tis a long time to wait. Perhaps you are more patient than you realize."

"Perhaps so," he fairly growled at the thought of the delay. Could Kathryn be persuaded to forget the foolish idea of waiting? What he'd been thinking, Neill was not sure.

"But since this will be the last Waryn wedding—" Geoffrey slapped him on the back, "—we ought to make it a memorable one."

Following his brother back the way they came, he thought again of the long days he would have to wait to see Kathryn, to touch her, to make her his in truth.

Could he do it?

Perhaps you are more patient than you realize.

Aye, he could. And would.

But Neill certainly did not have to like it.

"THEY ARE SO BEAUTIFUL!"

Guests had been arriving for days, and Kathryn had to admit she was becoming a slight bit overwhelmed. For so long, her family had comprised of two people: she and her father. Now she was part of something bigger. Part of the Waryn family and the clan with which they were so deeply intertwined.

Before the ceremony, all of Clan Kerr would be arriving here, at Kenshire.

The first guests to arrive were Neill's sister, Emma, and her husband, the Earl of Clave, who lived not far from them at all. Emma was both unpredictable and a joy to be around. Kathryn had taken to her immediately, and upon Neill's return from delivering the all-important message, the four of them had become inseparable.

Gillian and Allie, two sisters who'd grown up with Sara,

arrived with their husbands—Graeme deSowlis and Reid Kerr. If she'd thought Emma lovely, these sisters were no less so.

"Be sure to ask Lady Gillian of how she and Graeme came to be wed," Emma had told her before their arrival. "'Tis a most interesting tale."

Sara had given Emma a sharp look—only to break into giggles moments later. As the women entered the hall with their husbands, Kathryn glanced nervously at Sara. So many people she'd never met before. So much history that she was now a part of. It felt *right* . . . but it would require an adjustment, to be certain.

"You've grown . . . big since last I saw you," Emma exclaimed as Allie and her sister walked toward them.

"'Tis a wonder Reid allowed me to come at all," Allie said, looking down at her swollen belly. "I remember now," she chuckled. "He tried to keep us back, but . . ."

When the group of women laughed, it elicited a look from the men.

"I do wonder," Allie said, "if Reid wishes he wed a more malleable bride."

"I do not imagine," said her sister, whose own baby was back at home, "Reid would do well with . . . malleable."

From what Kathryn had heard, Reid had earned a reputation as a hard man to tame before he'd met Allie. But the tenacious lady had managed the impossible, and the chief's second was better for it, according not only to Neill but to Reid himself.

"Gillian. Allie. I am pleased to introduce you to my future sister-in-law, Lady Kathryn Wyld."

Kathryn smiled at the women, who did the same in return.

"I'm told your father was royal messenger to the king," Gillian said.

Allie added, "And that it was you who foiled the lord chancellor's attempt to waylay an accord between Alexander and Edward."

"I would not say that, precisely."

"Aye, my lady," called out a familiar voice from behind her. "I met Kathryn at The Wild Boar, where she bid her time before seizing the opportunity to confront the chancellor herself."

Neill told this story to every person who'd not heard it before. Soon he would have her winning the tournament that allowed for the king's reward too.

"If not for her, Caxton would not have been forced out of his position."

She rolled her eyes as Neill slipped an arm around her.

Word had spread quickly. Just days after Neill had returned from delivering the king's message, a new warden of the Middle March had been appointed. Douglas, Lord Warden of Scotland, had convened another council. Thankfully, it had been set after the wedding, a good thing since Clan Kerr would host it again. All expected for the border lords to agree on a return to the monthly Day of Truce meetings now that Caxton had been removed from power.

Order would be restored, and none too soon.

"If not for *us*," she clarified, ignoring the gleam in Neill's eyes. It had become increasingly more difficult to adhere to their agreed-upon wedding night. Stolen kisses did little to satiate them, and the one nighttime visit they'd risked had only served to frustrate them.

"How goes it at Highgate End?" Sara asked.

"Well," Gillian said, "though my maid Fiona was unable to make the journey. She hurt her shoulder—" she looked at her sister Allie, "—in an attempt to wield a longbow."

Allie winced. "I do feel badly about that. But Fiona was insistent on coming to the training yard with me. And she is not so old, after all."

"Is she not?" Gillian crossed her arms.

"Perhaps she is slightly advanced in age."

As the sisters traded barbs, Kathryn caught Emma's eye. She

would gain three sisters by marrying Neill, and though she'd not yet met Catrina, Bryce's wife, Kathryn had heard plenty about her from the others. From no siblings to . . . this. It felt like a gift.

"You look well pleased," Neill whispered in her ear. Grasping her hand as he did often, he pulled her away from the others.

"I've never had a sibling before, and now I will be gaining three sisters, two brothers, and a brother-in-law through our marriage."

Neill looked at his sister, who winked in response.

"They can be trying at times."

She followed his gaze. "Surely not Emma? She seems so sweet . . ."

Neill chuckled, squeezing her hand. "Sweet. Aye. And also troublesome."

"Nay. I do not believe it."

"Emma told the stable boy at Bristol that he could aspire to be king of England. He fashioned a crown from leaves and twigs and refused to take it off. She bowed to him whenever he walked by." Neill shook his head. "And he's likely wearing it still."

"That does not seem such a bad thing to do."

"The stable boy of a small northern manor will never become the king of England."

"Nay?" she argued. "What of Maximinus Thrax, emperor of Rome? He was a sheep farmer, if I recall my studies correctly."

"And if I recall mine, he led for just three years before he and his son were murdered by the same army who made him emperor."

"But still, he was the emperor of Rome." She raised her chin.

"You and Emma will get on well, I believe," Neill said. "My mother would have adored you."

Neill rarely spoke of his parents, and since she did not wish to press him on the matter, she simply smiled. He'd share as much as he liked—and she would be here to listen.

Kathryn could tell he thought of his mother, of her absence likely, with their wedding just days away.

"She fought them that day."

Kathryn assumed he meant the day she'd been killed.

Neill looked at Reid then, and Kathryn found herself wondering, again, how they'd found the strength to forgive the clan who'd taken their home. Killed their parents. Though the Kerrs had not done the deed themselves, their raid had taken everything from the Waryn siblings.

"I hated him, *them*, for so long." His voice was barely above a whisper. "But they thought they were doing their duty. Doing as their king bid them. Besides, Bristol Manor had once been a Clan Kerr holding. Bryce—" he looked back at her, "—by marrying Catrina did a service to both our families. We would be feuding still had it not been for his marriage. We never would have realized they're good people."

"So you've forgiven them, truly?"

"Aye," he said without hesitation. "They've served us well through these difficult times, and an ally is always better than an enemy."

This time, it was she who squeezed Neill's hand. "I am so very glad you came to the inn that day," she said.

"As am I, *Lady* Kathryn."

He said the title as if it were a private jest between them. And it was. Neill had seen right through her from the start. He'd known she was no common serving maid.

And she'd known from the start he was no common man. "Shall we rejoin our guests?"

He made a low sound, almost a growl, in his throat. "I can think of another place I'd rather be."

Her stomach flipped at his words. Three days. In just three days she would become his wife, in every possible way.

CHAPTER 34

*N*eill looked at the sky, thankful for the clear day as he waited on the church stairs with the priest. Father Simon, a man he'd heard much about since Clan Kerr's fate had interwoven with their own. Having dined with him for the past two nights, Neill could understand why the Kerr siblings valued him so. Soft-spoken yet firm, he'd led Neill and Kathryn through what they could expect of this day, yet Neill was more nervous than he'd ever been before a tournament.

Geoffrey, Bryce, and Garrick stood closest to him. The bride's maids would arrive with her, and as they waited, he tugged his new surcoat down, ensuring it was not creased. That he was prepared for his bride.

Neill was ready both for the ceremony that would tie him and Kathryn together forever and to make her his bride in truth.

All of Kenshire had crowded below the chapel, spilling into Kenshire's inner courtyard, so he was glad for the familiar colors of Clan Kerr, their chief standing not far from him. He was glad also for Peter and Faye, who acted as much as parents to his brother and Sara as they allowed, and Uncle Hugh, who'd returned from Camburg Castle near Wales just the day before. Allies like deSowlis were also present.

And though there were two important people missing from the ceremony—Adam and Cora hadn't had enough time to make the journey—Neill vowed to take Kathryn to Langford Castle at the earliest opportunity.

"They're coming." Geoffrey stood tall to see over the crowd gathered below them.

He watched as at least two hundred people moved to the side to create a path for Kathryn and her maids. Minstrels had been secured for the wedding feast that night, but now a single lutist played a lovely, familiar melody.

And then stopped.

It wasn't Kathryn's maid who walked toward him after all, but two people. A man and a woman.

And though he could not yet see their faces, Neill knew the couple well.

Throat scratchy, he swallowed, attempting to regain composure. "How?" he murmured to no one.

Geoffrey answered him. "Kathryn sent word to them before you left London."

Kathryn could not have known they would marry this day. If she'd let Neill have his way, they would already be man and wife.

"But . . ."

"She explained the date had not been set but they may want to leave 'posthaste.' They arrived last eve after you retired. It was Kathryn's idea for them to announce themselves now rather than earlier."

They smiled as if he were their son in truth rather than a boy whom they'd fostered. These two new guests were as dear to him as any in the world, and it felt right that they should be here. He knew Adam felt a special kinship with the Caiser family because of his connection with her father and grandfather, the man who'd bequeathed him Langford Castle. Bryce made space for them along the lowermost stone stair. Grinning at them, Neill collected himself as best he could, marveling at the surprise his future wife had managed to send to him this day.

Kathryn.

No sooner had he regained his composure than he spotted the first glimpse of color moving toward him through the crowd.

Bryce's wife, Catrina, followed by Emma and then Sara. They each wore a different color, but while they looked lovely today, it was the woman who was now coming toward him who nearly made his knees buckle. With her hair pulled partially back, her face completely visible, Kathryn's blue silk gown glimmered as the sun shone against the gold embroidery. Gold thread danced around her neckline, her sleeves . . . everywhere. And just one simple jewel adorned her neck.

Neill knew it well.

The necklace had been his mother's. And now, it was his wife's. Or his soon-to-be wife. He could not stop smiling at Kathryn as she finally joined him at the top of the stairs, and when Father Simon finally cleared his throat, loudly, Neill knew he'd been caught.

He attempted to concentrate on the priest's words, but it was a battle he could not win. He only processed the most important part: the recitation of his vows. Repeating after Father Simon, he said, "I, Sir Neill Waryn, take thee, Lady Kathryn Wyld, to be my wedded wife, to have and to hold from this day forward, for better for worse, for richer for poorer, for fairer or fouler, in sickness and in health, to love and to cherish, 'til death us depart, according to God's holy ordinance; and thereunto I plight thee my troth."

Kathryn said the same, and a short time later, it was done.

She was his wife. His heart felt like it had expanded to fill his whole body.

Cheers went up from the crowd as they made their way from the chapel toward the great hall. A wedding feast would last into the night.

"No more beautiful bride has ever graced this hall or any other," he said as they entered the front doors, which were held wide open. All would be welcome this day, Kenshire's hall filled beyond its capacity.

He'd seen it earlier in the day, the fresh strewn rushes and flowers everywhere, but it seemed somehow more vibrant, more decorative now. Everything seemed brighter and better now that they were wed.

"And you, sir, make an extraordinarily dashing groom."

Though their guests would sit at the extra trestle tables set out for the occasion, it would be some time before Neill and Kathryn took a seat. It was customary for the newly wed couple to walk among the guests first, and they gladly did so together.

Just before they arrived at the table closest to the dais, the one where Adam and Cora sat, Neill pulled Kathryn to the side.

"Before I introduce you to them, I want to thank you."

Kathryn smiled. "'Tis my wedding gift to you, husband."

"And a fine one at that. But how did you know the wedding would be delayed?"

"I didn't," she said. "In fact, I thought they would likely miss the ceremony, but I suspected they'd want to know . . . that you would be overjoyed to see them even if they arrived after the wedding."

"Thank you," he said again as they approached the table where Toren and Alex Kerr and their wives sat with the older couple. After a quick welcome to the others, he stood back as Adam and Cora rose from the table to greet them.

"Adam. Cora. It seems you've met my wife." Neill could tell

he grinned like a boy with his first sword every time he used that word. "Kathryn, Sir Adam Dayne and Lady Cora Maxwell."

"Of Clan Maxwell?" Kathryn asked. "I meant to ask you about it last eve."

"Aye, the same. But please do not judge me for it."

Her clan had been one of the first to boycott the Day of Truce more than thirty years earlier. A fierce lot of warriors Neill knew she loved dearly. Though it had taken some years, she confessed, for her Scottish family to accept her English husband.

"I met a man once, Fergus Maxwell, at The Wild Boar."

"My cousin," she said, giving her a wide smile. "So you've been to The Wild Boar? I was only there once. Do you remember, Adam?"

"Aye, I do," he said to her. "But wish that I could forget."

Adam turned back to Kathryn. "But that is a story for another day, as is yours. This day is for celebration, but I do hope we will have time to share stories before Cora and I must leave."

"We will ensure it," she said.

Knowing Kathryn would not do so, he pardoned them to the head table, where finally they sat.

Surrounded by family and friends and next to the woman he loved, Neill could think of no happier day. If his parents had been here to see it, they would have been well pleased. Even though Bryce taunted their sister, and Emma looked very much as if she were planning some nefarious deed, they would be proud.

Making them proud, wherever they were, had long been his goal, and he took a minute to savor the sensation.

"What are you thinking?" Kathryn asked, and he told her. They spoke of their parents then, and of the days that had brought them to this one.

They drank and laughed at Geoffrey's tales of his young

ones, warning the newly wed couple of how wee ones made a man turn into "nothing more than a simpering child" as they came into the world.

And Neill tried not to look at the ample cleavage Kathryn's gown displayed.

Tried not to remember her soft moans from a few nights past, on the eve they'd decided not to be alone in her bedchamber again if they wanted to have a wedding night in truth.

Neill tried, and failed, not to imagine his wife, fully unclothed, underneath him as she would be that night.

"What are you thinking?" Kathryn licked a bit of cake from her finger.

"I'm thinking—" he leaned toward her, ensuring his words were only for her to hear, "—I've been dreaming of slipping inside of you for so long that I fear I may not be able to control myself when I do."

"I . . ." Her lips parted and Neill watched as she thought more carefully on his words. "I look forward to . . ." Though she didn't finish, his suddenly shy wife did not need to say the words. He knew what she wanted.

He should not tempt fate, but would anyway. Knowing he tortured them both, Neill leaned in even closer.

"And I will give it to you. This night and every night, my lady."

"Can we leave our own wedding feast?"

He laughed, loudly enough to garner looks from those around them. Neill lifted his goblet in response, and their guests did the same.

There would be singing and dancing, a long night ahead.

But not for the newly married couple.

"Aye," he said. "We can."

CHAPTER 35

*S*he was ready.

Kathryn and Neill had left the hall at the same time, her cheeks flaming as the guests cheered and called out bawdy suggestions, but they'd been separated into their own private chambers so Kathryn could prepare for the wedding night. She was not far from the lord and lady of Kenshire, just one floor below them, in the same tower.

But that was not where she would be staying this night, or any other night henceforth. Neill would come to fetch her soon and bring her to their new chamber.

"You look lovely," Sara said, stepping back. The countess herself had fastened the clasp to the robe she'd gifted her that morn. Velvet, fur-lined, and exquisite. Kathryn had tried to refuse—the countess had given her so much already, gowns she claimed no longer fit and the kind of friendship that felt more like sisterhood—but Sara would have none of it.

"So tell us," Emma said as Faye tsked and left the room. Sara's maid had accompanied the ladies of the family to the chamber. She'd untied Kathryn's hair and brushed it until it gleamed. "Are you a virgin still?"

"Emma!" Catrina scolded her.

Kathryn knew Catrina the least of her new sisters-in-law, but she liked her just the same. These women were her family now, and if she could not speak of such things with family, then who could she take into her confidence?

"Aye," she admitted, fanning out her robe. Kathryn loved how it gathered around her feet, covering the equally as fine silk shift beneath it.

"You're nervous?" Catrina asked, her accent leaving no doubt she hailed from north of the border.

"Of course she's nervous," Emma answered for her, the chamber suddenly feeling quite crowded. She was grateful for their presence but felt quite ready to be reunited with Neill. "Do you know what to expect?"

"Aye. I know the first time will be painful. And after that, not as much so."

"Oh dear." Sara sat on the bed and patted the space beside her. "What about the ladies at court? What have they told you?"

Kathryn sat as the others gathered around them.

"Some," she admitted. "But none were widows."

"All virgins then," Emma blurted, which earned her a look from the others.

"Do not be nervous," Catrina said. "When there is love between a husband and wife—"

"Or even a man and a woman," Emma laughed at her own jest. "For who here was wed first?" She winked at Kathryn. "The Waryn women don't care to do things in the typical way."

That, she'd noticed. "I . . . may not have done so either. But we decided to wait . . ."

"An admirable feat, that." Emma looked toward the door as if Neill were to barge through it at any moment.

"Rest assured that you will be well taken care of. Neill is like our brothers in that way."

Both Sara and Catrina looked at her, their faces stricken.

"Gentle!" Emma blurted. "Large but, oh do stop. I meant their frames are large, but they are gentle still."

All of them burst into laughter at the way Emma had unintentionally phrased her words of comfort.

Which was precisely when Neill walked into the chamber.

Their laughter became even louder, and even Kathryn could not stop. She thought of what Emma had said and inadvertently looked . . . there.

Apparently the others noticed because, instead of gathering their composure, they did quite the opposite. They were doubled over in laughter, tears tracking down their cheeks.

Neill looked at his sister.

"Emma?"

Which only made the situation worse, since he had so easily predicted the source of their merriment.

"I . . . ," Emma managed, "claim my innocence in this matter."

"You can claim it—" Sara stood, "—but that certainly does not mean you're right to do so."

Neill smirked as the women made their way out of the chamber. Emma merely shrugged as she left the room.

"You'll pardon my sister," Neill said, holding Kathryn's gaze. "Though I fear you'll need to become accustomed to her. With Clave Castle so close to Kenshire—"

"She is a delight," Kathryn said honestly. She forgot whatever she'd been about to say next and took in the sight of her husband.

Divested of his surcoat, he wore only a loose linen shirt, its sleeves rolled to reveal thick forearms accustomed to wielding a sword. Her gaze moved up to his face, his eyes flickering with desire, which was when she realized this was finally truly going to happen.

"Are you nervous?" He took a step toward her.

"Aye," she admitted, wishing it were not so.

And then he did something unusual. Neill held out his hand.

Confused, she took it. Then, without a word, he unclasped her robe, laid it on the bed, and led her from her chamber.

"Are we going to your bedchamber?" she asked.

"Our bedchamber is located on the northeast side of the castle, and I'd not walk you there dressed this way."

He stopped, without warning, and kissed her hard. But he pulled back before she was ready, leaving her wanting much, much more.

"Then where?"

Neill didn't answer, but he did take a wall torch as they made their way down the circular stairwell. It was only as they walked through darkened corridors and down another set of steps that Kathryn realized where they were heading.

At this time of night?

When they exited the Sea Gate, Neill took off his leather shoes. Kathryn did the same. Wordlessly, he led her toward the water, which she could hear but not see. Everything in front of them was black with only the faintest glimmer coming from the moon.

Just like she had the first time, Kathryn twirled about as she reached the point where the saw grass around them became nothing but sand. The sight before her was spectacular. This time, instead of the castle, dots of lights along the wall-walks and atop each tower broke though the black night.

"Beautiful, is it not?"

"Aye," she said as he tugged her hand once more.

And then she noticed it.

A blanket spread out on the sand, and as they moved closer, Kathryn spotted a wooden slat with pieces of bread and cheese on it, along with a pitcher and two goblets.

"This is . . ." She had no words.

"Our wedding night," he finished for her.

SHE WAS MUCH MORE relaxed now.

Kathryn had not drunk much at dinner, and he'd seen her nibble a bite or two of meat and a small bite of almond cake. Now that they were alone, he'd lulled her into a discussion that would keep her mind free of worry. She'd eaten a few bites of bread and cheese, drunk two goblets full of red wine, and finally forgotten that she wore nothing but her shift.

At first, she'd worried they would be seen by the guards, but Neill had assured her the men atop the wall could see nothing but the light from the torch he'd stuck in the sand.

His wife looked out into the darkness, and though he couldn't see her face, he had memorized every feature and could easily imagine it. If she but turned her head, their lips would be close to touching.

"Go on," he said as she told a story of her childhood at court.

He lifted the mass of waves over her shoulder and pulled the string he'd been looking at for the past hour. The one that loosened the top of her shift. He was able to pull it off her shoulder, exposing the bare skin to his touch.

Kathryn stopped talking, but she did not turn around just yet.

When he kissed her first on the shoulder, and then on her neck, Neill hardened immediately. He was ready.

But she was not.

Not yet.

When he pulled back the errant strands of her hair this time, they fell back, as if in protest. To ensure they stayed put this time, he grasped as much hair as he could and held it.

Turning her head toward him.

Guiding their mouths together, Neill kissed her with the knowledge that, this time, they would not stop. Hungrily, he caressed her with his lips, his tongue. His hands slipped under her shift, which she aided him by lifting up, and he removed the fine but offending garment in one swift movement.

Standing, he quickly removed his own clothing as she watched.

"Are you afraid still?"

He sat, and his wife's eyes followed his movement, resting between his legs.

"It will hurt for but a moment."

And then she surprised him by laughing.

"'Tis not the reaction a man hopes to elicit from his wife when she sees him for the first time."

He groaned as her body taunted him. Her full breasts, the mound of hair peeking out from between her legs as if to taunt him.

"'Tis just something your sister said."

"If we cannot talk about her just now . . ."

She smiled, the corners of her perfect lips rising just enough that he could see the white of her teeth.

A tug in his chest made him impatient.

He laid her down and climbed over her in one quick movement. This time it was his turn to laugh at her look of surprised delight. Instead of lowering his mouth onto hers, Neill kissed his way down her chest toward her breast, taking it in his hands first. He gave the perfect hardened nipple the attention it deserved as his fingers entered her without warning. Pressing his palm against her, he grazed his teeth gently on her nipple. Kathryn's gasp was a welcome sound.

With the waves as their backdrop, the warm summer night licking their naked bodies, Neill used everything he had to ensure Kathryn would forget the tales she'd heard about the pain of having her maidenhood taken away.

When her hands started clawing against his back, Neill moved to the second breast but did not relent the sweet torment of his caresses down below.

"Neill . . ."

A sweet sound, but he was aiming for an even sweeter one.

So he circled and pressed until her rapid breathing was the only thing he could hear.

And still, Neill did not relent.

When her wetness covered his fingers and her moans filled his ears, still Neill continued to pleasure her.

Lifting his head, he removed his hands and watched her return to him.

Lips parted. Cheeks flushed.

His wife looked thoroughly ravished. But she was not.

Not yet.

Without giving her time to consider anything but the afterglow of pleasure, he positioned himself inside her.

And thrust, hard. Hard enough to break the barrier.

"Ahhh."

Not pleasurable. Not yet.

Neill propped himself over her, motionless, and watched her face.

"That was the worst of it."

"Aye?"

"Aye."

His cock throbbed in protest, but still he did not move. He'd wanted so badly to be inside her, and now that he had what he so desperately needed, Neill had to attempt to ignore it. Because if he thought of them joined, of her tightness, of . . .

"Are you well?"

Nay.

"Aye, love. Tell me when it no longer pains you."

"It no longer pains me."

Groaning, Neill did not wait for further confirmation.

He pulled out slowly, just to be sure.

"That . . . feels . . . different."

"This is just the beginning."

Out, and in. Just slightly deeper this time.

"Ahhh."

"By night's end . . ." This time, he circled his hips as he moved. "You will come again, as you did beneath my fingers. And will know the pleasure of joining this way."

Her hands fled from his back and grasped the blanket beneath them.

"I believe . . . I believe I know the pleasure already."

He moved slightly faster now, one hand moving down her stomach.

"Nay, wife. I do not believe you do."

She was tight, slick, and able to take him fully. So he did not hold back, and teased with his fingers too. Small, quick circles at odds with the deep, slow thrusts that claimed her as his wife each time.

"Neill . . ."

Ah, yes. That was better.

"Aye, love?"

Straining to hold himself back, Neill knew his voice must sound pained. And though he'd imagined this very moment over, and over, and over again, he was determined she would come first.

Now.

He thrust hard but rubbed his thumb softly. By the look on Kathryn's face, he could tell she was overcome. Screaming into the night, she clenched against him. Neill removed his hand and let himself go completely.

His cries mingled with her own until he exploded, shuddering with her in one powerful moment that he'd remember for the rest of his life no matter how often they made love.

And they would. Often.

Collapsing and rolling her on top of him, Neill gathered her close, his hands resting on her buttocks. Her hair tickled his chest until she finally lifted her head. Pulling out, he groaned again and watched her expression as it turned from pleasure to wonder.

"Now that," he said, "is exactly what I was aiming for."

She tried to prop herself up, but Neill wouldn't let her. He wanted to feel her breasts against his chest. Feel every bit of her body pressing on his.

"Am I your prisoner?" she asked, turning her head to look up at him.

"Aye."

"Good."

He smiled, pulling her even tighter against him. They lay that way, listening to the waves, to each other's heartbeat.

"I would stay right here forever," she said finally.

"I love you," he murmured into her ear in response.

"And I love you, almost as much as . . ."

She lifted her head, Neill suddenly anxious about what she was going to say.

"Almost as much as?"

Kathryn glanced down between them, and then back up at his face.

"Almost as much as that." A wicked grin spread across her face.

"Worth waiting for?"

She nodded. "Aye. Very much so."

Much to his surprise, he agreed.

EPILOGUE

hey arrived at the inn just as the sun set, the smell of freshly baked bread wafting out through the open shutters. A familiar smell, and one Kathryn had missed. Kenshire's baker was as fine as any, but Magge made the inn's bread herself. She'd always bragged of it, saying an inn without good ale or bread would close its shutters before long. And as the third-generation owner of The Wild Boar, she would know better than most.

Kathryn and Neill had been married less than a fortnight, and he'd not wanted to leave Kenshire Castle so soon. But she had insisted on coming here to see Magge. To tell her she was safe and say goodbye properly. So they'd agreed to a visit to Brockburg with a stop at The Wild Boar on the way.

Kathryn took a deep breath as she stepped inside, immediately wishing she hadn't. While the smell of bread wafted out through the kitchen windows, the stench in the hall was one she'd gladly forgotten. No matter how often they changed the rushes or attempted to keep the floor free from bones and spilled ale, The Wild Boar had always smelled like any other inn.

A not entirely pleasant scent.

"Kathryn!"

Although Magge sounded overjoyed to see her, true to her nature, she sidled up to Neill first. The ladies at court could learn something of flirting from the aging innkeeper.

"Come here," she said, reaching for her next.

Kathryn tossed her arms around the woman who had harbored her, protected her, and squeezed tight.

"'Tis good to see you," she whispered. "I'm sorry we did not send word sooner."

Magge let her go, stepped back, and looked at her from top to bottom.

"You look as you did before. A true and proper lady."

"And my wife," Neill added.

Magge's eyes widened. Kathryn laughed as the innkeeper slapped first her and then Neill on the shoulder.

"I'd said you'd not be back. I won't deny I dared to hope."

"But here I am."

Magge made a noise. "To visit ol' Magge, and nothin' else."

That much was true.

"The wife of a Waryn. And this Waryn." Magge whistled. "I'll be hearing this story after I settle that." She nodded behind her.

How Magge could see through her back, Kathryn was not sure. But she'd always managed to sense fights before they broke out, and sure enough, two men behind her appeared to be squaring off. Neill stepped forward, but Kathryn stopped him.

"She'll want to do this herself."

"Show of strength?"

"Aye," Kathryn said, navigating them through the crowded hall to the very table where she'd first seen Neill some months ago.

She could tell he was remembering it as well.

They sat, Neill glancing Magge's way once more. As Kathryn had suspected, she'd prevented the fight and was already walking toward them with a pitcher.

"Servin' the great Neill Waryn and his wife," she said, placing it on their table along with three mugs. "And a pleasure to do it."

Magge sat with them, poured their drinks, and without preamble said, "So now. Go ahead."

Kathryn began to tell the tale, lowering her voice at times and letting Neill stop her at others. Only as she told the story did it strike her how very much had happened since they'd last left the Boar.

"And none of yer guests came here on their way," Magge tsked when she heard of the wedding.

"We gave them little notice," she said. "Neill wished to marry rather . . . quickly."

He nearly spilled the ale he'd just drunk when Magge slapped him on the back for the second time that night. "A right smart lad, just like his brothers."

Kathryn continued, but she noticed an odd look on Neill's face. He was no longer listening, his gazed fixed on something, or rather someone, near the entrance. She finished her story but could tell something was amiss.

"Ye'll be wanting some meat pies then, aye?" Magge said, standing after she'd congratulated them at least three more times.

"If it pleases you," Neill said.

"I miss some of this," she said, looking around the inn. "Perhaps I should join Magge for a time."

"Or perhaps not."

"Twould do no damage with you here to defend my honor."

"I'm not so sure of that," he said with a dark look at one of the men she'd noticed watching her.

Kathryn laughed then. "It seems, husband, we will not always agree."

Neill cocked his head to the side, looking at her for a long time before he answered.

"It appears not."

"But I still love you."

"As I love you." Neill leaned forward. "Would you like for me to show you?"

Aye, she would like that very much. "Later. I am quite hungry."

She glanced around the hall. The innkeeper was nowhere to be found.

"So now that the Day of Truce and hard-fought peace along the border have been restored, and my tournament days are in the past, whatever shall we do with our time?" he teased.

She looked for Magge and did not see her.

"Meat pies be damned."

This time it was she who grabbed her husband's hand. "I have a thought about that."

"And I'm thankful for it," Neill said, following her. "And for much, much more."

Love the Border Series and being on the inside? Join Blood & Brawn, a private reader group on Facebook.

ALSO BY CECELIA MECCA

The Border Series
    The Ward's Bride: Prequel Novella
    The Thief's Countess: Book 1
    The Lord's Captive: Book 2
    The Chief's Maiden: Book 3
    The Scot's Secret: Book 4
    The Earl's Entanglement: Book 5
    The Warrior's Queen: Book 6
    The Protector's Promise: Book 7
    The Rogue's Redemption: Book 8
    The Guardian's Favor: Book 9
    The Knight's Reward: Book 10

Enchanted Falls

Falling for the Knight: A Time Travel Romance

Bloodwite
    The Healer's Curse: Bloodwite Origin Story
    The Vampire's Temptation: Bloodwite Book 1

The Immortal's Salvation: Bloodwite Book 2
The Hunter's Affection: Bloodwite Book 3

New Historical Series, Coming Summer 2019

Blacksmith. Chief. Earl. Mercenary. Four men form a knightly order, sworn to friendship. . . and secrecy. Together, they will change the course of England.

BECOME AN INSIDER

Become a CM Insider to receive a bonus sexy scene to THE KNIGHT'S REWARD along with a free prequel novella and additional bonus scenes for other books in the series.

The CM Insider is also filled with new release information including exclusive cover reveals and giveaways with links to live videos and private Facebook groups so I can get to know my readers a bit more.

CeceliaMecca.com/Insider

ABOUT THE AUTHOR

Cecelia Mecca is the author of medieval romance, including the Border Series, and sometimes wishes she could be transported back in time to the days of knights and castles. Although the former English teacher's actual home is in Northeast Pennsylvania where she lives with her husband and two children, her online home can be found at CeceliaMecca.com. She would love to hear from you.

55025454R10165

Made in the USA
Middletown, DE
14 July 2019